REBECCA CHIANESE

PINNED

For my sister,
Sarah Francesca Chianese

REBECCA CHIANESE

PINNED

A Novel

MNP
Mt. Nittany Press

Lemont

Published by Mt. Nittany Press, an imprint of Eifrig Publishing, PO Box 66, Lemont, PA 16851.

For information regarding permission, write to:
Rights and Permissions Department,
Eifrig Publishing,
PO Box 66, Lemont, PA 16851, USA.
permissions@eifrigpublishing.com

Library of Congress Control Number:

Chianese, Rebecca
 Pinned, A Novel
 / Rebecca Chianese
     p. cm.

Paperback: ISBN 978-1-63233-399-5
Hardcover: ISBN 978-1-63233-400-8
eBook: ISBN 978-1-63233-401-5

    1. Pinned, A Novel
I. Chianese, Rebecca II. Title.

29 28 27 26 2025
5 4 3 2 1

Printed on acid-free paper. ∞

Three things that cannot be long hidden:

the sun, the moon, and the truth.

~ Gautama Buddha

Avalon, New Jersey
January 2025

Emmett Ainsworth found himself on the desolate January beach gasping. A gull screamed. Emmett's eyes widened, black spots filled his vision, he couldn't breathe.

He'd spent the past seven years getting out of wrestling holds and fighting to stay on his feet. No one was on top of him now, pinning him to a mat, while a crowd roared. He was on the beach. Alone. There was no whisper in his ear, no scent of cinnamon gum. Deep breaths, he thought, deep breaths and you can't hyperventilate. Slowly, he became aware of the salt and sand and sea and his heartbeat slowed until it was in concert with the waves.

He wondered how long he'd been there splayed open to the sky. He had no way of knowing.

No way of knowing. That phrase rang again and again like a bell, a call with no response, until he listened carefully and heard an answering ring from somewhere deep inside of him.

Yes, you did, it said, of course you did, you know exactly what you did, you knew it then, you know it now, you know, you know, you know.

CHAPTER 1
Three Months Earlier, October 2024

Olivia, Isa, and Delaney watched Kam Connover who was bragging about how he had used his highly priced, exceedingly authentic looking fake ID to pick up the keg. They knew, from past experience, that his parents' guesthouse was already well stocked with booze and pot. What they hadn't decided was whether or not they should go.

Olivia turned back to face Delaney who was making the argument to go, which was surprising because Delaney hated all things suburban including their grade's parties, and she hated Kam even more than she hated the rest of their grade.

"Kam's annoying." Delaney continued, "but…it is our last homecoming."

Olivia grimaced, "I have a bad feeling about it."

Delaney laughed, "The Connovers run this town, the cops won't break it up."

Olivia caught Isa's eye. It wasn't the cops that had Olivia worried.

Isa shrugged, which was how Olivia knew Delaney was going to convince them. The three of them had been best friends since they were toddlers, and Delaney was persuasive. Olivia just hoped they wouldn't all regret it.

Night fell, moonless and humid despite being early autumn. For a moment, as each partygoer stood on the crest of the hill overlooking the Connover estate, a tender breeze teased the air. They walked in pairs or small groups, their voices giddy, already feeling a desperate wistfulness for the night that hadn't happened yet.

Olivia and Isa made their way across the wide expanse of lawn. They walked huddled close together, in boyfriend jeans and cute tops, Olivia's gauzy and white tied at her midriff, Isa's a black St. Vincent's T-shirt, her favorite band, a drawing of the lead singer etched in pink, playing guitar, wings stretched behind her. Their arms pressed against one another, their legs in stride despite Olivia being three inches shorter, their heads bent toward the glowing square of light emanating from Isa's phone.

Olivia stopped, tucked her long dark hair behind her ear. "Wait, let me see."

Isa handed Olivia her phone to read. Olivia skimmed the onslaught of texts.

dont be like that
u want me
i can tell when u look at me
ur bodys rockin
I wanna rock u
im addicted to u
i just need to show you

"Ugh!" Olivia almost dropped the phone at the sight of an erect penis on Isa's phone. "This ends tonight." Olivia began marching toward the house, her long dark hair swaying. She looked ready for combat with her shoulders back and fists at

her side. Olivia was petite, curvy, and fiery. Her senior super-
latives were Best Dancer, Best Smile, and Hottest Temper.

"Olivia, don't say anything!"

Olivia stopped and looked at Isa. "Fine—I'll punch him
in the face."

"No—don't do anything—I'll handle it my own way."

It didn't sit well with Olivia to let Rory Lange get away
with his relentless nasty texts, but Isa was Olivia's ride or die,
and she couldn't bear the thought of upsetting her even more.

"You're giving me the look." Olivia said.

Isa kept her gaze steady. Her deep brown eyes were large,
tilted up at the outer corners with lashes so long and thick she
never applied mascara. The light from the phone accentuated
the curve of her cheek, fullness of her lips, dark smooth skin,
ink-black hair cropped and curling close to her head. Theirs
was a lifelong friendship and Olivia could tell how upset Isa
was, even if she looked calm and in control. And she knew
how much Isa hated a scene.

Olivia threw her hands up in the air. "Fine! I won't say
or do anything you don't want me to. But Rory can't just get
away with this."

"You know how this grade is, I am not about to become
their entertainment."

"I hear you. But, Isa, you know I've got you, right?"

"Always."

Kam's guesthouse was crowded with bodies. The room
was vibrating with House music and pulsing strobe lights. Isa
felt Olivia squeeze her hand, but before she could squeeze it
back, Rory Lange was standing in front of them.

Isa sidestepped him. "Get out of the way."

Isa wanted to push him but didn't want even that small

11

bit of physical contact. Isa couldn't remember a time when she and Rory hadn't been friends. Last year, when he'd confessed he had a crush on her since middle school, Isa, curious, wondered what it would be like to kiss him. So she did. It was disappointing. And then they'd hung out a few more times because Isa didn't want to accept the fact that it was so disappointing. Yet each time felt worse than the last. When Isa made it clear that there would be no more make-out sessions, the texts began. The first text had been coy: *see anything you like?* But they'd grown in urgency, how he couldn't stop thinking of her, what it did to him, and how much he wanted her to *see it.*

Isa thought if she ignored him long enough he'd grow bored and leave her alone. Instead, he'd escalated.

Isa glared at him. In the few weeks she'd avoided seeing him, he'd grown taller and started wearing his light brown hair slicked back, his face had sharpened, reminding her of a weasel. Isa repeated herself through gritted teeth. "Move."

Rory moved slowly, slinking backwards and grinning at her, a hungry look in his eyes. "Drinks are over there."

Isa ignored him and wedged herself into a space behind the kitchen counter where she plucked two cups from the pile, one for her and one for Olivia. When Rory attempted to get behind the counter, next to Isa, Olivia slid in between them.

Isa watched Rory's face as he clocked Olivia's intense glare. He reared back and put his hand up, the other one clutching his red solo cup to his chest. "Easy, tiger," he said to Olivia, "there's enough to go around."

"No one wants any, so back off." Olivia said and feinted stamping a foot at him, causing him to stumble backwards.

Isa laughed, turned away, grabbed the pitcher closest to her, and poured whatever concoction it was into two cups.

Olivia turned and winked at Isa, making her laugh again.

Rory walked over to Kam. The music was loud, but Olivia and Isa heard Rory shout *fuck those bitches* and Kam yell *forget those holes.*

Anger flooded Isa, burning her from the inside. She turned away so she wouldn't have to look at them. She already regretted letting Delaney talk them into coming. Isa scanned the room then looked at Olivia, "Where's Delaney, I'm gonna kill her."

Olivia smirked and accepted the drink Isa handed her. "Let's go find her."

They made a sweep of the party, weaving in and out of bodies. Isa took a sip of the warm, chemically sweet, green-Appletini mixture spiked with vodka, grimaced, and set it down. Olivia, who had already finished hers, picked it up.

"Don't." Isa warned, "That's a headache waiting to happen." Olivia shrugged and drank it all. "Let's dance."

The electronic thump of the music entered Isa's heart, thrummed through her veins, doing what alcohol never did for her. It relaxed her limbs, loosened her neck and spine, and pulled her away from the room of staring eyes. The beat of the music and Olivia's laughing face spinning around in front of her created a vortex of safety, and Isa slipped into it. No one else was on the floor yet and they were creating a spectacle in the small room, but Isa decided not to care. She'd let it be about this last party, the beginning of the end of high school, dancing with Olivia, and the music. Isa's father was a physics professor, but he loved music more than anything and he'd instilled that love in Isa. He kept a Bob Marley quote on his desk, *One good thing about music, when it hits you, you feel no pain.* Isa decided for the moment to let it be true.

Olivia was in the throes of the best part of being buzzed. That light, happy place before you realize how drunk you are and the merry-go-round begins.

The song changed and shouts of *hell yeahs* and *that's my jam* surged with the music. Suddenly the small dance floor was swarming with bodies. Olivia didn't remember at which point she and Isa became separated. She was dancing with Hunter Logan, who she low-key hated, but he was also the best dancer in their school, and Olivia loved to dance.

Hunter, Rory, and Kam were best friends and saw themselves as top dogs in their school. Olivia and Rory lived a few doors away from each other, were family friends, and had known one another as long as she could remember. Until junior year they had been as close as siblings. But things had changed and now they barely spoke.

Despite Olivia's mixed feelings about Hunter (bad that he was Rory's friend and acted like an ass whenever he was with him, good because best dancer and just being near him made her feel *more*. More exciting, more interested, more aware) she stayed close to him on the dance floor, their bodies in sync.

The heat from his skin released the scent of his soap and Olivia found herself wanting to press her lips against the curve of his throat. Hunter placed his arms loosely around the small of her back, pulling her in even closer. She felt her thighs brush his and desire flared. Soon their bodies were moving together the pulse of his heartbeat against hers. Two songs later, their bodies slick with sweat, Hunter pulled her off the dance floor promising a drink and some air. Instead of heading toward the patio and pool, he guided her upstairs, and she followed him.

Hunter was the only boy Olivia had ever made out with. The first time had been ninth grade during a stirring mortifying game of seven minutes in heaven. Then again when she'd agreed to go to the junior dance with him before their friend group had split up. Sometimes it seemed to Olivia and Isa that they were the only girls in their grade who weren't having sex, and they were fine with it. Yet, Olivia wished things were different. She wished Rory hadn't become a body-snatcher version of himself and that she and Hunter could have developed something. It seemed impossible now. Kam and Rory had become horrible, and Hunter was grouped in with them. She hadn't expected to spend five minutes with Hunter tonight, and yet, here they were alone in a room, and all she wanted to do was press her body against his.

Olivia registered the stocked cooler in the bedroom, the pop and fizz when he opened the can of beer, the bitter taste as she drank it, grateful for how cold it was against her dry throat. She was aware of Hunter taking the can from her, finishing it, holding her gaze with his.

"You're so pretty." He said it simply. Without smiling, his eyes roamed her face. He leaned in again and kissed her. She stood still, lost in her reaction to his touch; the burn on her skin where his fingers trailed against it, the shudder of her body when he pressed his lips against the space between her neck and her shoulder and then again across her clavicle and then lower still. She felt his fingers fumble with her bra and she helped him by reaching behind him and loosening the clasp herself. She felt the chill of the air-conditioned room against her skin. His lips were on her breasts, moving gently until his tongue was on the end of her nipple. She arched her body up and back, almost frantic with feeling. He held her with one arm, his other hand moving over her until he heard her breath catch. He was still fully dressed, and she longed for the heat of his skin against hers and began to lift his shirt over his head when she heard a commotion downstairs. Someone yelled "Cops!" and then she heard the sound of doors slamming and the thud of hurried footsteps.

Hunter helped her back into her clothes. Her cheeks burned as sobriety took the place of lust. He kissed her once, winked at her, and left.

She found Isa on the landing.

"Where have you been?"

"With Hunter."

"That's interesting."

Olivia rolled her eyes, "It's whatever."

"Someone thought the cops rolled up, but it was a false alarm."

"I don't feel so great."

"Let's get out of here."

Olivia felt nauseous from the boozy mixture she'd chugged and confused about how good her body had felt against Hunter's. All she wanted to do was get home and take a shower. She put her arm through Isa's as they made their way back to the car. "Did Delaney ever show?"

"No." Isa said, "Her mom made her babysit."

"She sucks."

Isa laughed and Olivia leaned against her as they walked back up the hill.

16

CHAPTER 2
December 2024

"I just don't understand why?" Beth Ainsworth tried to keep the plaintive tone tamped down. She was sure it would annoy Emmett as much as it had his father.

"I told you, Mom, it was interfering with my schoolwork."

"Ok, so it's a good thing you quit?"

"Yeah, I guess."

"It won't affect your standing?"

"I didn't get a scholarship for wrestling—I just made the team. It doesn't matter."

Beth tried not to obsess over the dullness of Emmett's response. "So how is everything else? Are you still seeing that girl? Marilyn? Marion?"

"Monica."

"Monica! Like Courtney Cox! Oh, why did I say that, now I'll think her name is Courtney!"

That elicited a small snort from Emmett, and Beth thought that was a good sign. Maybe her son wasn't as depressed as he sounded. "Eight days until Christmas break, I ordered dinner from your favorite caterer."

"Thanks, Mom."

Beth panicked again at the flatness of his thanks. He was

usually such a sweet boy, always so grateful for the smallest things. He sounded like he was underwater, his voice bubbling from a great distance. "So!" Beth exclaimed brightly, "Is Monica going with you to the Shore after Christmas?"

"Yeah, with a few of our friends."

"Has your father met her?" She tried not to sniff.

"No. He won't be there."

"No difference to me if he's there or not."

"I know, but he won't be."

"So, you'll have the place to yourselves."

"Yeah."

"Don't break anything. Or do. Actually, I don't care." She was rewarded with another slight snort.

"We won't break anything. And I'm making those animals chip in to tip the housekeeping staff."

"Is Monica an animal?" Beth tried not to sound alarmed. She'd met her once. Seemed nice. Pretty in a plain way. Not the type she thought her son would go for.

Emmett laughed outwardly this time. "No mom, I'm talking about the guys. Monica's awesome. It was her idea actually, about the tip. She thinks about things like that."

"Like what?"

"Tipping people. Workers aren't scenery to her."

"Workers aren't scenery to me either, Emmett! I treat my housekeeper like gold. Ask anyone. And as far as restaurants go, I always tip twenty percent no matter how subpar the service is!"

"That isn't what I meant—."

"Well, it's what you said."

"I was talking about the guys at school, and my friends from home. Monica's different. Not spoiled."

"You're not spoiled!"

"Forget it, Mom."

"Well, you're not!"

"Okay, Mom, I've gotta go. See you in a week."

"Wait—Emmett..."

He waited silently. Beth felt a desperate need to get some kind of reassurance from him. Her anxiety was skyrocketing. Why hadn't he mentioned his GPA?

"Don't worry, Mom. I'm fine. Everything's fine. Now that I've left the team I'll get more sleep. I've just been tired."

Beth knew Emmett was placating her, she could hear the flatness in his voice, and she just wanted to say something, anything to lift it. The trouble was, she couldn't find the words. "Okay, Son, see you in a week."

"Bye, Mom."

Beth sat in the silence and thought of all the questions she wanted to ask. What's wrong, how can I help, what happened to you, what should I do? All questions she knew would flatten Emmett's responses even more. All questions she was afraid couldn't be answered, or if they could, she wouldn't want to hear them.

CHAPTER 3

Olivia's mother, Indira Birnbaum-Irizzary, ran hard, "Zombie" by The Cranberries blasting through her ear pods. She began the descent down her road. Automatically as she ran past the Lange house she turned her head. It was decked out in Christmas revelry, giant nutcrackers at attention, their austerity frightening rather than welcoming. *Kind of like her former best friend,* Indira couldn't help thinking. Then she snickered. So engaged was she in her own snark that she nearly collided with Erica Lange, who seemed to magically appear from her driveway as if Indira's thoughts had conjured her. Erica seemed just as shocked and possibly dismayed to see Indira.

"Indira!" Erica plastered a smile on her face, "You're certainly full speed ahead!"

"Oh!" Indira stopped short and fought to catch her breath. "Was...um...noticing your Christmas decorations. Festive!"

Erica smiled a bit more widely and spoke in what Indira recognized as her fake voice, "Thank you! They're new! Felt like I needed some extra cheer, Rory is so focused on making weight for Saturday's match he's behaving like a bear." Then Erica surprised Indira by placing her slender manicured hand on Indira's arm and using her normal voice. "I just can't believe our babies are seniors!"

Indira felt the familiar warmth of years of friendship course through her in spite of herself. "Some days it feels like a lifetime. Some days, like a heartbeat." She immediately cursed herself for resorting to platitudes. Even accurate ones.

Erica removed her hand from Indira's forearm, "It was nice to literally bump into you." she laughed, "We need to catch up soon. Glass of wine?"

Indira played along, "Sure."

Indira decided to do another lap before going home. She picked up a slow jog to regulate her breath, and thought about her encounter with Erica. They'd known each other for almost two decades. Had been as close as sisters, or so she'd thought. Until Erica set her sights on a social ladder Indira had zero desire to climb. They had been a tight group of four, Indira, Erica, Joyce, and Margie. Forming a community during the messy, frantic, sublime years of early motherhood.

Indira made her way back up the hill, wondering at those women they had been and if they bore any resemblance to what they had become. Inexplicably, she found herself turning left at the top of the hill, taking herself out of the way of her usual run so she could pass the pool club where the four of them met, the sparkling place where their children became close friends. In December it looked forlorn, shuttered behind iron gates, the area desolate, so different from summertime. For years, Margie had declared it their *happy place*. Indira used to cringe at that description, thinking it sounded corny and kind of smug, but now it made her nostalgic.

A random memory flashed like a scene from a movie, the four of them sitting at the shallow end of the pool, watching their rising kindergarteners splash around. Erica's slightly older daughter Bailey (Rory's Irish twin as Erica was fond of saying) was taking diving lessons at the deep end.

"Bailey!" Erica yelled, unfortunately right in Indira's ear since they were sitting next to each other. "Point your toes! Give me a ten!"

Bailey startled, broke her diving stance, and looked over, squinting against the glare of the sun.

Indira could see all the way from their side of the pool the look of determined rebelliousness Bailey shot her mother.

"A ten Bailey! You've got this!" Erica shouted again.

Bailey gave her mother one last look then cannonballed right into the pool. The splash of her sturdy little body sent a shock wave across the pool and like an equal and opposite reaction, Erica was on her feet and marching over to the diving coach, her sleek, honey-toned ponytail high on her head, designer sunglasses flashing in the sunlight.

Indira watched with interest as the swim coach hastened away from the diving board and went to intercept Erica, speaking loudly enough for Indira to hear her on their side of the pool. "Mrs. Lange, please let us handle the instruction."

"Aren't you having them dive?"

"Yes."

"Then why did Bailey cannonball?"

Indira saw Bailey surface and expertly tread water while watching her mother. Her expression, Indira thought, could best be described as mutinous.

"It was swimmer's choice." Then she turned back to Bailey and yelled, "Excellent cannonball!"

Indira knew (because Erica had told her) that Erica tipped well because she wanted her children to have the best of the best. Indira wondered if that included protecting children from the ambition of their own mothers.

Indira turned her attention back to the pool and gasped. Delaney (six months older than Olivia and tall for her age) was moments away from drowning Olivia with her excessive hugging. Olivia was tiny, dimpled, and smiley, so Indira understood Delaney's enthusiasm, but Delaney's mother Margie seemed blissfully unaware of Delaney's antics; she was too busy giving Joyce a rundown of her responsibilities as newly minted class mom. Indira had noticed that Joyce's eyes had been glazed over pretty much the entire time Margie was speaking.

Indira jumped into the pool, unwrapped Delaney's arms from Olivia's neck and plopped Olivia onto her hip.

Instantly Delaney began scrambling up, trying to climb onto Indira's shoulders shouting, "Chicken Fight! Chicken Fight!"

Out of the corner of her eye, Indira saw Joyce jut her chin at Margie and say, "You might want to do something about that."

Margie shrugged and turned back to Joyce. "Indira's got it. Anyway—I've reorganized the entire..."

"Seriously, you may want to take care of that."

Indira really hoped Margie would listen to Joyce, but couldn't add her own two cents because she was trying to manage Delaney who had made it onto one shoulder while Olivia yelled, "Get off my mommy!"

Meanwhile Rory tried to convince Isa to climb onto his shoulders to take on Delaney and Indira, but Isa was now dog paddling as fast as her little legs could kick away from him and toward Joyce. Joyce bent down and scooped Isa out of the pool and onto her lap. Isa settled against her mother, turned her face from Margie's irritated stare, and wailed, "I don't want to chicken fight."

Joyce tightened her hold on her daughter, "You don't have to baby." Then she looked pointedly at Margie, "I don't think Indira wants to chicken fight either."

Delaney's small but mighty fingers were seeking purchase in Indira's topknot of curls.

Indira remembered how Margie had ignored the chaos with an impressive level of self-centeredness and how Erica had returned from the deep end of the pool, took one look at what was going on, and shouted, "Delaney Mary O'Shaugnessey! Climb down this moment!"

"Chicken fight!" Delaney bellowed.

"No!" Olivia screamed.

Indira had been exceedingly grateful to Erica who had jumped into the pool and lifted Delaney like a loaf of bread, deftly prying her fingers from Indira's hair with only a minimal amount of pulling.

Margie jumped from the side of the pool where she'd been sitting with Joyce and pushed her way gracelessly (to be fair, Indira thought, it was difficult to stride gracefully in knee deep water) over to Erica who unceremoniously dumped Delaney into Margie's arms.

Margie transferred her daughter to one hip and glared at Erica. "That was unnecessary."

Erica looked at her imperviously. "Actually, it was quite necessary."

"How about you handle your kids and I'll handle mine."

"Sure. As long as you do. Handle her."

Indira winced as Margie's face colored with anger. Margie drew herself up and pressed closer to Erica.

Indira however was used to circumventing toddler fights and realized she could use the same tactics here. "Who wants watermelon?"

"I do!" Delaney screamed from Margie's arms.

Margie glared once more at Erica who held a steady gaze before turning away.

They clambered from the pool and Indira remembered the amused look Joyce gave her and how they'd exchanged an eye roll before settling themselves in the shade of a linden tree where Indira happily handed out large slices of watermelon from a cooler.

Indira thought about that moment and how it rolled into one of the many, many days they'd spent together. How the proximity of their homes, and the close age of their children led to a decade and a half of friendship and how different things would be when June came and went and that connection dissolved as easily as it began.

Indira finished the additional loop she'd needed to recover from her surprise encounter with Erica and once again ran down her hill, this time when she passed Erica's house she kept her focus straight ahead.

Once inside she instinctively checked for Olivia's backpack and saw it sitting exactly where she'd dropped it yesterday. Indira forced herself to ignore the skydive sensation in her belly. She didn't have time to drag her daughter out of bed. In less than a year Olivia would be away at school and Indira would be an empty nester. How she hated that expression and yet she had no other way to reference it. Abandoned procreator? Finally-free progenitor? Indira didn't think she could handle another whole semester of senioritis. She had tried telling herself it was about time Olivia started acting like a teenager instead of the hyper-responsible mini adult she'd always been, but it was so out of character that Indira worried there was something else going on.

Isa had arrived early enough to get a coveted parking spot close to the gym entrance. She turned off the ignition and sank against her headrest for a moment. December cloud cover washed the day of color. Isa sighed and felt the shakiness of her breath inside her chest as though she'd just emerged from a violent crying jag. Yet she hadn't cried. She never cried.

Isa's phone trembled against her dashboard and a picture flared. She grabbed her phone, swiped away the repulsive image, and with a few practiced taps, immediately blocked him again. Isa now lived in a perpetual state of tamped-down rage.

Despite telling Olivia she would handle it, Isa didn't know what to do. She didn't want this to become a public drama, and she knew she couldn't turn to any adults because they would just make everything worse. Anything to do with sex and social media freaked them out. If her parents knew what Rory was sending her they would lose their minds and make a gigantic issue out of it. They would want to *sit down* with Rory's parents they would want to make it a *thing*. They still looked at everything from the lens of their own teenage years when Madonna was considered radical, and they worried about *girls' reputations*. But more than that, Isa knew it would fill her parents with shame and embarrassment, and the idea of causing that made it difficult for Isa to swallow or breathe. Her parents were careful about how they lived their lives. They protected their reputations fiercely and they raised her to do the same. It was implicit that being a Black family in a white community meant holding themselves to the highest of standards with no margin for error. If they discovered she was involved in anything this sordid it would crush them. And that would crush her.

Someone banged on her window and Isa jumped. She looked up in a moment of panic, it was just Delaney snapping her gum and laughing.

Isa made a face, but she was relieved to have a distraction. She opened the car door and the cold morning air rushed over her.

Delaney as usual was impossibly chic, wearing a pair of thrifted Dior baggy leather pants in dark green, thrifted Louboutin sneakers, and a sweatshirt from Target she'd expertly tailored herself. She didn't bother with a jacket despite the cold.

"Sweatpants, Isa?"

Isa shrugged. "Comfy."

"You don't even have gym."

"So?"

Delaney rolled her eyes, expertly made up with a thin line of green glitter, her halo of red gold curls giving her a deceptively angelic look. "You and Olivia. This place is a living hell, you could both give me a little fashion head."

Isa laughed.

"Party at Kam's this weekend. You going?"

"Nah."

"What's up with you?"

Isa shrugged. "Maybe I don't like bad music or people that suck."

Rory Lange blasted past them in his Range Rover, Yo Gotti's *Down in the DM* blaring.

"Speak of the devil." Delaney said sliding her arm through Isa's. "Douchey car, douchey music, douchey boy."

Rory Lange congratulated himself on his expert maneuver into a prime spot in front of the gym. He saw Isa and Delaney's heads swivel at the sound of his music pumping, he felt a surge of satisfaction that Isa's gaze landed in time to witness his smooth driving skills.

He felt the girls' eyes on him as he made a show of jumping out and greeting Hunter and Kam. The requisite chest bump and one-armed embrace was more aggressive and pronounced for the benefit of the girls. In sync, athletic bags over their shoulders, they loped toward the gym, chests out and eyes hooded as they passed the girls.

"Morning, Baby." Rory winked at Isa as he walked by.

"Fuckboy wannabes." Delaney taunted as the boys sauntered away. Isa laughed. Rory felt his neck and ears flush red.

Once inside the stifling heat of the locker room, after Rory pulled his jacket off and shoved it angrily into his locker, he noticed Hunter's phone lying on the bench. Hunter was facing the other way listening to Kam regale everyone with details of his last hookup.

Delaney's comment rang in Rory's ears, the way Isa had snickered. A lifetime ago Isa, Olivia, and Delaney had been his best friends, as close as family, now they'd turned on him, went on and on about *safe spaces*. They were too hypocritical to notice their radical, one-sided ideas had left him feeling isolated, disliked, targeted by the narrowing slits of their eyes and the flaring of hate in their nostrils.

Rory picked up Hunter's phone, punched in Hunter's passcode (all zeros), then went to camera and searched October 2022. There it was. The screenshot from the hookup video with Olivia.

Hunter had shown the picture to Rory the night it was taken and Rory had thought about it many times since then. Every time Olivia snubbed him or looked right through him he'd thought of it. Olivia with her back arched, Hunter hovering powerfully over her.

Rory felt a surge of rage. It was probably Olivia who had turned Isa against him. Olivia was always acting like she was better than him. She wasn't. With her busted up house and her stupid hippie-mom. Her dad was cool and had that whole grew-up-in-the-Bronx-Puerto-Rican thing going for him, but he drove a shitty Mazda and Olivia didn't even have her own car. She was always bumming rides. Rory thought about how he hated the entire Birnbaum-Irrizary family because he *used* to love them and now they seemed so far away. Without thinking it through he posted the picture on Hunter's snap and felt an instant release so good he felt intoxicated.

Suddenly the locker room burst into shouts and whistles. The guys were looking at Hunter and crowding around someone's phone.

Rory panicked for a second but calmed himself and handed Hunter his phone, "You're welcome."

Kam slapped Hunter's back, "Holding out on us, Brah?"

Hunter grabbed his phone, and his cheeks turned red. "Dude!" He quickly deleted the image.

Kam leaned in and whispered to Hunter, "That was a hot one dude—five flames!"

Hunter glared at him and looked around, "Shut up, man. We're not supposed to talk about it..."

Kam shrugged, "You already got your points for it—no one's gonna know, they'll just think it was a hookup. Play it cool."

Hunter glared at Rory, "That was messed up."

Rory clapped his hand on Hunter's shoulder, "Relax, bruh, it's not a big deal. Catch you losers later, got a meeting with Coach."

Kam pulled his pants down and thrust his jock at Rory.

Rory smirked and made his way toward Coach Walker's office, checking that his phone was still zipped into his pants pocket.

Rory tried to batten down the tightening of excitement in his groin and the flood of shame in his stomach. The shame was primitive, the first sensation he could remember. The tightening and excitement was newer, since puberty, but it flared often. Consequently, excitement and shame had become tangled together in his body, and one inadvertently elicited the other. Rory was aware of the sensations in a fleeting way, the same way he was aware that he was inhaling and exhaling. He tapped his phone again, absently reassuring himself it was still there, and entered Coach's office.

"Hey, Coach."

Coach Walker looked up from his desk and smiled at Rory. "My man! Right on time."

Coach Walker was easy for Rory to idolize. Still in his early 30's, he was adult enough to garner respect, but not old enough to fall into the dad category. He had a typical wrestler's build that hadn't yet gone to fat. Coach Walker was good looking in a way that guys appreciated: disarming grin, sly eyes, nose that had been busted a couple of times, and a jaw reminiscent of every cartoon superhero. His dating profile stated that he was: *White, Christian, Athletic, and looking for Love.* And he got the ladies. He'd shown Rory the women he'd matched with on dating apps, handed Rory his phone, so Rory could decide which ones to swipe right on.

It was a powerful feeling, one Rory would think of at night as he read the grade group chat or checked Instagram. As soon as Rory scrolled through comments or searched the flurry of pictures posted, he would get an odd sensation of himself growing smaller, and the space around him growing larger. The shrinking sensation was happening with greater frequency and it troubled Rory. He wondered if it was a residual effect of too much Molly, or if in fact, he was going crazy. Rory took his usual seat and waited for Coach to look up again.

Coach pushed his chair back and grinned, "What's good?"

"Just...chillin." Rory tried not to look at Coach's phone, so he wouldn't seem too eager.

Instead of handing over his phone Coach leaned back in his chair, his mouth pursed in what Rory had come to know as his concerned face. "Everything Ok, Lange? You seem—out of sorts."

Coach's office was the one place he felt understood. Every coach talked about the importance of valor and integrity on and off the field. Rory understood that the attributes that made you a great player were the same ones that made you a great man. But Coach Walker was the only one who made Rory feel he was truly achieving greatness. Coach believed in Rory, and that made Rory believe in himself. That's what he wanted to focus on this morning, his prowess. His manliness. All the things Coach instilled in him. He didn't like that he seemed rattled enough for Coach to notice.

"Nah. Just some bitch—"

"Careful, we respect the ladies."

"As long as the respect is mutual."

Coach nodded like he understood. "Tough weekend?"

Rory relaxed, "I did okay."

Coach smiled long and slow. "You're my star, can't have you losing your edge."

"Never."

"I'm counting on you." This time it was Coach who looked at Rory's phone.

Rory felt the tension slide away. What mattered most was his relationship with Coach. And the game.

Rory smiled, eager to show him that weekend's conquest. He was expecting to win an epic amount of points. As he reached for his phone images flashed unbidden into his mind. His last hook up with Isa, all those months ago. The way she'd become so distant. Coach had warned him about this, how girls sometimes pretended to hold back so the guy would have to fight for her. Coach explained that getting a girl aroused was like a reversal in wrestling, by using a defensive position to negate your opponent's advantage in order to gain control of the situation. You could use their bodies against them. Girls were easily aroused once they relaxed, so he applied all the techniques that worked so well with the countless other girls he'd hooked up with. He felt different with Isa, not just because they'd been close friends for so long, but he'd really liked her and he was sure she liked him, it should have been easy. But when he caressed her, gently, his touch light, his whispers sweet, she'd pushed him away, and when he tried talking to her, trying to make her understand how right she was for him, she called him cocky and entitled.

Maybe he was cocky. Why shouldn't he be? His grades were strong, he was in the top 5 percent of his class, but he never got credit for that. It was expected of him. He was white and male and lived in a high-income zip code. He got it, he was privileged. But what about the pressures it came with? What about the hours he put in on the mat? He had to beat out all the other privileged white guys and then take on the underprivileged black and brown guys. He deserved to be cocky, but he bristled at entitled. He worked harder than anyone and got less recognition than he deserved. Isa's rejection stung. He needed to forget about her and focus on all the action he *was* getting. Keep his head in the game.

Coach glanced again at Rory's phone, less subtle this time. Rory recognized the need in his glance. "Got some plays."

Rory watched Coach carefully, saw the telltale flare in his

eyes, the slight parting of his lips. The way his hand passed over his jaw. "Yeah? Anything we haven't seen before?"

"New plays, new results."

Coach smiled. "Results I'll like?"

"Money, Coach."

Rory felt a power surge through him. These were the moments he lived for, the mat, the game, and this office. He could be himself here. Didn't have to worry about every word, every action, even the music he listened to. He couldn't be a "poser white boy" who liked rap and he couldn't be a misogynist who "didn't get" how lyrics subjugated women. They were just lyrics! Just songs! He didn't write or produce or sing them. He just listened to them along with millions of other people.

Four years ago, the guys he looked up to didn't have to contend with all this shit. They were the leaders of the school. They called the shots. Suddenly, he was the bad guy. He'd done everything he needed to so he could rise to the top of the pack and all of a sudden the rules had changed. Coach got that. He understood. They didn't talk about it. But he could tell, from little things Coach said, that he got it. When he was in this office, Rory didn't feel small or confused. He didn't feel blamed for just being himself. He couldn't change the fact that he was white or a guy or had wealthy parents and he wouldn't want to if he could.

Coach Walker leaned back, "We got a big week coming up, Lange. You ready?"

"Ready, Coach."

Coach Walker nodded his head and Rory felt a surge of confidence.

"Alright, Lange, show me what's up."

Rory smiled and passed Coach his phone. Playbook time.

Isa was standing at her locker when the snap came through. Her first thought was how disappointing it was that Hunter was apparently as big an ass as Rory was. Her second thought was horror when she looked closer and realized it was Olivia in the grainy image. She quickly screenshotted it before it disappeared. He'd sent it to the grade group chat. Her heart raced and her skin burned as if she was suddenly running a fever. She forced herself to look at the picture again, something about it (other than its existence) bothered her, but she didn't have time to figure out what it was, she needed to warn Olivia that it was out there.

Olivia was still lying in bed when she heard Indira running up the steps. Olivia began praying to multiple deities. She started with Jesus, because, well, habit. *Please God. Do not let my mother come in here.* Then she moved on to her Tita's favorite, *O Holy St. Anthony, gentlest of Saints, do NOT let my mother come in here, please let her go into her room, please please please.* For good measure, and in deference to her Jewish grandmother who practiced Buddhism, Olivia squeezed her eyes shut and whispered to Kuan Yin, the Goddess of compassion, mercy, and healing, *Through seeing the Compassionate Mother in all beings, may we attain full awakening, and please let my mom go straight to her room.*

It worked! The pipes rumbled signifying her mother was in the shower. The frantic footsteps Olivia had heard were not to drag her out of bed, but she did need to get up and get ready so she could catch a ride before her mother left. Her phone pinged and Olivia saw a text appear from Isa.

this was on hunters snap

Olivia stared at the image of herself with her head thrown back, Hunter above her. Her breasts bare. It was grainy and no one would really be able to identify her because her face was pointed upward and away from the lens. But she recognized herself. It had to have been from that party when she and Hunter had hooked up in Kam's guestroom.

Anger rushed through her, setting her body on fire. She would kill him. How could she have been so stupid? She'd thought she liked him, thought he liked her. They'd even talked a few times since that night, in the hallways, or while they were waiting for class to start. He'd texted her multiple times about homework, and they'd had conversations over text, about the homework, but somehow it always felt like they were talking about other things too, about themselves in a way. She'd thought they might be building something, and she hadn't wanted to talk about it with anyone because it felt like it was theirs alone and strangely intimate. Now she was glad she hadn't told anyone, not even Isa. She felt so stupid. The shame was palpable—it had a taste, bitter on her tongue.

Olivia closed her eyes so she wouldn't have to look at it anymore. Her first rush of desire captured and distributed for the cheap thrill of every jerk in her grade. She knew with a sick certainty that no amount of praying would undo its existence. Some things were too much for saints or God to fix.

Olivia had no choice but to walk to school. She'd let her mother leave the house without asking for a ride. It was almost impossible to get out of bed and face going to school but the idea of lying there all day thinking about it seemed worse. So she forced herself to stand under the shower until the water ran cold. She blowdried her hair for warmth rather than style, put on layers, and trudged up her hill, thinking about the existence of the snap. Olivia was glad Isa had seen it and grabbed it. When she went to Hunter's to see for herself, it was already gone. Olivia hated Hunter for putting it out there. But she was glad she knew. Olivia felt another creep of shame, all those moments she'd thought about that hook-up, the secret hope that it would happen again, how the two of them couldn't seem to keep their eyes off each other in class. How stupid she'd been to fall for it. There was nothing she could do about it now. She'd just force herself to forget, not care. It was just a snap.

She heard a car pulling over and turned quickly her body poised to fight or flee. Then she relaxed when she saw who it was and smiled. "Hey!"

"Get in lady." Bailey said.

Olivia climbed into Bailey's jeep relieved to get out of the cold.

Bailey pulled back into traffic and smiled, "What's up?"

"Fuckery."

"That bad?"

Olivia slid her eyes sideways. "Have you forgotten?"

"I've had plenty of reminders. Can't wait for the dorms to reopen."

"That bad?" Olivia mimicked.

"Pure fuckery."

"Where are you going?"

"Yoga."

Olivia shot Bailey a surprised look. "I thought you hate yoga."

"I do. But I hate being trapped in the house with Erica and her relentless questions more."

"I'm going with you."

"What about school?"

"What about it?"

Bailey scanned Olivia's body. "You're wearing jeans, dude."

Olivia shrugged. "I'll sit in the lobby and read my book."

"What are you reading?"

"*We Are Completely Beside Ourselves*."

"Any good?"

"Yeah."

"What's it about?"

"A girl who's raised with a chimpanzee as a sibling."

Bailey laughed. "Sounds preferable, honestly."

Olivia gave her a look. Being Rory's sister was even worse than being ex-best friends. "I'm sure it does."

They were approaching the turn for the high school and Bailey looked at Olivia. Olivia shook her head, grimacing.

"You really want to come to Yoga?" Bailey asked.

"Anything's better than that place."

Bailey grinned and made an abrupt U-turn, causing three drivers to lean on their horns. Olivia was pretty sure some mom was whipping out her own phone to post a complaint about them on the local moms-group. *Teach your teens to respect the rules of the road!* Posted with a blurry pic of Bailey's car, which the mom would have snapped while behind the wheel of her Range Rover.

"Isn't the studio in town?" Olivia asked as Bailey sped in the opposite direction.

"I just realized there are other ways to escape Erica than yoga."

Olivia laughed, "Your mom's not so bad. You should hear mine in the morning freaking out because I might be late. For *homeroom!*"

Bailey rolled her eyes, "There is no way you can compare an Indira freak-out to an Erica freak-out and you know it. Hungry?"

"Starving."

"Rockies?"

"Fuck, yeah!"

Bailey laughed, blasted St. Vincent's song, "Savior," and stepped on the gas toward their favorite deli.

Olivia watched the winter landscape rush by. "It feels like forever since we've done this."

"You ok, Liv? You don't seem like yourself."

Olivia wasn't herself. Or maybe she was. Maybe this flat feeling was her new self. But she didn't know how to explain that to Bailey. So she just nodded. Then she looked over and gave Bailey a sly look, "Floor it."

Bailey had been the first one to get her license. Isa was the next oldest, so she always rode shotgun while Olivia and Rory had sat in the back, thrilled to be in a car without parents. Back then going to Rockies Deli was tantamount to jet setting around the world. Olivia closed her eyes and remembered Rory the way he was then. He must have used the same shampoo as Bailey because they both carried a vague scent of green apple, except Rory also smelled of weather, air in the fall, sweat in summer, and fire in winter. She'd known Rory her entire life. She couldn't remember a time without him.

Olivia resisted the impulse to turn around and look at the back seat. As if she could watch an old movie of Rory and her back there, his thumb covering hers, as they played round after round of thumby-war. He always won by swinging his thumb around and capturing hers. She'd howl that he cheated, and he'd get that mischievous slow smile which made her laugh. Back then she forgave him everything because of that smile. Everyone did. Now Olivia knew better. Her stomach clenched and Olivia told herself it was just hunger. Olivia thought about the Rockies menu and decided on a bacon egg and cheese with a whipped vanilla cappuccino. Bailey was perhaps the one person who could help them, the one who could tell them what to do. She always seemed to have the answers.

Not only that, but she had the guts to do something about it. Yet it wasn't only Olivia's story to tell and she couldn't betray Isa. Olivia watched the road loom up in front of them and wished for the hundredth time that morning that she could close her eyes and everything would disappear.

CHAPTER 4

The week before the winter holidays was always frantic at the high school. There were concerts and sporting events to attend, holiday parties, club meetings, and exams to cram for. For the seniors and their parents it was bittersweet.

Joyce Davies was walk-running toward the auditorium, still dressed in her work suit and heels, her computer bag banging against her leg. It would be Isa's last holiday concert and she didn't want to miss a moment of it.

"No running in the halls, lady!"

Joyce turned to see Margie coming from an adjacent hallway. "Hey, Marge. Are we late?"

"Nope."

Joyce slowed and took a breath, "The halls are so empty I thought I was late."

"You're early, it starts at 7."

"Oh!" Joyce stopped abruptly. "It's always been 6."

"We changed it this year." Margie and Joyce were now walking in time, Joyce's heels clicking against the tiled floor, Margie's Tory Burch flats cushioned and silent.

"Huh."

"You must have missed the emails and texts. You should download our district whatsapp."

"I'd rather stick a fork in my eye."

Margie laughed, "We'll get good seats at least."

They walked toward the gymnasium where the thump of bodies against mats and a piercing whistle echoed through the hallways. The gym doors opened and Coach Walker stepped out, his whistle glinting in the fluorescent light, an ever-present clipboard in his hands.

Coach Walker smiled at them. "Hey, Margie, Mrs. Davies, nice to see you both."

Margie stopped so Joyce did as well. Margie smiled back, "Hey Coach. Getting some air?"

Coach gave what Margie frequently referred to as his blonde George Clooney look, dipping his head, looking up through tousled locks, and grinning. "Sometimes it's hard to think in there and I'm working up stats."

Margie nodded, "I'm sure Rory Lange is at the top of your list."

Joyce looked at her watch.

Coach must have clocked her impatience because he turned his smile toward her. "We'll miss Isa next year. Girls softball won't be the same without her."

Joyce smiled the same smile she used for opposing attorneys, polite. "I'm sure Isa will miss everyone as well."

Margie placed her hand on Coach's arm for a brief second. He turned toward her, the bashful grin back in place.

"Coach," Margie leaned in conspiratorially, "how are we looking for states? Cal said he has high hopes."

Cal was the athletic director and no one except Margie was on a first name basis with him. Coach called him Boss and Joyce never called him anything.

Coach nodded. "A lot depends on the January match. That's why we're going so hard in there."

Margie dipped her head in recognition, "Cal thinks Rory

will bring us to states, says he's following in Emmett Ainsworth's footsteps. And from what I hear you've done a great job of team building this year, they seem tighter than ever."

The cheerleaders had a nickname for Coach Walker. They called him Ice. Named after a heartthrob fantasy character in a series they all loved whose eyes were blue and cold as ice.

Joyce no longer seemed impatient, but looked increasingly uncomfortable as Coach Walker and Margie stood gazing at one another.

"Margie," Coach said, dipping his head and pinning her with his eyes, "You have no idea how much your words mean to me. I've worked hard to make sure my guys understand that although they go man to man on the mat, it's the team bond that will carry us to the states. To know that effort is recognized…" Coach placed his palm on Margie's arm, "Words can't express how that makes me feel."

"It's true dedication on your part as well as hard work from our boys. If we get to the states again we all win." Margie turned to Joyce, "As Board President, I can't express how much that means for our district." Margie winked at Joyce, "and our brand."

Joyce looked confused. "Brand?"

"Our schools are our brand and we are the best of the best. That's what drives property values. You can thank Coach for his part in that."

Joyce looked at Margie. "I think we should get to the auditorium."

Margie smiled and clapped her hands, "You're right! Vamanos!"

Joyce gave an almost imperceptible eye roll and was about to begin walking away but Margie had turned back to Coach Walker.

PINNED

"Coach, for the team bonding dinner at the Connovers—you know Ginny Connover and I are good friends, right?"

Coach nodded enthusiastically, "Of course. And Kam is a true leader on this team."

Margie's voice rose an octave, "He's a powerhouse on those mats."

Coach agreed, "Strongest in his weight class."

"Anyways, I've worked it out with some of our local vendors, and not only will they be sponsoring the tournament, they're also sending food for the party, and I was hoping I could count on you to be there for the delivery and set up. I'd do it myself, but Delaney would kill me. She said they don't want moms there and they especially don't want school-board-president-moms there!"

Coach beamed, "Of course. How very generous of you! Thank you, Margie!"

"Oh, they've donated! It's very generous of them!"

"Well, I'll be sure to thank them." He grinned, "And thank you as well, for all you do."

"Of course!"

Joyce cleared her throat, "Tik tok, Marge."

The halls were beginning to fill with people, and Joyce began walking so fast Margie practically had to jog to keep up.

"Joyce, don't worry, we have plenty of time!"

Joyce looked at her, "Don't you think it's a little weird?"

"What?" Margie looked genuinely surprised.

"Coach Walker having all those parties at the Connovers?"

"Not at all! You just aren't involved in boy's sports—I mean obviously I'm not either. Delaney hates sweating and the twins aren't showing any athletic prowess, I'm sad to say—but as school board president I keep tabs on our athletic teams and our wrestling team is stellar! Honestly, when Emmett

Ainsworth graduated I despaired we'd lose ground, but Rory Lange and Kam Connover are just as good, thank God they're in different weight classes or…"

"I don't care about wrestling stats, Marge. I'm talking about Walker being over at the Connover's for all those parties."

"You misunderstand! He's not there for the house parties! He's only there for team bonding parties."

"It's a slippery slope, Marge."

"Joyce! All the towns have these team bonding parties. We just happen to be the crème de la crème. Best coach, best wrestlers, and the best parents! It's so generous of the Connovers to let the team use their guesthouse. Ginnifer said Coach has them clean up after themselves. Her housekeeper compliments them!"

"There is never any supervision there. If I didn't trust Isa as much as I do, I wouldn't allow her to go to those parties."

Margie gasped, "Joyce! That would be social suicide! Isa, Delaney, and Olivia are the most popular girls in the grade. Of course they're going to Kam's parties. Nothing bad happens there! We have good kids!"

This time Joyce rolled her eyes right to Margie's face.

"Anyways, Coach isn't at all the parties! He's only there for the team bonding ones, and they're on school nights! The whole thing is over by 9PM!"

"Like I said, Marge. Slippery slope."

"Look, we're not trying to get athletic placements for our kids, Isa's a shoo in for valedictorian and Delaney's—well she's Delaney—but Rory, Kam, and Hunter, they need those spots at D1 schools—and Coach is the guy to get it for them."

"I hear you, but—."

"Joyce, please *do not* say a word against that man. You have no idea how valuable he is to our district."

Both women were saved from further discussion as Indira and Jimmy Birnbaum-Irrizary intercepted them at the auditorium doors.

Joyce smiled at Indira, a full warm smile. "Indira! It's been too long."

Jimmy bent to kiss Joyce then Margie on the cheek and the four of them walked into the auditorium for the first of the last school events they would ever watch together, strains of "Winter Wonderland" already stirring nostalgia for every parent in attendance. Margie looped her arm through Joyce's. And Joyce, who did not ever do arm looping with anyone other than her husband, allowed it.

CHAPTER 5

Emmett buried himself deeper into his jacket as he walked across campus. The sky felt low and oppressive, and the layers he wore seemed futile against the damp blustery day. He thought about the warmth of the dining hall and picked up his pace. The promise of a steaming cup of terrible coffee with half and half and a mountain of sugar was the only thing keeping him alive.

Emmett walked with his head down against the wind but lifted it once he joined the throng of students hurrying toward their breakfasts. He wondered if he was too late for a chocolate croissant (they were the first to go) or his other favorite, cheese and pineapple. They weren't as popular, but that meant there were fewer available. He decided to pin his hopes on a chocolate chip muffin, they were purchased in bulk in their cellophane wrappers and could be found as late in the day as 4PM. One of the best things about quitting the wrestling team was eating whatever he wanted whenever he wanted.

Emmett's head turned sharply, he'd caught something from the corner of his eye. There. The familiar shape of a head, dark blonde crew cut, broad shoulders…

Emmett stopped and turned, he felt a terrible vertigo overcome him, his breath quickened, his heart pounded in his ears.

What could Coach be doing on campus? A recruitment meeting? Why hadn't he reached out? Did he even want him to reach out? Emmett's vision blurred, so that all he could see was a tiny pinpoint in front of him, he felt the world tilting.

"Hey, man, you OK?"

Was it Coach asking? No, it was a kid from his History class. His name started with a J—Justin? No Jackson!

"Emmett, Dude, you OK?"

"Yeah man, thanks."

"You sure." Jackson still had his hand on Emmett's arm. Emmett didn't want it there, but he was afraid to pull away. He felt unsteady.

"Yeah, man, I'm good. Just a little light headed—guess I forgot to eat yesterday."

"Ok—I'm headed to class, but I could go back in—"

"Nah, thanks, I'm good now."

Jackson took his hand off his arm and looked him over. "Yeah you don't look as pale, you looked like you saw a ghost, it was freaky."

"Blood sugar."

"OK, man, see you in class later."

"Yeah, thanks."

Emmett searched the area but there was no sign of Coach. Maybe he'd never been here. Maybe Jackson was right, and he'd been seeing shadows that weren't there. Ghosts that lived in his mind.

CHAPTER 6

Keith Lange hustled toward the 6:30 train out of Grand Central. He took a moment to mourn the loss of drink carts, chugging past the spot where his guy used to be. Never mind, he thought, one less drink would help his waistband. It was a lie he told himself every evening, because after his second drink following a heavy dinner, he always had a third, rationalizing that the drink cart was now defunct and he was one down.

His trench coat flapping behind him, Keith scrambled to make the third car, *The New York Post* tucked firmly under his arm. He felt a twinge of pain in his hip, an old sports injury that had developed into arthritis, but he pushed forward, anxious not to be hemmed into a middle seat.

He felt his phone blowing up in his pocket. Erica. Like clockwork, each evening, trying to catch him in that window between the subway and no service once the train propelled him further into the tunnels.

Calculating the risk of facing her passive-aggressive wrath if he didn't answer her, he pulled out his phone and tried to answer as he walked.

Broccoli or green bean as a veg...either is fine

he answered, instead of I DON'T CARE, then ignored the rest of her texts.

He felt a vague satisfaction in being a few minutes late as he ran to catch the train. He wouldn't have service for at least fifteen minutes, a respite from the monotony of hearing a litany of her day: where she'd shopped, whom she'd talked to, Rory's game stats, Bailey's snarky comments. And then she'd repeat every blessed thing at dinner. He knew he was required to respond to every one of her texts or she would later accuse him of ignoring her. And if he let his gaze drift during dinner she'd punish him by setting her lips in a straight line, paste on a wide, fake smile and proclaim loudly that caring for a family and a home must be as boring to hear about as it is to do. Keith felt his phone buzz for the fifth time in a row and thought about throwing himself under the train. He was pretty sure it would be less painful.

Keith made it onto the train and realized the only seat left was the middle of a five-seater. It would be a long, uncomfortable forty minutes. He felt an unreasonable surge of anger at Erica, as though it was somehow her fault he was late. Holding onto his phone he silenced it and shoved his trench coat onto the overhead rack. Then, with a sincere apology, he climbed over the elderly woman and hipster guy filling the rest of the seats, and settled his large frame as comfortably as he could while the other four people shuffled around him.

Keith had just made it out of the jammed up parking lot and was about to rev the engine of his sleek orange Porsche when he saw his neighbor Jimmy Irizarry, tall and athletic, hatless despite the cold, his dark hair shining from the light mist leftover from the earlier rain.

Keith pulled over and waved his hand out of the window, watching until Jimmy caught sight of him, and waved back.

Keith saw Jimmy hesitate, then pick up his stride, his long legs closing the gap toward Keith's car. Keith snickered, he bet Indira forgot to pick Jimmy up. It was ludicrous, Keith thought. They had three drivers in that house and only two cars. Keith had multiple cars, one for each driver and several for himself, cars served different purposes, for instance, he couldn't take this beauty to the golf course, his clubs didn't fit!

"Hey, man, been a while." Keith greeted Jimmy with a wide smile. "Did Indira forget to pick you up?"

Jimmy laughed, "Sort of, I told her I'd walk if she wasn't here, but thanks for the ride."

"Did you just get back in town?"

"Yesterday."

Keith pulled into traffic without looking and a series of horns blared at them. He waved an insincere apology and turned to leer at Jimmy. "Someplace hot?"

"Barcelona. And the temperature is moderate, but it's still winter there."

"You're a lucky son of a bitch."

The two men had been having some version of this conversation for the past fifteen years.

Jimmy shrugged. "It's not as glamorous as it sounds. Long plane rides, and we're holed up in conference rooms all day."

"Yeah, but, the evenings." Keith waggled his sandy eyebrows at Jimmy.

"Long dinners with the same guys we spent all day pitching to."

"The nights then. Come on, brother, throw a guy a bone! I've gotta live vicariously."

"Nah. You'd be sorely disappointed."

Keith shook his head. "All that freedom and you're just wasting it." Then he laughed and clapped Jimmy's thigh.

Keith pulled into Jimmy's driveway. "It was good to see you, Buddy. It's been too long."

Jimmy smiled, "Yeah man, good to see you too."

Keith watched Jimmy walk to the side door of his house. The only home on the block that hadn't been renovated beyond recognition, kitchen and bathrooms never updated. He felt slightly embarrassed for Jimmy, until he thought of how he and Indira were constantly touching one another, the way they looked at each other when they laughed, how Olivia still called Jimmy "Daddy," and never seemed to chafe at anything he said. Maybe Jimmy's house sucked, and Indira was an airhead who forgot to pick him up at the station, but Jimmy walked toward his kitchen door like a man who couldn't wait to get home. Keith shrugged and backed out of Jimmy's narrow beat up driveway. *Ah well,* he thought, *if I got to travel as much as that lucky fuck, I'd probably be happy to get home too.*

Looking forward to the buzz from his first cocktail, Keith shrugged off his trench coat and hung it on a peg in the pristine mudroom. He waited a beat, taking the temperature of the house. For years he'd advocated for a dog, enjoying the idea of a loyal greeting when he walked in the door, a companion who loved him unconditionally. But Erica reminded him that he was home almost never, and half the time he was home he spent sleeping. He'd tried again last week, mentioning that in September they'd have no kids at home and what would she do to fill her time. She gave him a withering look and reminded him that she planned to be at every one of Rory's wrestling matches and she couldn't be tied down with a puppy. Keith sighed. He barely remembered the woman he'd married. She'd been at the top of her class at Brown and could go shot for shot with any of his fraternity brothers. She was smart and hot and fun when he married her. Now all she talked about was the kids, the house, and her myriad projects, none of which took any brainpower other than basic organizational skills. Christ, she did the same shit his administrative assistant did. Except his assistant knew better than to regale him with the minutiae of every little thing.

Keith closed the mudroom door loud enough to alert everyone, straightened his shoulders, attempted to pull in his abdominals beneath the bloat of his belly, and went in to face his family.

"I'm home!"

No one answered, but he heard a pause in Erica's monologue. He walked into the kitchen, which was bright and sparkling with glass and electricity, sleek white cabinets and gleaming sugar marble. Keith's eyes lit up at the well-stocked bar in the butler's pantry.

"How is everyone?" He asked as he made his way to the bar.

Erica came over and pecked his cheek, leaving an imprint of her lips behind. He swiped at his cheek, rubbed away the gloss. Tried not to feel irritated. His friends at the club were always talking about how hot Erica was. Keith couldn't deny she was in good shape. Hours spent on the tennis court and spin class paid off. Astronomical bills at the medi-spa kept her face as smooth and unlined as a 30-year-old, and her wardrobe filled with expensive tiny dresses and designer shoes with heels that could puncture a lung if she ever came after him with one of them kept her firmly in the hot category. But it seemed her personality had been carefully erased, just like the lines on her forehead. There was nothing left but a smooth, controlled, artificial surface. Keith dropped a couple of cubes into a highball glass.

He felt Erica pretending not to watch how high Keith filled his highball glass with straight gin and another wave of irritation swept through him, *can't even have a drink in my own house without her hovering.*

"Dinner's almost ready." Erica trilled. "Beef stew with those little red potatoes you like and some lovely carrots. Broccoli as a veg. Oh! And Bailey made a glorious salad and a side of quinoa."

Keith looked at his daughter and watched as she fought the urge to roll her eyes. It was discernible. He could almost see the eyeballs fighting to stay still in their sockets. He could read her bubble and knew Bailey was as irritated as he was by her mother's incessant prattle. He gave a conspiratorial smirk and Bailey narrowed her eyes at him.

Keith smoothed his face into a jovial approximation of happiness, "Sounds great."

Keith wondered why he and Bailey weren't allies like they used to be when she was a tiny thing. He could tell Erica drove Bailey crazy, and she could be terribly cutting when she'd had enough of her mother, yet he caught a side eye from Bailey if he showed even a modicum of frustration. When she was little and wanted to be rescued from Erica's latest exploit—Erica was always trying to get bows to stay in Bailey's hair or get her to wear clothing plastered with rainbows and sparkles—she'd crawl into his lap or put her arms up for him to lift her to safety. She'd been his girl and he'd relished it. When had things changed? He couldn't remember. "How long till dinner?"

"Long enough for you to wash up and check ESPN scores." Erica smiled kindly at him, and he smiled back appreciatively.

Keith made an exit like an actor finally getting off stage after he'd forgotten all his lines and escaped to the family room where the lure of ESPN and a respite from conversation awaited him. He felt Bailey's eyes burning the back of his head and he wondered what transgression he'd committed this time or if it was simply that she could read his mind, a thought so uncomfortable, he took a gulp of his drink, letting the burn of the gin anesthetize his train of thought.

"Hey dad." Rory lifted his head.

Keith nodded at the television where two sports pundits were predicting the Super Bowl. "49ers?"

"They like the Ravens for it."

"Never gonna happen."

Rory shrugged, "You never know."

"I know."

Rory laughed, "Well you have a fifty-fifty shot at being right."

"Your mother wants us for dinner."

"Now?"

"Yeah."

"Okay."

But neither of them moved.

"How's the team shaping up?" Keith asked.

"A couple of promising juniors. Coach thinks I look good."

"Yeah?"

"Thinks I'll bring us to States."

Keith nodded, his eyes on the television, but his mind wandered back in time. Rory had been so young when Coach Walker plucked him out of modified football and brought him up for varsity pre-season. Keith remembered one summer day when he went to the practice field to check it all out. It was rare for Keith to take off from work except for the occasional golf outing. Rory had just entered 8th grade and wouldn't be thirteen until November. "Lange!" Coach Walker yelled, "Bring it in!" It was a hot, clear day.

Keith couldn't take his eyes off his son, towered over by the high school athletes. Rory raced to Coach's side. Coach pulled him by his helmet, locked eyes with Rory, and said something. Rory nodded, turned, and ran back onto the field.

Keith tried to identify the reason for the unease he was feeling. The obvious cause was how small Rory looked. Yet Coach had reassured Keith that Rory would be riding the bench most of the time, he wanted him on the team to condition him. Rory was fast. He'd use him for plays where his speed would keep him out of harm's way and give the team an advantage. Besides, Coach had said with a wink, Rory's real talent would be wrestling. Coach told Keith about watching Rory in a modified match and realizing he was the kid who could follow Emmett Ainsworth's footsteps and bring them to glory at the States.

Suddenly Rory was down, underneath the body of a kid outweighing Rory by about 80lbs. The urgent shriek of the whistle pierced the air.

"Carlisle!" Coach roared, "Get over here!"

The tangle of limbs unfurled until Carlisle loomed into a vertical position, another kid extended his arm to Rory and lifted him to his feet.

"Think that's cute, Carlisle?" Coach roared, "Get down and give me twenty—no thirty—thirty suicides." It looked as though Carlisle was about to protest when Coach bellowed, "NOW!"

Keith watched with a swell of pride as Rory stayed focused and kept pace with the team. He took hit after hit. Keith wondered if some of it was retaliation for Carlisle's punishment. Keith glanced over at Carlisle who was still laboring away. He wondered about Coach's judgment. Setting Rory up as his pet wasn't going to win him any favors with his teammates. Keith watched as Rory took another hit. He was holding his own, but barely.

Keith's own high school career had been stellar. In fact it had catapulted him to play Division 1. There had even been talk of getting drafted by the major leagues. Keith credited his high school and college athletic career for the success he'd found when he left Connecticut and made his way on Wall Street. Sure, his father had been there before him, paving the way, but Keith knew nothing really gave you an edge, everything was a liability, a house of cards that could tumble around you faster than you built it. Yet he'd done it. He'd built his house of cards, and it was sturdy.

Keith knew the inner price he paid. The copious amounts of alcohol he'd consumed to mitigate he long list of *what ifs* that lingered perpetually in his consciousness.

What if: He lost his edge, or worse was edged out by someone better, there was always someone better. And someone lesser. The antidote: Use the someone lesser as a leg up, stay ahead of the someone better any way you had to.

What if: Bad luck. There was always bad luck. An injury. A deal gone wrong. Something beyond his control. The antidote: Have a contingency plan. Steroids for an injury. Any means necessary to salvage a deal.

What if: He grew weary. The antidote: Keep going. At any cost. Rest is death.

And there it was. The niggle of worry in his gut. Did he want his boy to live by these same rules? Sure it had served him well, but there had been an invisible cost, a constant burn in his stomach, rising up and flooding his chest, searing his gullet. Keith placed his hand over his belly, which had grown large and hard from years of too much alcohol. Here he was standing on the sidelines, watching his boy about to enter the same life. Keith's hand lifted away from his stomach where it had failed to soothe him and reached for a brief moment toward Rory before he shoved it in his pocket.

There was no way to protect Rory from the fears of inadequacy, of losing something before he'd earned it, of losing something once he'd given up everything to get it. Rory would have to learn for himself. There was no way to do it for him. And how could he stand in Rory's way? Keith tried to imagine if his father had told him not to go for the brass ring (not that Big Keith would ever have told him not to go for it. He'd been groomed since conception, the deal cinched, when he was born male and had his father's moniker stamped on his own birth certificate.) He'd had no choice but to fling himself again and again at that brass ring and hold onto it at all costs, he wouldn't have had the courage to refuse and his father wouldn't have let him, and if his father had offered him a choice, he would have interpreted it as a lack of confidence and resented him for it.

The idea of Rory resenting him seemed worse than any other thing that could happen. No. He'd have to lead by example. But he'd try to give Rory what he'd never been given. He'd try to let him know he understood. That he wasn't alone in this. That was the thing. Keith had always felt so very alone. Even when surrounded by his friends and coworkers and family members, he'd felt as small and isolated and insignificant as a dot of light in the sky.

On their way home from the field that day, the familiar smell of shoulder pads damp with sweat permeating the car, Keith listened to Rory talk about plays, who was good at what, who sucked.

Keith listened and made encouraging noises. As they turned onto their road, Keith asked as casually as he could,

"What'd Coach want, when he pulled you off the field?"

"Oh," Rory smiled, "He told me not to worry—that my size was my strength—that I could outrun all of them and that even if they caught me, it wouldn't hurt going down."

"Huh." Keith looked over at his son.

Rory smiled a dazzling smile. "It's like he knew I was scared. And he knew what to say."

Keith looked away. Wondering that Rory could admit to being scared and he didn't sound like a wuss. He sounded brave.

Rory smiled again. "And he was right! They could hardly catch me and when they did, it didn't hurt."

Keith nodded. "He's looking out for you."

"Yeah."

"And you're enjoying it?"

"Yeah."

"Good. Good."

They were pulling into the driveway. Before turning off the ignition, Keith paused, "Rory, I'm proud of you—because you're going for what you want."

"Thanks, dad!" Rory was gathering his gear, one hand on the door handle.

"But—"

Rory looked at him. "Yeah?"

"I only want this because you want it, you know? If that changes—if you just want to play JV, hang out with kids your own age, you do that, okay?"

"Okay." Rory smiled again, wide and bright. "Thanks dad."

Keith nodded.

"Don't worry, dad. It's all good."

Keith nodded again. Rory flashed him another smile and hopped out of the car. Keith watched him go. Then he turned off the ignition and sat for a few minutes. Trying to figure out if the doubts had subsided. They hadn't. Keith knew, from experience, there was no respite. Not for him. And not for Rory. Rory just didn't know it yet. And he didn't know how to tell him.

"Dad! Rory! Dinner!" Bailey shouted. Keith's reverie broke and with it came relief. That underlying feeling that maybe something was wrong had crept back in with his thoughts. Keith put his palm on Rory's head for a moment, feeling the softness of his son's hair, "Ok, Kid, let's eat."

Erica had the table set in the kitchen and was at the stove ladling the stew into bowls. It smelled like heaven and Keith happily took his seat at the head of the table, thanking his lucky stars that at least he'd married a woman who could cook.

Keith chewed and swallowed. "Delicious." He thought of what poor Jimmy would be eating at the Birnbaum-Irrizzary's, tofu masquerading as meat and a mess of soggy vegetables. Indira couldn't cook, but she was a sweetheart. Jimmy may not be getting a hot dinner tonight, but he wouldn't be eating it with a side of bitterness and resentment either.

"Glad you like it, he gave me the prime cut."

Bailey and Rory focused on their plates.

Keith tried again, "Gave Jimmy a ride home."

Bailey looked up.

"That's nice." Erica nodded absently, then her eyes lit up. "By the way, the gala is Saturday night. Rory, you and Hunter are still able to valet for us, right?"

"Are Jimmy and Indira going?" Keith interrupted.

Erica gave him a confused look, "It's the Club gala."

"Oh, I thought it was that school thing."

"That's always in April."

"Right."

Bailey took a tiny bite of the brown pile of what looked like grass seed to Keith, and asked, "How come you guys never hang out with Indira and Jimmy anymore? I can't remember the last time we saw them."

Rory looked down and shoveled food into his mouth as though an invisible hand was waiting to snatch it away.

Erica sniffed. "We just travel in different circles."

"What does that even mean?"

Keith threw Bailey a wary look and wished he hadn't brought their neighbors up at all. He'd just been making conversation. He watched as Erica's eyebrows drew a millimeter closer.

"It means, dear daughter, that Indira and Jimmy have a different group of friends than we do, and they spend time with them. There are no hard feelings. Whenever Indira and I see each other we're happy and we always chat and catch up."

Keith knew whenever Erica referred to Bailey as "dear daughter" it meant she was irritated and trying not to show it. He registered a tiny flare of validation, Bailey may not be his little girl anymore, but they didn't have conflict. It was Erica she fought with. That kid could get under his wife's skin like a bad tattoo.

"But…" Bailey said, "They were our best friends."

Rory rolled his eyes and swallowed, "Who cares?"

Erica saw the gleam in Bailey's eye at Rory's comment and rushed to diffuse it. "Bailey, we weren't *best friends*. We just spent time together because we lived on the same road and had children the same age. We never had much in common."

"I don't know." Keith took a chance, "We vacationed with them, spent holidays together. We were more than neighbors, for sure."

"Oh for heaven's sake." Erica declared, "People change. They move on."

"Indira and Jimmy didn't change." Bailey said, "We did."

Erica brightened, "Exactly!"

"So who do you consider your close friends now?"

"Oh. You know." Erica said, waving her hand with a fluid motion through the air. "Other members of the club."

"But who specifically?"

"Oh—I don't know—lots of people. The Connovers, the Logans."

"So, Rory's friend's parents?"

Erica looked up and to the right, "Well, yes, I suppose that's true."

"Do you vacation with them?"

Erica made a sour face. "When does this family have time to vacation? Between your father's work schedule, Rory's sports teams, and my charity work, we can't find time." Then, as if she'd become aware of the less than perfect image of her life she had inadvertently portrayed, she smiled and regrouped. "Anyway, we have The Club. We don't need to vacation together. That place is like a vacation every day and no wasted moments traveling!"

Bailey leaned forward. "So let me get this straight? You ghosted your best friends because they didn't belong to an exclusive country club. I guess the community pool where we went all of our lives wasn't a place to help Rory social climb?"

"Shut up, Bailey!" Rory yelled.

"What? It's a simple observation."

Rory glared at her. "It's not that deep. You're just stirring shit."

"Language," Erica said, but it was half-hearted. "Bailey, I didn't ghost anyone. We grew apart. It was as much Indira as it was me."

Bailey looked at her mother. "That's dishonest, *dear mother*, and you know it."

Keith remembered the hurt, confused look on Indira's face when Erica had, for the third time in a month, dismissed Indira's suggestion that they go over for Friday night pizza the way they always had, because there was a *thing* she couldn't miss at The Club. It was the first summer their family had joined. The Logans and Connovers had offered to sponsor them after years of languishing on a protracted and not very ethical waiting list. If it weren't for Rory becoming the heir to the wrestling team throne, and Erica using that to ingratiate herself with parents who had influence on the membership committee, Keith was fairly certain the Langes would still be in a state of humiliating club limbo, and they would probably still be friends with the Irizzary's.

Keith agreed with Bailey but knew if he didn't do something to deflect, there would be no way to enjoy the rest of his dinner in peace, "B, pass me a roll, would you?"

Bailey passed the basket of rolls without breaking eye contact with her mother.

"Babe," Keith tried again. "This stew really is delicious."

Finally, Erica broke eye contact with Bailey and shrugged. "Bailey, I invited Indira and Jimmy and the kids up to the club many times. She was the one who didn't feel comfortable. She was the one who made cracks about whether or not Hispanics and Jews were allowed in. It was quite insulting, really."

Keith looked surprised. "Really?"

"Yes. Really."

"Huh. Well, Indira's kind of touchy. But Jimmy's not like that at all."

"Like what dad? Sensitive to the reality of racist antisemitic country clubs?"

Keith put his hands up in mock surrender. "Don't drag me into this."

Bailey narrowed her eyes at him, and Keith knew she was about to move in, but then he noticed Bailey glance at her mother. Erica's face looked pinched and anxious and she'd placed her fork down, her food untouched.

"Whatever," Bailey exhaled. "I was just wondering. I guess I miss them, that's all."

Erica's shoulders visibly sagged, "We have many happy memories. And they're right down the road. I'm sure they'd love to see you. Why don't you pop over there tomorrow?"

Bailey pressed her lips together and nodded.

Keith relaxed. Crisis averted. Rory had the look of a trapped animal, so Keith winked at him and was rewarded with a smirk. Another five minutes and he would be able to mix himself another drink and escape to the family room and the respite of the television.

Erica sighed with relief. She'd worked for hours on what seemed like a simple stew, and she couldn't bear the thought that dinner would devolve into recriminations and door slamming. Desperate to avoid any more land mines she fearlessly iterated the mission of the Save the Wetlands Fund, because she knew Bailey would approve of it and Rory wouldn't scoff. After all, who could be *against* wetlands? On safe ground again, Erica wrested control of the evening, gratified when Bailey stayed behind to help her clean up. Rory, like the angel he was, cleared the table before going to his room to finish an essay and Keith mixed himself a third cocktail and took it to the family room to watch his favorite sports channel. A sense of well being settled over Erica as she loaded the last of the dishes and inspected Bailey's wiping of the countertops.

Satisfied, she kissed Bailey, oblivious to the stiffening of her daughter's shoulders, and climbed up to the third floor master suite to wash up and put on her pajamas.

It was after 9:00, so Erica opened the silver Tiffany pillbox she kept on her nightstand and popped a tiny white Ativan under her tongue, allowing it to dissolve along with any residual worries she had about her family. She focused on the sublingual burst of bitter, then a release of sweetness, secure in the knowledge that it would hit her brain faster this way and combat the normal state of anxiety in which she spent all day. Erica's physician had advised her to use imagery to help her relax, but she couldn't control the images flitting across her eyelids. Keith mixing his third cocktail of the evening, the slight tremor in his hand, the sunburned complexion of his face even though it was midwinter and he hadn't felt sun in months, the protrusion of his belly over his pants like a heart attack about to manifest. Bailey at dinner, her angry dismissive tone, the rigid set of her jaw, the dull look in her eyes. Erica saw Ginnifer Connover and her twin daughters. Their three shiny, blonde heads close together, all of them in tennis whites, happy, perfect.

Erica had been so excited to have a daughter, certain they would be best friends. Yet Bailey had been ornery from the start, a will so impenetrable it was impossible for Erica to impose upon. As a toddler, Bailey balked at the adorable shoes Erica tried to dress her in, screaming, "Pinch!" at the top of her lungs. Erica didn't know how Bailey had even learned the word "pinch", and she applied it to anything she didn't want to wear: hair barrettes, tights, dresses, all of the things Erica found beautiful. Other mothers brought their toddler daughters to the nail salon where they would sit as if in a drug induced state while the manicurist massaged lotion onto their tiny hands and feet and painted rainbow colors and sparkles on their seashell-nails. Meanwhile Bailey would refuse to enter, holding her nose and shaking her head. Erica was mortified. Once, Bailey had even kicked her. Erica lost her temper and twisted Bailey's little arm as they left. She strapped her mutinous daughter into the car seat and threw herself into the driver's seat, grateful to have a reprieve from Bailey's big, gray, accusatory, eyes. She loved Bailey with everything she had. And she knew Bailey loved her despite any actions to the contrary. It was just so much easier with Rory.

It was as if Erica and Rory communed from the start. He was a fat, happy, compliant baby, and he renewed Erica's faith in her parenting. She breathed a contented sigh at the thought of all of his accomplishments. It had been such a long competitive road, but he'd never wavered, never complained, just kept plowing ahead, racking up newspaper articles and awards, toughing it out through injuries that would have benched a lesser player, never letting his grades slip, all while managing to retain a popular status at school.

The anti-anxiety medication Erica took was working and her breathing felt even and relaxed. Yet, as soon as she floated blissfully into the nothingness of sleep, she startled awake, vigilant. Her heart pounding, listening for ice cubes in a glass. Not Keith's, but the sounds of her childhood. The heavy stumble of her father in the den downstairs, the quiet murmur of her mother, then a roar from her father, the thwack of an open hand, a stifled outcry, the thud of a body against a wall, bedtime stories of her youth.

One memory in particular intruded, breaking through the gauze of her anti-anxiety medication. The clink of ice against the glass, a shuffle, and a bang.

Erica, small in her bed, had been sound asleep. Her eyes had sprung open and the darkness had taken familiar shapes. Her dresser, high and wide and squat in the small room had loomed above her. She could make out the panels of her bedroom door, the knob turning.

A slice of light had cracked the darkness. Erica had listened to the ice cubes move in the glass and had waited for the shadow to fill the room.

Erica had watched as her mother slipped into the room, forced herself to check her mother's face in the brief moment of light. One time it had been painted red with blood. Another time her mother's left eye had been replaced by a raised purple slit. It had frightened Erica. But that night there had been no blood, no discoloration, or swelling, just a glisten of tears and a twist of pain.

Erica had moved over, her mother closed the door as carefully and quietly as she could while holding her glass, which she had drained before setting it down on the dresser. She had crossed in two steps to Erica's bed. Erica had slid against the wall and held the covers aloft. She had smelled the scent of her mother at night (what she would later come to recognize as gin) mixed with the scent of her mother during the day (the vanilla body lotion her mother had rubbed into her skin every morning and would rub into Erica's own much smaller hands if Erica sat very still and very quietly while her mother got dressed.)

"Shh, baby, mommy's alright."

"I know, mommy."

"He doesn't mean it."

"I know."

Her mother had lain still and flat against the pillow. She had been so slight that the narrow bed still had enough room for Erica if she squeezed sideways with her back flat against the wall. From this position, Erica had been able to cover her mother, and keep watch over her as her mother's face had grown slack with sleep. Erica had listened to the familiar night sounds of her father lumber down the hall.

The clink of ice, a shuffle, and a bang. They were sounds, which would repeat throughout the night, and they meant different things. That time, it had been the final drain of his glass. The shuffle hadn't been two bodies colliding but her father struggling toward his bedroom door, the bang hadn't been her mother's body hitting something hard, it had just been his slamming of his bedroom. Erica had patted her mother's shoulder. *Sleep tight*, she had whispered into the quiet room while she had waited to fall back to sleep.

The next morning, when her father had left for work and her mother was her daytime self again, moving around the kitchen with quick bright movements, making Erica breakfast, stopping for a moment to smooth Erica's hair from her face, softly humming along with the radio permanently fixed to a country music station, Erica looked out of the window where the small dining table was pushed against the wall. Erica saw a chipmunk scampering at the base of the large oak tree outside their kitchen door. Woods loomed dense and dark yards away but in their yard the sun was rising casting a warm glow over the chipmunk busily collecting acorns from the ground, suddenly the chipmunk froze in its tracks. Later, Erica realized it must have sensed the hawk about to swoop from the sky. It had shocked Erica. The sudden violent flapping of wings, the sharp scream, then silence as the hawk stilled, the intensity of its gleaming eyes as it squeezed the life out of the tiny chipmunk trapped in the it's talons, before lifting from the ground in a swift motion, soaring into the air, the limp body of the chipmunk hanging. The way that chipmunk had grown so still reminded had Erica of her mother at night.

Her heart pounding despite the Ativan, Erica looked around her opulent bedroom, as her eyes adjusted to the dark. She told herself that everything was okay now. Her children's childhoods were so different from hers.

Maybe Keith drank a little too much maybe he bullied his way through life at times. But he would never hit her or lift a hand to her kids. And Erica knew, if he did, she could leave. Their wealth protected her now, but it could protect her if she left as well.

Erica reached for her pillbox and slid another tablet under her tongue. Then for good measure she reverted to her childhood trick to put herself to sleep. Squeezing her eyes shut she mentally recited the Lord's Prayer over and over until it was all she knew. *Our Father who art in heaven, hallowed be thy name. Thy kingdom come. Thy will be done, on earth as it is in heaven. Give us this day our daily bread; and forgive us our trespasses, as we forgive those who trespass against us; and lead us not into temptation, but deliver us from evil. Our Father who art in heaven, hallowed be thy name. Thy kingdom come, thy will be done....*

CHAPTER 7

"Hey," Monica dragged the word out as she stood on her toes and wrapped her arms around Emmett's neck, "Get in here!"

He laughed and bent forward kissing her, tasting just her, no lip gloss or minty things. They stumbled together into her dorm room. They had it to themselves. Strings of fairy lights gave the room a soft glow, easing the harsh fall of night.

Monica let go of him long enough so he could shrug out of his heavy jacket then immediately pressed her body against him, kissing the smooth skin at the top of his chest where she'd successfully managed to unfasten three of his buttons. "You smell good," she whispered.

"I've missed you."

Monica laughed, "I saw you this morning."

"It was a long day, and we were in that workshop. It's not the same."

"Well, I'm here now." Monica unbuttoned the rest of his shirt, grazing his skin with her lips until he shivered and pulled her closer. Soon they were on her narrow bed, their clothes scattered.

"Are you cold?" he asked.

"No." Her hair slid over his face and he wrapped his arm around her. He felt her breasts, soft against him, the hard point of her nipples sending a shock of desire through him, freezing him.

Monica felt the tensing of his body. "You okay?"

Emmett swallowed, kept his eyes closed, "Mmmhmm."

Monica lifted her head and looked at him, "Yeah?"

He nodded. But there was a pallor in his lips and his nostrils flared.

"Are you feeling sick?" Monica asked.

His arm tightened around her and he shook his head no.

Monica brushed the hair away from his forehead. "You feel kind of clammy...it's okay we don't have to do this right now."

Emmett's eyes flew open, he looked panicked, "Did I move too fast..."

"What? No!" She laughed. "Did I?"

He shook his head.

Monica sat up, her breasts swaying above him, "Hey, what's going on?"

Emmett looked at her. "I keep thinking about the training."

"The one today? On consent?"

Emmett nodded.

"Okay?"

"Have I ever...you know?"

"No! Babe, you're great, you're considerate." She grinned, "and sexy as fuck. Besides, I'd never be with a guy who wasn't. Trust me."

Emmett squeezed his eyes shut. "What if..." He whispered, "How can I tell—if I'm the kind of guy...."

"Emmett, you're not, at least you haven't been...I mean it's pretty clear. Was there any new information in there for you today?"

His eyes flew open. "All of it."

Monica nodded. "Can you be more specific?

"The idea of doing something without your consent. It makes me feel sick."

"Okay. Well that's an easy one. You won't. Right? If I'm passed out or too drunk to know where I am, or not in the mood, you would respect that. I know that about you. You wouldn't touch me without my consent. I mean if anything— I'm the assertive one here." She smiled, "and that's not a complaint by the way."

Emmett smiled, but he felt weak. He tried focusing on Monica, on her features, the way her eyes sloped down a tiny bit, softening her gaze, the light brown almost amber, color, the prominence of her nose, giving her face strength, the way it creased at the top when she laughed, her smile so wide and bright it made him instantly smile back. Her lips were full and all he wanted to do was kiss them and feel how soft they were against his, but he couldn't. He didn't dare look at her breasts visible between the curtains of wavy dark brown hair. His penis stirred against her thigh and the sensation made him choke. Because ever since that day last week…when he'd thought he'd seen Coach…the feeling of arousal made him feel sick to his stomach. Emmett stared at Monica, willing himself to see only her, but he couldn't block out the images, it was as though he was being forced to watch a film he couldn't turn off, couldn't close his eyes against, Coach's face hard as he knelt beside Emmett who was doing pushups in the rain, the ground muddy, Emmett's face meeting it.

You wanna win, Ainsworth? Ten more! Faster. Harder. Coach's whisper in his ear…*You wanna get laid this weekend? Are you a man or a boy? A man or a boy? Faster! Harder!* Images flitted across Emmett's vision, a party that weekend, soft skin against his fingertips, the unhooking of a silky bra, the falling away of thin fabric and the loosening of breasts, all of those images whirring until his vision blurred, making him dizzy. Until his stomach churned and his breath felt trapped and he was pinned down, not by an opponent, but by the inability to move his own limbs. He couldn't breathe, he couldn't see, his chest felt like it was about to burst. Maybe it would. Maybe if it did, it would all end. He wanted it to. Then, against his will, his body forced air into his throat, his lungs, and he was still alive.

"Babe, Babe, hey. Are you okay?" Monica was there, above him, her face worried. But solid. No other images superimposed on hers.

Emmett nodded, tried to smile. "Yeah, yeah. I'm fine. Just a little lightheaded—may be dehydrated."

Her face relaxed. "Okay, Mister, let's go eat." She jumped up, shimmying quickly into her clothes. Emmett looked at the beauty of her body, wishing for a respite from the longing he felt.

He got up slowly, relieved that he was no longer dizzy, the spots in his vision had dissipated, and the room looked normal again, the rushing in his ears receded until all he heard were the sounds of a Thursday night in the dorms.

Monica tossed him his shirt and winked. "Let's get a Murph Burger, that's almost as sexy as you are."

Emmett grinned and pushed all the other thoughts away —that he was going crazy, that he was a terrible person. That he should die. Maybe he could just go with his girlfriend who he really, really loved, and have a burger. Maybe that would be okay, at least for tonight.

CHAPTER 8
January 2025

Still on winter break, Bailey was back at her childhood desk, lost in her work. Erica knocked on Bailey's bedroom door at the exact same time as opening it and stuck her head in, making Bailey jump.

"Sorry, B!" Erica's cheeks were still flushed and there was an almost imperceptible halo of frizz around her hairline, the only telltale sign that she'd clocked an hour and a half of rigorous, heart pumping, competitive spinning.

Bailey lifted her hand in greeting and gave a half-hearted wave before turning back to her computer.

Erica ignored Bailey's dismissive body language and engaged a cheerful tone, "What are you working on?"

"Finishing a paper."

Erica brightened. "About?"

Bailey narrowed her eyes. "The Liar's Paradox."

Erica laughed. "No reason to look so suspicious. Can't a mother be interested in her daughter's intellectual pursuits?"

Bailey sighed, "It's for *Poetry and Philosophy.*"

Erica took a sip from her water bottle then launched into a recitation, "The Cretans always liars, evil beasts, idle bellies!

But thou art not dead: thou livest and abidest forever, for in thee we live and move and have our being."

Bailey stared at Erica who winked and said, "Cretans and liars. Perfect for dinner with BK this evening. He's both."

Bailey's mouth gaped and Erica pointed her finger at her. "If you say I said it I'll deny it."

Bailey shook her head. "I uh…just never knew you felt that way about Grandpa…."

"Would it be asking too much to just ignore anything that comes out of his mouth tonight?" Erica asked hopefully. Her father-in-law had been the bane of her existence since the day she met him. He insisted she call him BK (short for Big Keith) and kissed her right on the lips (which she found disgusting.) She told herself repeatedly that Keith was nothing like his father. Besides, her own father was worse, so who was she to judge. She'd been lying to herself for decades. She thought Bailey would have figured that out by now. Sensing an opening she tried again. "What do you think, B? We just ignore anything that comes out of his mouth?"

Bailey looked like she might be considering it. "Unless it's misogynistic or racist."

Erica thought about it. Calling Letitia James an angry Black woman was both misogynistic and racist and he'd been yelling exactly that in the background while Erica was on the phone with her mother-in-law. "Bailey, have you met BK? Every other word out of his mouth is one or both of those things."

Bailey shrugged, "Don't start none won't be none."

"That's a double negative."

"Yep. Pick your battles, Erica."

"After you finish your paper will you run some errands for me?"

"Sure."

Bailey put her head back down, and Erica took the silent cue and left the room without saying anything more. Her own dad had been a gambler. He didn't know when to fold them or how to quit while he was ahead. Erica knew how to do both.

She glanced at her Fitbit. 5,000 steps and that didn't count her early morning spin class. She'd been the first to arrive not just to fight off the other women for her favorite spot, but it also gave her time to tell the other women about Rory. He was now deciding between Duke and U Mass at Amherst where he'd received a full ride and had been offered a spot on the football as well as the wrestling team. Erica was fervently hoping for the Duke bumper sticker, *but,* as she would proudly announce to her spin-class friends, she wasn't one to interfere. It was entirely Rory's decision. Satisfied that her caloric intake (black coffee and a smoothie) had been offset according to her fitbit, Erica headed downstairs to get ready for the arrival of her in-laws.

This dinner was, for Erica, an unfortunate turn of events. BK and Kitty Lange had a sudden desire to see their grandchildren before leaving for their season in Key Biscayne. Erica wanted to tell Kitty to be careful what she wished for. Erica could barely keep Rory and Bailey from sniping at each other. She had no idea how she would handle adding Big Keith and his *big mouth* to the mix.

Erica paused at the bottom of the stairs. Something was wrong. But what? There was a shadow on the front door. An enormous round shadow. Erica stared in horror at it. She ran to the door and wrenched it open, the enormous wreath swinging from the force of Erica's brute force against the door. How could she have forgotten this? It was two days after the Epiphany! A day after *all* Christmas decorations needed to be removed. And this wasn't a simple seasonal wreath, which she could easily have left up until Valentine's Day. This wreath had a bright red bow wishing the world a Merry Christmas! It had sparkles and battery operated lights, which would shine like a beacon in the evenings.

Erica wrestled the thing off the door and began to drag it to the curb, where she laid it to rest gently against the tree she'd dragged out yesterday. Erica looked up and down the block. No one, it seemed, had done the same. Except her neighbor across the street who had inexplicably taken hers down on January 2nd (why rob yourself of five more days of light?). Not to mention that her neighbor's tree was an artificial one, which Erica did not approve of. Where was the smell of Christmas in an artificial tree? Erica had asked her about it once and she'd had the nerve to say she sprayed it with pine scent. Pine Scent! As if that made it any better.

Erica brushed tree needles from her hands and surveyed the road. That other neighbor a few doors down would be dragging her fire hazard of a tree to the curb two weeks from now, claiming she was *so* busy. That was even more unacceptable than an artificial tree. She also left all of her Christmas decorations up through April. It disgusted Erica. The other three homes on the road were Jewish families so...no lights or trees, although they each had lovely menorah is the window and one of them made quite a nice effort with a giant sparkling dreidel on the front lawn. Erica felt sorry for them not having the fabulousness of Christmas to brighten up all of December. Yet here they were for the next three months, in the same boat, with bare trees and gray skies, lawns rutted from the interminable rains of early winter.

Now that she'd solved that horror, she marched back into the house. She needed to Big-Keith-proof the house and make dinner, which would take the rest of the day.

Kitty and BK filled the large kitchen with their presence. Kitty sniffed at the elaborate display. "Are we serving ourselves this evening?"

"Fine by me!" BK shouted, "I'm starved. Took forever to get down here. Your traffic situation is worse than ever! Must be all those commie hipsters flocking up here from Brooklyn." He guffawed. BK often amused himself with his own observations.

Erica placed a prime slice of beef on BK's plate and ignored the commie hipster comment. "I made your favorite, BK," she said, trying to placate him. She'd already hidden the Ruth Bader Ginsberg biography that Bailey bought her for Christmas to de-liberalize the house and blocked all the cable news channels on the family room smart TV. She knew to neutralize any potential conflict between Bailey and her in-laws.

Dinner, Erica thought, despite all of her fears, had actually progressed quite nicely. BK raved about the food between forkfuls and Kitty had even nodded curtly in agreement. Keith stuck to wine instead of his usual cocktails, which Erica took as a good sign, and Rory was regaling his grandfather with highlights from their last match and discussing strategies for Saturday's tournament.

Erica slid her glance toward Bailey, who looked like she was in physical pain. Maybe it was BK's loud chewing that was getting to her daughter. Erica wished she'd turned the din-ner music piped in from their sound system a bit louder.

Rory took a moment to swallow, creating a sudden lull in the conversation.

"So," Big Keith pronounced.

Bailey took a sip of water.

"This mayor you've got down here—him—it—you know the whole Bruce Jenner thing."

Erica made a valiant attempt to speak over him, "More peas, BK?"

Keith grunted.

Rory looked up with interest.

"No politics at the dinner table, dear," Kitty spoke firmly.

"I'm not talking about politics, Kitty! I don't care whether he's a democrat or republican, but I'm asking—he's a Bruce Jenner thing, right?"

Bailey placed her fork down. "She is the mayor, BK. And with all due respect to your no-politics rule, Grandma, just for information purposes, she's an Independent.

"Yeah, but he's not a she, right?" BK smirked.

"Her pronouns," Bailey said calmly, "are she/her/hers."

BK sputtered, "Pronouns! What does that even mean? He's a tranny right?"

Bailey looked at him. "I know it's new information, BK. But our mayor is a woman. She's a woman. Whatever sex organs she was born with aren't really any of your business."

"He's the one making it my business! Wearing wigs and ladies dresses!"

"Well, BK, how would you feel if your employees demanded to know what your dick looks like? You made it their business by wearing suits and ties signaling you have one."

BK slammed his fist on the table. "How dare you talk to me like that?" He looked at Erica, "Is this what they're teaching them at that school?"

Rory snorted, "Turned her into a feminazi."

Bailey ignored Rory and stared at BK.

"You know," Erica said, "She/her. He/his. They/them. It takes some getting used to, but it isn't really that difficult if one tries. After all, I'm sure you would agree, Kitty, that etiquette would dictate we at least try."

Kitty looked at Erica as though a second head had sprouted from her neck.

BK pushed his plate away and pointed his finger at Keith. "You allow this nonsense in your home? You allow your daughter to speak that way to me?"

Keith looked at Bailey and sighed. "Apologize to your grandfather."

"I will not." Bailey said.

"Bailey." Keith's teeth were clenched so hard it came out as a whisper yell. "You will not disrespect your grandfather over some stranger. Apologize."

Bailey looked at her father. "I'm not sorry, so I won't apologize." Then she looked at her grandfather. "You are the one who should apologize for saying such vile nasty things about another human being just because you're afraid of things you don't understand."

BK's face turned red and he shouted at Bailey, "Do you think you can bully me, little girl? You and the rest of the woke socialists?"

Bailey looked back at him steadily. "You're the one shouting and pointing your finger. I'm not feeling the whole bullying accusation right now."

Keith banged the table. "Apologize to your grandfather or leave the table."

Bailey laughed. "That's an easy one."

Rory's face turned red. "That isn't punishment! She wants to leave. She hates us!"

Erica stood up, "She doesn't hate us! She loves us! Right Bailey? You love your grandparents. You love BK!"

Bailey looked around the table. "I don't hate any of you." Then she looked at BK. She looked straight into his eyes. She searched them. If she saw any sign of contrition, any sign of vulnerability, she wouldn't say it. He was a human being, her father's father. She was *of* him. She owed him that. She searched. He stared back at her. His pale blue eyes a laser focus on hers. Devoid of all emotion. Flat as paper. "I don't love you, BK. You are everything that is wrong with this world."

With that she began to clear the plates.

"Leave them!" her father shouted. "Leave them and get out!"

So she did.

Isa turned onto Olivia's road. She took the turn slowly and tried not to glance at Rory's house. She couldn't stomach the idea of seeing him and wished she didn't have to pass it every time she came to pick up Olivia. If Bailey didn't live there, Isa would torch the place with her mind.

Despite wanting to avoid looking at Rory's house, Isa glanced over at the Lange house and was shocked to see Bailey throwing a duffel bag into the trunk of her car. Isa felt a rare pulse of happiness, she pulled over, and rolled down her window. "Hey, lady!" she shouted.

By the time she'd finished throwing her clothes, books, and laptop into a bag, Bailey's tears had dried. They'd been the angry kind that seeped out of corners and rolled down her face without her knowing.

Bailey's head snapped up when she heard Isa's greeting and, in spite of everything, she smiled and walked over to the car. "Hey."

"What's up?"

Bailey shrugged.

"Going back already?"

"Already? It felt like a lifetime."

Isa looked sad. "We didn't get to hang out."

Bailey caught Isa's gaze and held it. Bailey's gray eyes captured the light from the street lamp transfixing Isa, as if there were secrets Isa was supposed to discover. Isa wondered if Bailey could see the truth in Isa's, the secrets she wanted to keep hidden. Bailey spoke, breaking the spell.

"Next time?"

"Cool." Isa said. "So, how's college life?"

Bailey shrugged, "The work is good—but the people…"

"Meet anyone cute?"

"Define cute."

"I don't know… a guy you think is cute."

Bailey looked at Isa a while longer. "I don't find any guys cute. I thought you knew that."

Isa held Bailey's gaze. "I guess I didn't know-know."

Bailey stared at her. "So now you do."

"Yeah." Isa looked away. Her heart was pounding. She found her eyes moving back to Bailey's lips. The way one corner turned up. They were thin and wide and Isa wondered what it would be like to kiss them and found that confusing.

Bailey nodded toward Olivia's house. "Picking up Liv?"

Isa nodded.

"Guess you better get going then."

"I guess." Isa was reluctant to leave, but couldn't think of anything to say.

Bailey smiled, "If you want to come visit some time…"

Isa brightened, "I'd love to…I mean we would…Olivia and I."

Bailey grinned, "Ok, then."

Isa smiled, felt her face burning, and lifted her hand as she pulled away. As soon as she was out of sight she rolled her eyes at herself. *Seriously.* She thought. *How's college life?* She wasn't sure why she was suddenly so nervous and awkward. She'd known forever that Bailey was gay. No one had ever said it out loud. But Isa knew. So why was she suddenly so enthralled? And why on earth did she ask if Bailey met any cute guys? Was it a way for her to force Bailey to tell her directly? Things were messy enough because of Bailey's horrible brother. Was it possible Isa was attracted to Bailey? Had Isa had a crush on Rory because in her world girls didn't have crushes on other girls? Not because anyone thought it was wrong, but there just weren't many people who did. Her mother's college roommate Nina was gay, and Isa couldn't remember a time where Nina wasn't in her life, but Nina said she'd known all her life she was gay. And Isa couldn't remember ever feeling that way. Only when she was around Bailey. Could she be bi? Is it because she knew Bailey was gay and had always looked up to Bailey, sought her attention? Had she thought she had a crush on Rory when all along it had been Bailey? Is that why it felt so wrong when she and Rory had kissed? But there were no other girls Isa was attracted to. She loved Olivia and Delaney but the thought of kissing either of them was gross. Yet, there weren't any guys Isa was attracted to either. Rory had been the only one. And look how that had turned out. Isa thought for the hundredth time about telling Bailey what was going on, but the idea made her sick to her stomach. So she did what she always did—buried the thought and turned the music up.

Bailey watched Isa's car until it was gone, wishing she could have thought of a way to make her stay longer instead of sending her away. But that was what she always did when faced with a chance she'd be rejected. Reject them first. It was a supremely effective way to evade humiliation. It was also an extremely effective way to remain lonely. Shrugging off the feeling of longing, she went back to her car, blasted "Baby Hoop Earrings" by Gilanares and peeled out of the driveway away from everything, the memory of BK's angry face and cold blue eyes slipping from her mind as she sang about a girl who'd been broken then found a way to repair the cracks with silver not gold.

A couple of hours later, Isa sat up in bed, exhausted, in need of sleep, but unable to commit to the process of shutting down her phone and disconnecting from the simultaneous conversations she was having.

She and Olivia were monitoring the gigantic fight happening on the grade group chat between Team Prom Committee and Team Everyone Else, while at the same time Olivia was making her case for doing something about Rory.

> **maybe we should tell Bailey,** Olivia wrote
> **NO**
> **she would shut it down**
> **we will handle it ourselves**

Meanwhile on the grade group chat Rory was leading the Team Prom Committee charge,

> **the bus is dope yo**
> **buck fifty first come first serve,** Kam Connover chimed in
> **elitist,** someone from Team Everyone Else answered
> **so woke,** Rory answered
> **ur an ahole Rory**

Isa agreed that Rory was indeed an ahole, but she was only reading the grade group chat in order to keep up in the unlikely event something important happened. She knew that if she didn't keep up, somehow she or Olivia might be called out and she didn't want to be late to that game either. Isa kept scrolling and reading, locked in a horrible state of nodding off, only to be awakened with a racing pulse when her phone pinged. Olivia's name flared and her comment appeared below it: **STFU Rory.**

Isa scrolled up to see what she'd missed. Rory was channeling Machine Gun Kelly in response to Delaney because they were now arguing about the DJ.

suck my dragon balls bitch

STFU Rory, Olivia had answered

suck your own tiny balls, Delaney said

your mouth is so much sweeter tho

Isa's thumbs moved rapidly over the surface of her phone as she texted Olivia privately.

he needs to stop

Isa watched the bubbles as Olivia typed.

We can shut him down for good

how

kams party we end this

I thought we weren't going

Change of plans

Isa thought about it. Maybe Olivia was right. Maybe she could do something besides incessantly blocking and ignoring him. Neither were effective and only seemed to be grinding her into a state of exhaustion. Maybe there was a way to fight back.

And with that thought she felt a bubble of anger and a surge of confidence which allowed her to turn off all notifications on her phone, set her alarm for 6:30, and submit to an unconscious state, where, if she was lucky, she wouldn't remember her dreams.

CHAPTER 9

Hunter Logan watched as morning dawned pale and silent. He'd been startled awake by the incessant buzz of his phone, which had slipped from his hand as he'd fallen asleep at some point in the night. Hunter mistook the buzzing vibrations against his pillow as a call and he'd woken with his heart pounding and his mouth dry. It hadn't been a call. Just a constant barrage of texts from the grade group chat, a continuation of the fight, as people woke up and caught up, took sides and weighed in.

> fuck you both we'll take our own ride, Delaney wrote
> lol did i hurt your feelings
> did I hurt yours piss baby
> rory shove your buck fifty up your ass ridin with you Delaney
> yeah
> same
> yeah fuck off Rory
> lol the party or the woke bus take your pick
> this is stupid we cant have two busses
> yeah we can PARTY BUS
> you mean the douche bus

Hunter turned it off and rolled over, his eyes gritty from lack of sleep, his stomach growling, gnawing with hunger. He had to make weight for Saturday's big match, so breakfast would be a single hardboiled egg and black coffee. As hungry as he was, he couldn't force himself out of bed, so he laid on his side, his back to the wall.

Get. Up. He commanded himself. Yet he couldn't make his body move. It wasn't until he heard his mother shout from the bottom of the steps that he was able to drag himself out of bed and into the shower. He allowed himself 30 seconds of hot water streaming over his body, loosening the tight muscles in his neck and shoulders. He hurriedly soaped himself, then turned off the hot water, letting the shock of cold sluice the soap and sleep from his body, invigorating him. Toughening him.

Cece Logan smiled at Hunter and offered a bowl with a singular egg sliding around inside it. She turned away after he accepted it and poured a mug of black coffee setting it down with a clank against the slate counter.

"Thanks, mom." He sipped his coffee, feeling the jolt he needed.

His mother appraised him. Hunter met her eyes then looked away, hoping she wouldn't talk to him or ask him anything.

"You okay, honey?"

Hunter did his best to smile through the dry yolk of the egg like glue in his mouth. He nodded.

"You sure? You look tired."

He shrugged.

"Everything all right at school?"

Hunter took a sip of coffee in an attempt to swallow the yolk and tried to think of something to appease his mother so she'd stop assessing him. "I got an A on that history paper."

She nodded and smiled, but Hunter recognized the vague reflex for what it was. She wasn't interested in his grades. She knew they were strong. She was after something else. Hunter felt his stomach clench.

"How is everything —else?"

"We've got the big match Saturday, I'm focused on that."

His mother pursed her lips. Unlike Rory and Kam's moms and all of the dads, Cece Logan didn't care about wrestling. In fact she didn't approve of the starving and weight making and it had taken her years to stop trying to ply him with food he couldn't have when he was trying to make weight. She would have been happier if Hunter had been a musician or a theater kid. But he wasn't. And his younger brothers were both following in his footsteps, which brought on an uneasy feeling Hunter tried to dispel by not thinking about it. Cece cocked her head in a way that made Hunter nervous.

"Is there something— bothering you? I just feel like you're not yourself lately—like there's something you aren't telling me."

Hunter popped the last bite of egg white into his mouth, chewed, swallowed, and drained his coffee cup. He got up and put his hands on his mother's shoulders—something he still marveled at, that despite her care giving and mom-like behavior he was so much bigger than she was. It made him feel like an adult with a kid brain, and it was disconcerting. His mother was more perceptive than Rory's and Kam's moms, and she was far more perceptive than any of their fathers. He needed to placate her, throw her off track. He smiled his most charming smile, making sure it crinkled his eyes. It was easy to be sincere. He loved her. And didn't want her to worry. And… he needed her not to focus on him. He needed to get through the rest of this year and make it to college. Far away from this town and all of the people in it.

"I'm good, mom, I promise. It's just intense right now." Hunter saw his mother's hands flutter and rushed to stave off whatever worry was coming toward him. "After this match I'll get more rest. Love you!" He kissed the top of her head and fled without turning back, as she stood, her hands going to her shoulders, one arm crossing over the other, landing in the place his hands had rested.

CHAPTER 10

Delaney pulled up in front of Olivia's just as she emerged, feet shoved into ancient Ugg boots, legs encased in leggings, bundled into a hoodie emblazoned with their school logo.

"Really, Olivia?" Delaney said, when Olivia hurled herself into the passenger seat. "You need to start giving a shit. Just a little. For my sake."

Olivia looked at Delaney's red-gold curls framing her face, her winged eye-makeup that must have taken fifteen minutes to apply. "I don't know how you find the energy, but thanks for the ride."

"Anytime, Sweets." Delaney turned the radio up. It was one of Olivia's favorite Kendrick Lamar songs. She reached over and shuffled it to the next song.

Delaney gave a sideways glance to Olivia, "Not in the mood or…"

"I know it's stupid but…"

"What?"

"It just reminds me of…"

"Hunter?"

Olivia nodded.

"Did you have a thing for him? I kind of thought it was just a hookup."

"It was."

"So?"

Olivia shook her head. "That snap."

Delaney smirked, "It was hot. Honestly if that was mine I'd put it up on OnlyFans."

Olivia laughed. Delaney wasn't being hyperbolic. She had an OnlyFans site and made more money on it than she could in any other job. It funded Delaney's love of all things vintage-couture. For the site, Delaney wore lingerie and made up her face with so much glitter and artistry that she was virtually unrecognizable. She placed a tiny mic on her wrist, covered it with vintage rubber bracelets, and used rhythmic movements to scratch her head, resulting in a vaguely hypnotic, extremely erotic, effect that fetish customers paid dearly for. Olivia was the only one privy to this information. No one else, not even Isa or Bailey, knew about it. Olivia found it shocking. Delaney was outrageous and it was what Olivia loved about her. But it also meant that Delaney would never understand how hurt she was by Hunter posting that picture.

Delaney turned to look at Olivia and the car swerved.

"Watch it!" Olivia said.

"You really are upset about it—I'm sorry, Liv—did you not know about it?"

"No! I wouldn't have agreed to it—ever."

"That's not right. I'm gonna kick his ass."

Olivia liked that idea. Delaney would kick Hunter's ass for her, she would kick Rory's ass for Isa, and Isa could kick Kam's ass for the hell of it. "Ha, let's mess them up at Kam's party Saturday night."

"I thought we weren't going."

"Change of plans."

"Isa too?"

"Yep. We need to figure out what those slimebags are up to."

"Ugh. I don't know if I can stand seeing Kam's face."

"You're not still hooking up with him are you?"

"Nope. Not since he sent me this…"

Delaney thrust her phone at Olivia. Olivia tapped Delaney's code in and went to Kam's last text. It was a video of Kam naked from the waist up, the edges of his pubic hair visible as he sang Machine Gun Kelly's lyrics into the camera about how he'd banged her again and they would never be friends. Rude.

Olivia dropped the phone, "No!"

Delaney nodded, "I can never unsee that so I can never hook up with him again."

"Disgusting."

Delaney shrugged. "Honestly he was hot, our thing was hot. But he had to go and ruin it with his juvenile douchebaggery."

Olivia shook her head. She would never understand what happened, how everyone had changed so much, she felt a tightening in her chest, rolled down her window, picked Delaney's phone up and found Mitski's "Nobody" and let the song fill the car and ward off everything else.

Saturday morning broke with driving rains lashing through trees, pounding on rooftops, creating swamps across suburban backyards.

Rory opened his eyes, disoriented for a moment by the thick rivulets of water slamming the windowpane. The staccato beat ominous in its force. The gray light behind the water made it impossible for Rory to tell the time and he shot up in bed, adrenaline coursing through him at the thought that he may have slept through his alarm. Jabbing at his phone until the screen brightened revealing it was only 6:15.

Rory slumped against the wall behind his bed, resting his head against the cold. He still had half an hour before he needed to get up, but he would never get back to sleep and the idea of lying there alone with his thoughts was too much.

Today was the biggest match of his career. The determining factor of whether or not he'd be a contender for the states. It didn't matter for college, he had the offers he had, but it mattered for his legacy.

He was hungry but couldn't eat until after weigh in. He got up and stretched, letting the hunger go, focusing instead on the acuity of his mind. It was as though the hunger sharpened his ability to evaluate and strategize. Maybe it was primitive DNA showing him the way to food opportunities, taking him on the hunt.

Maybe that's what wrestling was. A modern day man vs. man, man vs. animal, man vs. the environment, man vs. everything.

Rory stood naked in front of his mirror, assessing the definition in his muscles. Making weight had the added benefit of delineating every line, every swell, of his body. The word swell was too much for him and he felt the familiar stirring, the tension of pleasure and shame, and watched himself grow. He felt powerful. Magnificent. Euphoric. Intruding on the euphoria was a small familiar voice telling him to stop. That he was filthy. Wrong. He waited a moment and the other voices took over, drowning the small one out. Telling him this was his birthright. It was natural. He had nothing to be ashamed of, but should feel proud. He was put on earth for this very reason. It was not only his right, but also his duty to be virile.

He reached for his phone.

By 8 am the high school campus was buzzing with cars and people. Erica stood at the entrance of the cafeteria where half a dozen moms stood in hairnets and team jerseys, doling out food to the boys who made weight. Erica saw yearning in their eyes as they stood in line, and she felt an intense maternal surge of pride. These boys sacrificed so much to wrestle, their dedication and commitment would make them leaders in the world, and Rory would be in the front of that pack, just as she was in the front of the pack of moms, working tirelessly behind the scenes to make trays of protein and nutrient rich food for them. All the years of carpooling, scheduling, locker-room laundry (with the amount she spent on dryer sheets she could easily have bought herself another Birkin) keeping her son on task, herding the other moms and players into fundraising efforts, the countless team dinners she'd hosted. She'd done her share to launch these young men and felt her own sense of pride and accomplishment. Their win was her win. Their loss was her loss. There was so much riding on today she could barely breathe.

Erica felt a light tap on the back of her shoulder and positioned her face into her most helpful smile, eradicating any anticipation of the match, it wouldn't do to show her own anxiety, she needed to be a rock for these boys.

She turned ready to help and came face to face with Indira. "Hey, Erica."

Indira's smile was an irritant. Couldn't she see how busy Erica was with her clipboard and the long line of hungry boys she was checking in? "Indira. What are you doing here?" Indira never went to sporting events. How many times had she heard Indira say sports just weren't her thing? Well, sports weren't Erica's "thing" either. She went to support her children and their school district.

Indira smiled wider, "There's a poetry slam in the auditorium, but I cut through the cafeteria and here you are."

"Oh. Yes. Well enjoy the poetry slam. Is Olivia participating?"

"She's one of the organizers."

"Oh, well—have fun." She leaned forward in what she hoped was a conspiratorial, inclusionary manner. Erica prided herself on making everyone feel important and tried never to be rude. "I'm a little busy here—not sure you know, but this determines where we seed."

"Oh! No I didn't but—good luck!"

"Thanks, sweetie. I'll tell Rory you wished him luck." And with that she turned around waiting until she felt the mugginess of Indira's body heat move away and the flow of air around her loosen.

Indira continued toward the auditorium, coming to a stop as she rounded the bend to an empty hallway. She could still hear the noise of boys and trays and mayhem, but she was fairly certain no one would come upon her here. Leaning for a moment against the wall, she tried to lessen the tension behind her breastbone, the feeling that it was difficult to breathe. It was an actual physical pain. Indira mustered the courage to identify the source. Rejection. Perhaps it was the throwback of walking through the hallways of a high school (although Indira had attended school in Brooklyn, which couldn't be more different from this suburban setting with sports teams and PTA moms). Indira thought back to her high school days, wondering if there was a similar feeling of rejection. She couldn't remember anything specifically. Sure, there were arguments among her girlfriends, they had periods of being on the outs with one another, but for the most part Indira was the peacemaker. And although she remembered a pervasive sense of anxiety whenever there was tension among her friends, she couldn't remember specifically feeling iced out. Sure, she felt insecure at times, but she couldn't remember that physical pang of rejection. Even with boys—because Indira was too afraid to like a boy, she never expected them to like her back, and so rejection wasn't a real thing. She remembered watching with awe the girls who had boyfriends. Observing with anthropological interest the way they would hold hands, sit on their boyfriend's laps (sometimes quite brazenly straddling them), wearing their boyfriend's jackets, or making out under a street lamp. Why a street lamp, she often wondered. Did they want an audience? They were an alien species to Indira, these loud confident girls. She half-admired, half-feared them. And she had been a little bit obsessed with them. She was also grateful to them for showing her a window into their lives. But she never wanted to be like them. She was happy with her circle of friends, she had filled her weekend nights with uninterrupted studying and a few sleepovers when her friends had dragged her out of the apartment. She had a couple friends in her neighborhood. But they tended to see each other during the day. They walked along Sheepshead Bay, or lathered themselves in baby oil lying on old bed sheets on the hot sand, taking intermittent dips in the greasy waters of Brighton Beach. At night, there were parties on the beach, but she avoided them since they were fueled with pot smoking and vodka-soaked watermelon. Indira was known back then, in the lexicon of their times, as a good girl. A generation before that she would have been a square. It was a role she was comfortable in. She went to the social events she wanted to and skipped the ones she didn't. She talked to the boys she felt comfortable with (non-threatening intellectual boys who shared the same interests as her—boys she didn't have to fend off or worse, feel attracted to).

In the interest of self-awareness, Indira had to admit to herself that the pain behind her breastbone, the humiliation of rejection, was not a residual feeling from high school or some ancient childhood wound. It was current and present and very real. All the platitudes she's told herself about Erica just being busy, or getting more involved with the club, or the fact that their kids were older and they didn't need to spend time together whiling away the hours, hadn't been a rejection of her, Indira. It had simply been a consequence of busy lives, a confluence of events. But there was no denying that Indira had allowed a false hope to grow after their brief encounter the week before Christmas. The casual *glass of wine* comment that Indira knew wasn't sincere but clung to anyway. She needed to face the fact that the dissolution of her friendship with Erica had nothing to do with being busy or the kids growing up, and everything to do with the way Erica felt about her. She had been dismissed.

With this realization Indira felt (with a certain amount of horror) a prickling behind her eyes and the fullness of a sob tightening her throat. She pressed her eyes until she saw flashes of white. Swallowed. Then said to herself, that over-used phrase she hated until this moment when she realized the full impact of the truth behind it. *It is what it is.*

With that thought she allowed herself to let go of Erica Lange and their old friendship. She would think of it fondly, in sepia tones the way she thought of her child-raising years. Something she'd loved and relegated to happy memories. Trying to hold on to an elusive past was a sure path to suffering.

And Indira had no wish to suffer. She focused on putting one foot firmly in front of the other, letting the din of the cafeteria fade behind her.

Jimmy Irizzary watched the minutes tick by with a familiar pang of regret. He'd promised Olivia and Indira he would try to make the poetry slam. He listened to the drone of voices coming through his phone. It was on mute because there was nothing he needed to contribute to this call. Yet here he was in the converted home office above the garage, listening to his team carry on and on about a presentation they were giving on Monday. If Jimmy was honest with himself, he knew he could jump off the call and make it in time for the poetry slam. Yet he *almost* preferred to stay on this call and listen to the posturing of his sales associates rather than listen to earnest poetry recited in spoken word cadence by a bunch of privileged suburban high school students who burned through their parent's credit cards with expertise far surpassing their spoken word skills. Jimmy knew his thoughts about this were mean and possibly unwarranted, but he couldn't shake them.

He was finding his life in the suburbs increasingly frustrating. Earlier that month Jimmy mentioned something to Indira about moving back to the city when Olivia graduated. She'd looked at him, her light brown eyes sparked with anger. "Great, for the price of our house, we'll find a one bedroom in Murray Hill, Olivia can sleep on the couch. You can convert our only closet into a home office."

"It would be a change, I get that, but the city would be at our fingertips."

"I didn't realize you were so unhappy here."

"I'm not—it's just…"

"What?"

"Doesn't it ever feel stifling? The same friends, the same small talk?"

Indira looked as if she'd just warded off a physical blow. "Am I stifling you somehow? Because it seems to me you do pretty much whatever you want."

"It was just a thought…"

"Apparently it's something you've given a lot of thought to."

"I get it. Olivia going to school is going to be a big change, maybe you're not ready yet…but in the future."

"I don't want to move to the city, Jimmy. I'm okay with discussing a change. But it needs to make sense."

He saw the defeat in her eyes and that wasn't what he wanted. He didn't know what he wanted. Maybe that was the problem.

He checked his watch. Almost 10:30, too late to make the poetry slam. A profound sense of relief mingled with regret at Olivia's potential disappointment, he placed the phone with its irritating stream of babble on his desk, resisting the urge to throw it against the wall. He thought to himself, not for the first time, that despite what everybody thought, his mother, Indira, Olivia, his team, every client he'd ever wooed, his friends and neighbors, that he was not such a happy-go-lucky guy. He was, in fact, filled with an inexplicable rage.

CHAPTER 11

The announcer had just finished welcoming the teams to the mats when Emmett Ainsworth, former state champ and alum, now a sophomore at Dartmouth, walked through the gymnasium door. Rory's teammates saw him first and sent up a rousing cheer, which went through the gym in a wave of sound. Emmett, looked slightly taken aback, as if he hadn't expected such an overwhelming response.

Honestly, Erica thought, *Emmett had his moment, he needs to take a seat.* Erica leaned over to the woman next to her, "Shame Emmett quit the team. Dartmouth must have proven more difficult than he expected."

The woman turned to Erica with wide eyes, "Why did he quit?"

Erica shrugged, "Who knows? Could be grades, could be he was outmatched."

"Well, that doesn't bode well for our boys if a kid like Emmett dropped off the team."

Erica sniffed, "I don't know about Christopher, but Rory won't have any trouble, he's at the top of his class. And he's no quitter."

The woman turned away and bit her lip. She looked worried. Erica felt a moment of remorse but let it go. The woman's son was a middle of the pack wrestler, and he was a middle-of-the-pack student. There was nothing Erica could do about that. She was still irritated. Right now instead of Coach focusing on Rory, he was hugging Emmett and whispering something in his ear. She watched them closely and felt slightly mollified when she saw Coach nod at Rory, a look of pride on his face, Coach's broad handsome smile visible even from the fan section. She couldn't be sure but she thought Emmett paled a bit. He stared at Rory for a moment before turning away. *Jealous,* she thought. *Rory's poised to beat Emmett's record. Washed up by his sophomore year of college.* Erica leaned forward. Rory was stepping onto the mat. He looked determined, like a winner. Suddenly she felt more charitable to Emmett Ainsworth. It seemed having him there was good for Rory, his focus intensified, and his desire to win and prove himself to one of his heroes, was going to work in his favor. She could tell. She had no doubt that he would lead his team to victory.

Emmett stood next to Coach during Rory's bout. The boys readied themselves in standing position. Rory's stance was strong, balanced. His opponent was using a lot of energy to mean mug, but it didn't seem to faze Rory. His opponent lunged forward, took a leg shot, but Rory blocked him easily by putting his head down, then moved quickly for a takedown, his opponent escaped, Emmett was close enough to hear Rory grunt and the slap of bodies against the mat, Rory grappled his way and attempted a tilt but his opponent blocked him. Mere seconds passed, but Emmet recognized the strain on their faces and knew that for them time was standing still. Rory went in for a redirect tilt and rotated his opponent across his chest in a bold move. They grappled until

Rory moved into a cradle position. The gym hushed as his opponent pushed back, but Rory was patient, keeping his chest high, trapping him in a lock, then knocked him onto his far hip, sending him to a near fall. The crowd got to their feet, Emmett felt them roaring, he watched Rory's opponent try his escape, but Rory's hold was firm. Emmett watched as the guy's shoulders hit the mat and Rory leaned in for the pin.

The noise was deafening. Emmett felt Coach move closer, smelled the unwelcome familiar smell of Coach's aftershave, the cinnamon gum he always chewed. His breath was a fleeting moment of heat against his ear, then the whisper, *he's the new you.*

Emmett forced himself to stand in place and watch the machinations of the winner being declared, the requisite chest bumping, back patting, and ass slapping. Emmett made sure he found his moment to congratulate Rory who looked into Emmett's eyes with a mixture of pride and deference, which made Emmett's stomach drop. As soon as he could, Emmett slipped away from the gym, walking along the echoing halls of his former high school, feeling slightly nauseous and disoriented. *He's the new you, the new you.* The words seemed to follow his footsteps. A terrible refrain.

Emmett barely remembered when Rory joined the team. He remembered being surprised. He'd seemed so young, so slight. He wasn't any more. Rory was as tall as Emmett was now, and if he met him in a bar he would mistake Rory for a college student.

The roar of the crowd dimmed as Emmett walked, but the nausea grew stronger. There had been a time when he'd lived for that sound. All it did now was make him uneasy. He strode quickly toward the exit. Soon he'd be on his way to pick up Monica and head down to meet a bunch of their Dartmouth friends at his father's beach house on the Jersey Shore. Emmett loved the beach in the winter, and he was pretty sure he loved Monica. Emmett told himself he just needed to get away from the gym and this town, and everything would be okay. *Rory will be okay*. Emmett told himself. After all, he'd survived his years on the team. Rory would as well. And if Rory didn't like wrestling in college, he could always quit.

Erica had cheered louder, longer, and stronger, than anyone in the stands when Rory pinned his opponent. Coach whooped, the crowd roared, and Rory had solidified his path to the states.

The excitement in the gym washed over and around Erica, she basked in it as she made her way through the stands, there would be pomp and circumstance in the next few minutes, but she wanted to be near Rory for this moment. He was surrounded by a pile of wrestlers, so she just stood nearby, pride bursting, when she felt a frisson of electricity and the solidity of a body next to her, the familiar scent of aftershave and cinnamon gum. She turned to face him, "Coach! You did it!"

"Your boy did it, Erica. He's a star."

"He couldn't have done it without your guidance and support." Erica looked up at Coach. The pulse in her throat gave an extra beat when his eyes met hers. So blue, Ice, the cheerleaders called him, but Erica saw only warmth. And he was adorable, the bashful way he dipped his head, his slow grin. Erica placed her hand briefly and lightly on his bicep. His arm was solid, strong, buzzing against her palm. "I'll let you get back to your team, I just wanted to congratulate you."

Erica lifted her hand and walked back to the stands, reveling in Rory's success and wondering briefly if Coach was watching her walk away and if he felt the electricity she felt whenever she was near him. She smiled to herself, every girl needed a secret of her own, and if hers was the low-key attraction that would never ever be acted upon, then in the history of secrets, hers wasn't so bad. Sometimes Erica felt this town was full of secrets, and they didn't feel as benign as a teeny tiny crush on the man who was going to be responsible for Rory's ascendance to a D1 school. Erica went back to the stands to accept the enthusiastic congratulations that would be coming her way, walking tall, an extra sashay to her hips, and one more toss of her luxurious ponytail, raising her arms and shimmying just as the refrain from the Black Eyed Peas song, "I Gotta Feeling" boomed through the gym, thinking that it would indeed be a good night.

CHAPTER 12

Saturday evening came with a blast of excitement exacerbated by relief. Several events celebrating the heady combination were taking place.

For the parents of the winning wrestling team, it meant three couples, the Langes, Connovers, and Logans, would celebrate in the club dining room with several rounds of cocktails. Gin martinis for the men, tequila and lime for the ladies, because as Ginnifer Connover often said, tequila was a low calorie stimulant and God knew they didn't need any more calories or depressants. Many bottles of wine would follow, each one carefully curated by Don Connover, who surpassed even the best sommelier for knowledge of fine wine. Preprandial cocktails (yes, Don referred to cocktails before dinner as preprandial) would take place in the elegant bar room, which seemed to Erica to be straight out of a Fitzgerald novel.

Erica, despite her penchant for trendy couture, loved everything and anything from the Jazz Age. It began in 8th grade when she was 12 years old and read *The Short Stories of F. Scott Fitzgerald*. "Bernice Bobs Her Hair" became a formative piece of literature for Erica. She took the lessons to heart and decided to live her life as if it had already happened to her. The thwarting of social conventions dictated by her parents, the realization that she felt like an outsider looking in, and the subsequent understanding that the best solution was to emulate the ones who did fit in, preparing herself for the inevitable attempt at retribution by the very individuals she was emulating. Erica determined upon finishing the story that she would cut off anyone's braids before she bobbed her own hair. She'd throw them in the face of any boy who displayed traitorous fickle behavior. She'd win the game before anyone even knew it was being played.

When Erica finally worked her way up to *The Great Gatsby*, she committed to memory Daisy's line referring to her infant daughter … *the best thing a girl can be in this world, a beautiful little fool.* Erica thought at the time that Daisy was nobody's fool and didn't fully understand why she would wish that for her daughter. By the end of the story, Erica understood that a beautiful fool was an effective weapon in the arsenal of life. Beautiful fools reaped the benefits of delighting everyone in their path while having the opportunity to experience the unspoiled joy that only a fool can have. Erica somehow understood that the juxtaposition of innocence and knowledge it would take to perpetrate such an act required an expertise she did not possess. It was not a role she, Erica, was born to play, it was however, an archetype she enjoyed observing. And so began Erica's lifelong fascination with beautiful fools. One of the perks of this fascination was that no matter how tedious an event was, no matter how tired she was or how much her feet hurt in high heels, Erica could always distract herself by looking for the beautiful fools. In this room alone, Erica could spot five of them. None were at her table. Ginnifer was too healthy and outdoorsy and didn't suffer even the approximation of a fool. Privately, Erica thought Cece Logan too bland and mousy to be a beautiful fool. Everything about Cece screamed conformity, from her navy blue shift and cornflower blue cardigan to her shoulder length ash-blond hair, tasteful makeup, and uninspired if well-constructed flats. Cece, while beyond reproach, went unnoticed in a room. But what she lacked in zest and beauty she made up for in lifelong pedigree, resulting in an innate, unshakeable confidence Erica envied more than anything or anyone else in the room.

"This particular vintage is for the ladies, lush and full." Don Connover was in the middle of his dissertation on the wines he'd selected.

"Bite your tongue!" Ginnifer joked, "We're all smooth and svelte." Everyone laughed, yet it wasn't lost on Erica that elegance and breeding dictated that Don should serve an exquisite wine without making mention of it because no one in his world would expect anything less. Erica found it gauche the way he went on and on. Erica searched for a trace of Ginnifer's embarrassment or irritation, or failing that, at least a whiff of condescending indulgence. But to Ginnifer's credit, Erica couldn't detect even a flash of any of those things. She seemed perfectly at ease, allowing Don to pontificate. The gleaming wood-paneled room lit by ornate sconces and a sparkling chandelier served as a fitting backdrop to Don's lengthy, mannered speech.

Erica didn't mind because it gave her ample opportunity to observe the beautiful fool at the other end of the bar from her. Erica watched the power the beautiful fool wielded over the men in their group, the way they bowed their heads closer to her when she spoke, the almost deferential way they looked at her whenever they had the opportunity. She watched how the women seemed to form a protective circle around her, touching her hand here, her shoulder there. The way her musical laugh lifted and floated above the room, settling over everyone like a shimmering veil of happiness. It was astonishing to behold and Erica was delighted by how delightful she was and how much she enhanced the roaring twenties ambience of the bar room. With a narrowing of her eyes, Erica could almost imagine the men's boxy, ill-fitting, expensive suits were instead elegant dinner jackets, and that her own body-skimming Balenciaga was actually a flapper dress resplendent with fringe and silk.

Erica whiled away the remaining minutes this way until members of her party were properly drunk and they could all move into the dining room, where she could pretend to eat her dinner, sample Don's carefully procured wine selection, and bask in the glow of Rory's resounding success on the mats that morning.

Don Connover placed his hand at the small of Erica's back as they came up to the table. She allowed him to pull her chair out for her, before he turned to slide the chair in expertly for his wife. Ginny sat down effortlessly. Erica took note that Keith failed to pull Cece's chair out on his other side, and he was sitting before both of them. He may have been born with a silver spoon in his mouth Erica thought, but her husband was a boor. "Thank you, Don, always the gentleman."

"My pleasure." He winked at her. Erica felt vaguely repulsed, but she played along and smiled slowly back at him. Lifting her glass and holding it to her lips.

"So what are we expecting in this glass?"

He leaned closer, "Smoke and blackberry."

"Mmm." she murmured and averted her gaze from his, allowing him to take in the curve of her lips, the line of her neck, and the smooth expanse of décolletage.

Then she turned her attention to Ginnifer, "Tell me Ginny, the food pantry?"

"Thank you for asking! Do you realize there are nearly 200,000 people living with food insecurity in Westchester County alone?"

"I told Keith to make a donation, we hope it helps."

"It was so generous, Erica, really. Maybe a few less people will go to bed hungry tonight." Ginny took a tiny bite of her salmon, then proceeded to cover it up with the mashed potatoes.

Erica sawed a tiny piece of filet mignon away with her knife and tucked it under the green beans. Then she cut a green bean in thirds, stabbed the smallest one with the tines of her fork and lifted it off with her teeth, leaving her lips as shellacked as a shiny red Corvette. She pretended not to notice Don watching her lips move.

Erica had the thought as she carefully chewed, that for this moment in time, there was nowhere else she would rather be.

The Birnbaum-Irizzarry's were not having as elegant an evening, although they wouldn't trade places with anyone. U2's *How To Dismantle An Atomic Bomb* was playing. Jimmy was sprawled on their large battered couch in front of the fireplace with Indira's feet in his lap. She was wearing yoga pants and Jimmy's SUNY Binghamton sweatshirt from 1992. He had on threadbare Diesel jeans and a Nirvana T-shirt, which Indira suspected were also from 1992. The remnants of their take out Thai food were scattered across the scratched oversized coffee table and they were each on their second beer. Olivia and Isa had just left the house and the room still resonated with their sound, sparkle, and perfume.

Jimmy pressed his thumb into the arch of Indira's foot causing her to promptly relax. She tried not to let his sudden desire to ask her questions about the morning distract her.

"I take it the poetry thing went well."

"Mmm."

"Was Olivia happy with the turnout?"

"Seemed good—I mean not like the wrestling tournament." If Jimmy noticed the unusual bitter tone he didn't react to it. Indira decided to concentrate on his hands on her instead.

"Students mostly?" Jimmy pulled his hands away.

"Don't stop."

"Only if you pay attention."

"Yes. Kids from all over, even other towns. It was a huge success and they raised a lot of money for a local battered women's shelter."

"It was a charity thing?"

"In part."

"Oh." That information caused Jimmy to feel like an even bigger heel for not going. "Did we contribute, I hope?"

" I bought two tickets, even though I knew you probably wouldn't make it. "

"That's it? No cash donation?"

"Oh. I don't know. No one asked me for one."

"Make sure you make one."

"Ok." Indira wondered briefly why Jimmy was suddenly so interested in something as mundane as Olivia's school activities. While he took obsessive notice of grades and class standing, the extra-curricular activities were usually relegated to a perfunctory interest at best. Then she relaxed into the sensation of his hands on her feet.

Jimmy smiled at the way Indira threw her head back against the couch pillow, the line of her throat alabaster in the glow of the fire. He focused on the spot beneath her jaw he knew made her sigh when he pressed his lips against it. Slowly he moved out from under her legs and over her, pressing his lips against her skin, her scent familiar and comforting, helping her wriggle out of her clothes, sliding out of his.

He closed his eyes and sought redemption in his lips over hers, and like the song suggested, lost himself in the sensation of honey on his tongue. He moved over and into her.

Indira felt the sudden intensity of Jimmy's body, the shift in his movements. She'd been pleasantly drifting, enjoying the sensation of him, the music, the beer buzz, and the illicit nature of sex not in their bedroom, but she felt the shift and opened her eyes to find him looking at her. She smiled and kissed him, he smiled back and kissed her, but she'd seen something there... an intensity she hadn't seen since their earliest days together. When they had been falling in love. Was that it? Was he falling in love with her all over again? And if so, was it because he'd fallen out of love with her? Was that the shift she'd been feeling these past months? Indira tried to pull back and look once again into his eyes, search for whatever it was she'd seen. But he was smiling his sexiest smile at her now, and moving against her exactly the way she needed. She arched higher, losing herself in him, until it was all that mattered.

CHAPTER 13

Olivia and Isa parked on the road at the end of a snaking line of cars. They had to walk a quarter of a mile to make it up the road and across the property. It was a cold moonless night, and neither of them had dressed warmly. Their feelings of dread about attending the party shifted to relief when they entered the warmth of the guesthouse. The place smelled like lavender and vinegar (organic cleaning fluid Kam's mother insisted her cleaning staff use), beer, and vape. One of Kam's rules was they couldn't stink up the place with weed or cigarettes, because his mother had the nose of a bloodhound and even if she didn't enter the guest house for three months she would *know*. All of his friends had access to medical marijuana pens and most of the nicotine smokers had never even tried cigarettes, going right for e-sticks. For the time being, it was a sanitized world to come of age in.

Olivia looked at Isa. "If Rory comes near you I swear I will knock him back."

"What are we going to do about Hunter—the photo?"

The image flashed in Olivia's mind, her head thrown back, her breasts exposed.

"I hate Hunter for taking that. Hope he chokes on a dick."

"That's the thing, I thought you understood, I mean I didn't think you thought he literally took it. He obviously planned it and distributed it."

"And took it."

"Liv…the angle. He couldn't have."

"He had to. No one else was there—"

And then, just like that, the miasma Olivia had been experiencing lifted. It was visceral, a splintering and shattering of shame replaced with a white-hot nuclear rage.

"I will murder him."

"We have to be smart about it."

"I'll bash his head in. How's that for smart."

"Seriously, Liv. We have to be strategic."

Isa watched as the color came back slowly into Olivia's face, flooding her lips and cheeks. Her nostrils flared, her eyes narrowed and glinting. Her chest was moving up and down as if she'd just raced. Isa waited patiently waiting for Olivia to come back into herself. "Liv. We're going to get them. But we can't get *ourselves* in the process."

Olivia nodded. "Then what?"

"We act like nothing's wrong. And we bide our time until we find out what those dirty little toads are up to."

"We already know."

"We know about Rory and Hunter. But who took that picture?"

"It had to be Kam." Olivia paled, "Or Rory?"

Isa shook her head, "I was dancing with Kam that whole time you were upstairs. And Rory was watching us like a creep. He never moved."

"Then it was one of their asshole buddies."

"Most of the guys were away, remember?"

"There were seven guys there that night."

"Lee and his friends! The four of them were getting high on the back porch. I could see them through the sliders. And none of them would do that."

"A girl?"

"Olivia, they were all on the dance floor."

"You've really thought about this."

Isa looked at her, "I knew you never would have consented to that pic—so yeah—I've thought about this."

"Any chance you're wrong?"

Isa gave her another look. "You know I'm not."

Olivia nodded.

"You were only up there for about 15 minutes, but I was nervous for you. Kam can't dance. He kept stepping on my feet. I'd had enough and was about to get off the floor when Lee and those guys got paranoid and started yelling about cops."

"So, who was up there with us?"

Isa looked at her. "I can't figure it out."

Olivia felt her arms prickle. "I'm asking Hunter."

"He won't tell you."

"He *will* fucking tell me. You'll see."

Isa followed Olivia into the heart of the party looking straight ahead, pretending to ignore the avidity in the stares and whispers of their peers.

Olivia looked around. Aside from more bodies and an extra hum of testosterone from winning the match that morning, it was the same bullshit party as ever. The room was littered with canned margaritas and half eaten boxes of pizza. The guys were shirtless even though it was January, girls stood in clusters uncomfortable without their usual party trick of taking selfies (forbidden at a Connover party), the familiar smell of vape and the constant thump of music. A pervasive boredom mingling with rage was a socially lethal combination for a place like this, and Olivia could feel Isa's careful gaze on her back.

Olivia and Isa made their way over to where Delaney was standing with a group of girls casually sipping fizzy, overly sweet faux margaritas from cans, which had grown lukewarm in their palms.

Delaney looped her arm through Isa's. "Thank God you bitches are here. This party sucks filthy ass."

Olivia watched Hunter Logan register their presence. He looked nervous. She waited for him to make eye contact. When he did, his eyes held hers. He didn't waver, or smirk, or look away. It was as if they knew one another in a way that was both strange and familiar. As if a mystery had been unlocked somewhere inside her, a flood of heat and knowledge and longing and hate. The picture popped into her mind and for the first time she thought of it without feeling shame. There was something pure and cleansing about the frenzy of rage boiling inside her. Olivia smiled at him. Maybe he read her, or maybe it was something else, but he didn't smile back.

Isa gave Olivia a quizzical look and Olivia laughed.

Isa laughed too, but Olivia could tell she was worried about her. Olivia wondered if Isa was right to be worried. She did feel slightly unhinged.

"What's going on?" Delaney asked.

"This party's bad vibes." Olivia said.

Delaney shrugged. "Obviously."

Isa laughed.

The song changed and it was once again *everyone's jam.*

Bodies filled the dance floor and once again, Olivia was dancing with Hunter Logan.

At least, Isa noted, he had his shirt on, unlike the other bros piling around her. She saw Rory's face appear and suddenly his hands were around her waist. She removed his hands and took a step away. "Get off me."

He moved toward her, "Come on Isa, don't do me like this." His words were pleading but his smirk was demanding and his eyes greedy. He came toward her again, this time getting so close her knee was in a position to lift and do real damage. She leaned in, repulsed by the heavy cologne and something else, pheromones maybe, and whispered close to his ear, "Back off, or I'll smash your balls so far up you'll choke on them."

Rory dropped his hands like her body burned and went palms up, backing off, but smirking the whole time. "Can't blame a guy for trying," he yelled into the music.

Isa moved closer, "Stop trying, you sociopath."

This time he backed off for real, his smirk disappeared, and she saw something else fill his eyes. Isa recognized it because she felt it too. Hatred. *Good.* She thought. *Bring it.*

Olivia watched Isa and felt her adrenaline surge, pulling her away from the magnetic heat of Hunter and the music. He felt the change in her body and swiveled his head around to see what Olivia was looking at. He turned back to her and bent forward whispering urgently in her ear, "I need you to know—I didn't send that snap—one of the guys pranked me."

Olivia pushed his face away from her ear. "Fuck you, who took it?"

"Huh?"

"Who. Took. It."

"I did—I mean…I'm sorry I shouldn't have…"

"You're a liar. Who else was there?"

"No one—look I'm sorry, I shouldn't have taken it—"

"Tell me who took it."

"It was just a selfie set up—I'm sorry—Olivia—wait." His hand reached for hers.

She shook him off and walked toward Isa. Groups of kids turned their way and moved closer. They smelled drama and were circling. Isa and Delaney closed ranks around Olivia. Delaney grabbed a bottle from the counter and the three of them strode out of the room, leaving hungry eyes and gaping mouths, the disappointment palpable, the tantalizing morsel dangled and swept away before they'd had their fill.

The frigid air felt good after the heat of the party. Delaney led them to the other side of the covered Olympic-size pool. They found a wrought iron patio set at the far end of the grounds beside a grove of evergreens. Delaney passed the bottle to Olivia who took a burning sip then tried to hand it to Isa who refused. Olivia set the bottle down with a satisfying clank against the table.

The music was a distant thump and four acres of woods lay dark and impenetrable before them. They were only about 40 yards away from the guesthouse, but it felt like they'd entered a different world.

Delaney pulled on her vape and exhaled a fruit scented stream. "Should the ass-kicking begin?"

Isa and Olivia caught each other's gaze, but neither of them spoke.

"He had no right to send that snap," Delaney said.

Olivia began to cry. Not an angry tear that she could push back with her fingertips, but full body wracking sobs. Her knees hit the ground. Isa dropped down and put her arm around Olivia. "Hey, now."

Delaney knelt down so she could catch Olivia's eye, "Those guys are dickheads. No one judged you. Hunter's the fittest guy in our grade, everyone was jealous. And you may not care—but you did look hot and you really can't see anything, his head is covering most of your boob."

Olivia cringed and Isa glared at Delaney who rolled her eyes, "What? It was like an art photo. Everyone said so."

"Fuck that!" Olivia's voice sounded like she was strangling. "That was invasive and exploitative. And creepy as hell."

Delaney pulled out her phone, her thumbs whirring. "Huh. I just kind of assumed it was a selfie but unless Hunter's a fucking contortionist…"

"You have it on your phone!" Isa yelled.

Delaney shrugged again. "It's no biggie."

"Seriously?" Isa glared.

"It was days ago! Everyone's forgotten about it."

Olivia swiped at her nose. "Ugh."

Delaney put her hand on Olivia's shoulder. "The question is…who took it?"

Olivia looked at her.

Delaney stared at Olivia like she was dense, "Well, who else was in the room?"

"No one!"

Delaney looked irritated. "Obviously someone was. The hookup was months ago, right? Maybe you forgot."

"No one else was there. He said it was a selfie set-up."

"Bullshit," Delaney said.

"Delaney, we were alone in the upstairs bedroom."

"The one with the balcony?" Delaney asked.

"No, the smaller one. At the top of the stairs."

Isa looked toward the house. "Let's go look."

Delaney jumped to her feet and tried to pull Olivia up.

Olivia gripped the wrought iron, the cold stinging her hands, "No way. I'm not going back there. Especially like this."

"We'll go through the secret entrance," Delaney said.

"What are you talking about?" Isa asked.

Delaney tried for nonchalant, but even in the dark, Olivia and Isa could see her blush. "Kam showed me last summer. When we were hooking up."

The girls stared at her.

"What?" Delaney asked.

Isa made a face, but there was no sting in it. "Show us."

They walked in single file, following Delaney and wisps of vape, the frozen grass a delicate crunch beneath their boots. They maneuvered around the hulking covered pool furniture, and instead of going into the cabana where they'd changed countless times over the years, Delaney led them through a door they'd never noticed before. It was behind a trellis and shorter than the other massive doors everywhere else on the Connover estate, and it had a number key padlock. Delaney tapped a series of buttons and the door clicked. They stepped inside and light flooded the room. The girls stood blinking in a utilitarian workroom, garden equipment stored along the walls in clinical uniformity.

"I know, " Delaney said, "Looks like a serial killer's lair."

Delaney turned around to check that no light illuminated them from outside but the door was solid and caulked and there were no windows. She slipped her vape into her pocket.

"This way."

Olivia and Isa followed her through a narrow door into a space that felt more like a tunnel than a hall. Isa was last through and when the door shut behind her it seemed to disappear against the wall.

Delaney came to an abrupt stop, and the girls bumped into one another. Olivia let out a soft oof. Isa's eyes adjusted to the darkness, and she watched Delaney patting the wall in front of her. A moment later Delaney let out a small breath of satisfaction, and she pushed a panel and they were in a small mudroom with boots and jackets. There was no light sensor, but there were windows and the moonlight was bright enough to reveal a door with a key panel on it.

"Let's hope they haven't changed this code either." Delaney punched in some numbers and jiggled the door handle. The door swung open, and the three girls were standing in the back mudroom off the kitchen.

Delaney smirked. "Rich people—they do it cause they can," then led the way up the back stairs and down a narrow hall, which opened onto the second floor. She stood aside and put her hand out, Olivia walked past her to the open door at the top of the steps. She peeked in and nodded and the girls quickly slipped in.

Olivia closed the door and leaned against it. "Well, that was a lot of drama.

"This is the room right?" Delaney asked and waited for confirmation in the form of Olivia's nod. "Okay, show us exactly where you were.

Olivia walked over to the bed and perched on the end of it. Then she pulled Delaney over to sit next to her. We were sitting together here and he reached over like this…"

Isa scanned the room then walked over to a louvered door and pulled it open to reveal a large closet containing a few shelves stacked with fluffy white towels, a hair dryer, and a tray with miniature bottles of lotions and perfume. A brand new white robe was the only item hanging on the pole. Another symbol of wealth, a home with so much square footage that an entire closet could be dedicated to a guest robe and towels, and large enough for a full grown adult to stand comfortably in. Isa took in the expensively crafted louvred doors, designed so that the closet had air circulation while preventing closet dust. Isa stepped inside and pulled the door closed, then whipped out her cell phone and positioned it. She turned on her camera and captured Olivia and Delaney on the bed with an unimpeded view.

"Can you see me?" Isa asked.

"Nooo," Olivia drawled.

"How about the light on my phone?"

"Nope," Delaney confirmed.

Isa stepped out and showed Olivia and Delaney images of themselves staring at the viewer from the bed.

"Maybe," Olivia sounded tentative, "there was a hidden camera?"

Delaney pointed to the closet, "Or more likely some perv was in here."

"But who?" Olivia asked. "Isa said everyone at the party was downstairs the whole time."

Delaney looked at Isa, "There's no way you could know for sure."

"I'm sure." Isa said.

Delaney snorted, "You can't be…" Then she stopped. "Ohhhh that thing."

"Highly superior autobiographical memory with quality and quantity of retention over time." Isa rattled off. "How do you ever doubt me?"

"Her *mind* is a camera." Olivia said.

"No one was missing," Isa explained, "except Olivia and

Hunter. When someone yelled *cops* everyone scattered and I went upstairs to find Olivia. Hunter passed me on his way down and she was coming out of this room."

"So who was in the closet?" Olivia was afraid of the answer, but more afraid of not knowing.

"I don't know." Isa looked at Delaney, "but whoever it was knew about the entrance from the pool. Which means Kam showed them."

"And..." Olivia said in a tight voice, "Hunter knew too."

Delaney looked at her, "Did you ever have any doubt about that?"

Olivia looked away. "I didn't—but having it confirmed..."

Olivia thought of the image that circulated, Hunter hovering over her bare breast, her head thrown back. She tried telling herself it didn't matter, *it was just sex. Just tits.* She felt the rage build, *but they're mine. My tits. My sex. They won't get away with this.* She ignored the whisper in her mind *they already have.*

Isa put her arm around her. "Nope," she declared, as if she'd read Olivia's mind. "They will not get away with this."

"So," Delaney said, putting her hands on her hips. "What are we gonna do about it?"

The guest room window was easily visible from the woods beyond the pool house. Light flooded through chinks in the drapes. Coach Walker had been standing frozen in place, watching from his place in the woods, ever since the three girls disappeared into the gardening room. His movie-star features contorted with fury. No one except Kam, Rory, Hunter, and himself were supposed to know about the secret entrance. Turning to face the woods, shielding the light from his phone with his body, he stabbed at the screen, texting instructions for the remainder of the evening.

Rory felt his phone buzz in his pocket. He was dancing with a sophomore and was confident of where it would lead. He thought about the guest room but remembered the rules. No underage girls. Only seniors. He figured he could sneak her up to the other bedroom instead. He'd lose points but he was horny and he'd blown his chance with Isa. He couldn't handle any of the junior and senior girls right now. The way they looked at him—like they were superior to him. He'd stick to the freshman and sophomore girls—just for tonight, which meant no video so no points. He was so far ahead he could afford a night off. The way this one was looking at him right now—like she adored him, like she was *grateful.* He needed that and a hand job more than points tonight. He ignored the buzz of the phone in his pocket. He knew he'd pay for that, lose points and maybe even a level, but he'd claim his battery died and he hadn't realized. He'd be in trouble, but he didn't care. He needed a night off. He *deserved* it.

Rory wasn't answering his phone, which was completely against the rules and meant Coach going in was too risky now. The only option left for him was to melt back into the woods. In all the years of the game, there had been no breaks in the rules. And tonight there had been multiple transgressions. Punishments would be meted out, they would need to be subtle, but they would hurt.

CHAPTER 14

Erica Lange took as long as she possibly could in the bathroom. Removing her makeup, combing out her hair, applying serum and night cream. Listening by the door she still didn't hear any snoring, so she slipped back into her dressing room. She wanted to update all her social media posts with Rory's big win, but she couldn't risk Keith seeing them and figure out she was avoiding him, so instead she reorganized her perfectly organized cosmetics drawer. Then she reorganized her Louboutins from nudes to blacks. There were 13 pairs. She vowed that first thing tomorrow she'd get a 14th pair so as not to have bad luck. Creeping to the edge of her dressing room, she listened, still no snoring. Was the man dead in there? She'd never known him to consume that much alcohol without passing out immediately.

She was still flying high from Rory's win that afternoon and she didn't want to ruin the warm glow she felt with Keith's two and a half minutes of huffing and puffing on top of her. She was also starving. She thought about sneaking downstairs for one of her Jenny Craig bars. She'd barely touched her dinner and had only two sips of wine, so the only calories she'd taken in were tequila and three bites of green bean, one bite of rice, and two bites of steak, which she cut into tiny pieces and ate one by one to make it seem like she was eating her dinner. She figured she could eat the Jenny Craig bar and still be down by 500 calories for the day. Then she thought about how flat and empty her stomach felt and decided to wait until the morning and have it with her coffee. Erica didn't need to tiptoe anymore. She could hear Keith snoring even with the bathroom door closed. He was sleeping sitting up in bed with his light on and his phone on the mound of his stomach. Good thing she hadn't posted yet. Taking her phone and bottled water she tiptoed into her sitting room and curled up on her chaise under the white fur blanket she kept for exactly that purpose. She swiftly updated all her sites with action shots of Rory, team vernacular, and a plethora of exclamation marks punctuated with smiley sunglass emojis. With a sigh of contentment, Erica switched off her light and settled against the satin pillow. If she curled her legs up and slept on her left side, she'd preserve her mink lashes *and* her blowout.

Jimmy slept peacefully beside Indira, who was rereading *One Hundred Years of Solitude* for the third time. She needed to stay awake until Olivia got home. She was so engrossed that she hadn't heard the garage door open, but she heard the kitchen door close and Olivia come up the stairs. Indira thought about going in to find out how the party went. Olivia hadn't seemed herself recently and Indira felt a hollow anxious feeling whenever she thought about it. Indira almost slipped out of bed but imagined Olivia's shuttered face, the clipped answers, and decided she didn't have enough strength to handle the anticipated rejection. Consoling herself with the knowledge that Olivia was home safe from harm, she turned back to her book, promising herself she'd close it after one more chapter.

Isa slid the key into the lock as silently as possible and tried tiptoeing past the living room to no avail.

"Sa, is that you?"

The use of her nickname and the light tone of her mother's voice suggested that her parents were relaxed. Isa smelled the wood fire when she pulled into the driveway, and she imagined her parents snuggled on the green velvet couch in front of the fireplace with glasses of cabernet in their hands. She could hear the strains of a Wynton Marsalis tune, and she longed for a moment to curl up next to her parents on the couch and put her head in her mother's lap the way she did as a child.

Isa moved instinctively toward them before remembering the litany of questions they would be sure to ask her. She didn't have the energy to ward them off so instead she poked her head in, smiled widely, and said, "Hey, parents—looking cozy," in as breezy a tone as she could muster.

"Hey, baby girl." Her father patted the couch next to him.

Isa smiled, "Love you guys, gotta get up early to study so...."

She saw her father's face fall and her mother's smile falter. Hardening her heart against it, she blew them a kiss and scooted up the stairs.

Joyce and Thomas Davies looked at one another. Joyce smiled, "Teenagers."

Thomas swept his thumb across her cheek. "You look like one yourself in this light."

Joyce swatted at him, but settled back against him.

The music ended and seconds ticked by with only the sound of the fire before the mournful notes of trumpet filled the room. The beginning notes of "I Got Lost in Your Arms."

Joyce sighed, "It was a lovely weekend, wasn't it."

"You're lovely." He pulled her closer and bent over to kiss her, his face, inexplicably sad.

"What is it, baby?" Joyce cupped his cheek.

"Must be the music," he said and kissed his wife.

CHAPTER 15

Emmett picked Monica up at her parents' place in Pali-sades Park before heading to the Garden State and the quiet beauty of Avalon in the winter.

Emmett had debated whether or not to bring Monica home during the Christmas break and was glad he'd decided against it. He imagined her at the high school wrestling match and a flush of shame crept up the side of his neck. The way the gym erupted like he was some hero coming back from war. No one seemed to care that he'd quit the wrestling team at Dartmouth, bragging rights for Coach Walker circling the drain and sliding out of sight. His mother had seemed fine with it too, and his father didn't register enough to care. After six years of living and breathing wrestling, it was over without a word.

He was glad his father was out of the country so he could bring Monica and their friends to Avalon for a long week-end before school began again without worrying that his dad would show up with a girlfriend Monica's age. He dreaded the day when he'd need to introduce Monica to his family. The day would come; it hadn't gone unnoticed that he was a regular fixture at her parent's home, but she had never met his father and had only met his mother briefly, when she'd come up for a quick visit during parent's weekend.

Monica came from a large, noisy, gregarious family. She had four sisters, and she was smack in the middle. Whenever he'd visited their crowded home he was treated to food, laughter, arguing, and more hugging than he'd thought was humanly possible. The contrast of his mother's sad, cold, five-thousand-foot home seemed depressing. A visit to his father's empty beach house in the dead of winter was as much as he was ready for Monica to witness.

"This is nice," Monica whispered.

The balcony overlooking the dunes was pitch black with a dome of stars above them. They could hear the lashing of the waves and the roar of the wind. Dinner had been made and eaten and cleared away and the group of nine sat on chairs passing a joint, drinking Emmett's father's excellent red wine, braced against the cold.

Monica's mittened hand was tucked against the side of Emmett's thigh and he held her close against him. The rowdy laughter and conversation of his friends washed over him. "I'm glad we're here."

He smiled and kissed her.

"Hey, hey, get a room!" one of the guys shouted. "There's plenty of them."

Emmett ignored him. He wished he hadn't brought the rest of their friends.

Monica just laughed and kissed him again. Then she picked up his phone, shuffled his playlist. Mary Nelson's cover of "Let's Groove" began and Monica pulled Emmett to his feet. The other two girls got up and began dancing, climbing on top of the picnic table, swaying to the slow funk, their arms reaching toward the stars.

Monica took her mittens off and placed one hand against

his cheek, her palm warm against his cold skin. He turned his face and kissed the tender mound beneath her third and fourth fingers.

Maybe, he thought, this was what happiness is, the difference between feeling numb and feeling alive.

The end of the weekend came too quickly, and before he knew it, Monica caught a ride with their friends who were on their way back to school. They all had early classes the next day and it was a seven hour ride to Dartmouth. He didn't have any classes until the next evening, and he had promised his father he would stay and make sure the house was locked up properly.

As Emmett walked onto the desolate beach, he imagined Monica driving further away, mile after mile while the maids cleared away the detritus of their weekend, scrubbing human filth from the porcelain and marble, making the beds with luxurious linens, treating stains, washing and drying and stacking perfectly folded sheets neatly away in closets. Emmet wanted to wait until they finished, to tip them personally, to see that his father's house was as his father had left it. He had hours to kill and was spending them walking the windy beach, watching the silver-bellied gulls lit by the sun swoop and dive above the waves.

Emmett walked with his back to the wind, the ocean roiling alongside him. Without Monica and his friends and the steady pursuit of entertainment, Emmett found himself once more warding off an unsettled anxious feeling. Emmett wondered, not for the first time, if he'd made a mistake leaving the wrestling team. He'd expected to feel relieved, giving up the early hours, the food, and alcohol restrictions, the academic pressures that mounted alongside the wrestling commitment. Yet Emmett had lived that way for so long; he found himself continuing many of the rhythms he'd developed over the years. He'd also expected to miss the camaraderie of being on a team, yet he'd slipped away without feeling anything. No relief, no loss, just the same emptiness.

Except when he was with Monica. He'd never met anyone he could have such long conversations with. Sure, he and his buddies could dissect a football pool for hours. They had lengthy debates over the merits of a specific player or analyzed each team's strategy. They could also spend hours listening to songs and breaking them down the way they would a team, comparing beats, instrumentation, lyrics, and vocals like they were sport. But he'd never met anyone he could share ideas with. Explore thoughts and events outside the realm of evaluating and competing. Suddenly a gaping hole he'd never known existed was full, and he couldn't get enough or be enough. At times, it made him feel ill, the longing to be near her, the bang in his stomach as though his heart had dropped from its rightful place.

He was happier than he could remember being. So why—he wondered—did images keep flashing in front of his eyes bringing him back again and again to that gym. Not his college one, but his high school gym. Emmett walked with purpose along the ocean's edge, not caring if the water lapped his boots. He needed to drown out the images flashing unbidden behind his eyes, even when they were wide open, staring at the sea.

The beach was noisy with wind and waves and the call of the gulls. He let the sounds fill his head, replacing the image of the high school gym. He tried to stay on his feet and not loose himself, but the images intruded, and he could no longer hear the waves breaking on the shore, only the roar from the home team fans where they sat shoulder to shoulder, the familiar smell of mats and androstenone, creating a scent consisting of sweat, piss, and sugar. The smiling faces of the team on the bench, half of whom he'd mentored, the others who looked at him like a celebrity. Teachers and the principal, friends of his mother, students who knew him but were now young enough that while their faces may be familiar, had no personal connection to him.

Emmett saw the room over and over again from that vantage point, the rush of noise, sense memory flooding him, this time in a full embrace from Coach. Pulling back from the backslapping macho hug, until they were eye to eye, and there it was, that knowing gleam in Coach's eye, a remembrance. Coach nodded toward one of the wrestlers standing in the same spot Emmett had been many times ready to step onto the mat. "There's your replacement, Ainsworth."

Emmett had stared at Rory Lange's face. Trying to make sense of it. When Rory had joined the team he'd been so young. Had seemed happy, open and trusting. Emmett tried to reconcile how different Rory looked now, feral and stressed, readying himself for the match.

Coach whispered in his ear again, the familiar scent of cinnamon gum, *he's the new you.* Then images of all the girls, smooth expanses of throats, breasts, small and high, large and bell shaped, belonging to friends of his, classmates, relegated to images on his phone, Coach's flush, his quick breath, a hooding of his eyes, a thumbs up.

Emmett's world tilted. He felt his legs swoop from under him but when he hit the ground it was wet and gritty and smelled of rotting seaweed. The gym became the wide pale sky, the mats a roiling ocean. His throat was closing, something was squeezing his lungs, and he found it impossible to breathe. Then the world went dark.

When Emmett came to seconds later, he couldn't tell if it had been a moment or a lifetime that he'd been gone. The words *you know you know you always knew you know you knowyouknowyouknow* sounding in his head.

He sat up and breathed deeply, marveling at the way his lungs expanded, his throat dry and painful but no longer constricted. He sat for a while, his head in his hands, staring at the packed damp sand. He felt the damp against his skin. He was cold, his bones ached. He wanted to stand up, brush himself off, get on with his walk, get back to the house, close it up, and drive as quickly as he could back to school and Monica. He just couldn't get his legs to comply. So he sat, lifted his gaze, and watched the ocean.

He had been a junior in HS when it had started. When the coach had first approached him. "So. Kid. I hear there's some trouble going down at home."

Emmett's first instinct was to shrug it off. But Coach knew. He understood. So Emmett nodded.

Coach put his hand on the desk and spoke softly, making Emmett pay closer attention. "Divorce sucks. I know. My parents split when I was a freshman in high school. The crying, the fighting... it tears you up. You feel sorry for both of them but you're pissed off that they can't get it together."

Emmett listened carefully. That was almost exactly how he felt. Except he wasn't pissed at his mom and he didn't feel sorry for his dad. But feeling torn up inside, the crying, and fighting, yeah.

Coach looked at Emmett as though he were trying to decide whether he should say what he was thinking.

Emmett willed him silently. *Say it. Say. It.*

"Listen, Kid."

Emmett felt his limbs stiffen, then relax. He could feel it coming. Answers.

"You need to understand something about your dad, about fathers."

Emmett nodded.

"If their wives do their jobs right, it becomes almost impossible to stay married."

Emmett didn't understand. And it must have shown on his face because Coach looked like he was trying to come up with a way to impart this knowledge, and Emmett desperately wanted to grasp onto it.

"Look, you're a bright kid. But there are things about life that you haven't had the opportunity to learn about yet. So I'm gonna explain some stuff. And if it feels like too much, you've gotta let me know. Okay?"

Emmett nodded, tried to keep his impatience from showing.

"Here's the thing about men and women, and I want you to forget about your parents right now. I want you to think in broader terms. Men. And women. Now take it back a little to where it all starts, guys and girls about your age, got it?"

Emmett nodded.

Coach formed a steeple with his fingers and leaned back in his seat, the groan, and creak of the chair the only sound for a moment. "Sexuality is normal, puberty is a necessary part of development. But it happens differently for guys and girls. Guys are made ready for action. It's basic science. You're old enough now, and physically you're more developed than almost every guy in your year, yeah?"

Emmett tried as hard as he could not to blush, but he felt the stain rising up his body and into his cheeks. He nodded.

"Girls are made so that they aren't ready unless a guy helps them feel ready. It's just as important for them, but they have no way to get there without a guy. Also, we live in a sexist society, so they're conditioned not to want sex. Follow?"

Emmett hesitated and Coach saw that.

"Girls need a guy's touch in order to feel physically ready. And they also need to say no so that they don't feel they're doing something wrong. But they don't mean it. They want it as much as we do, but their bodies don't function as well as ours do for sexual pleasure, so it's our job to do it right, to help them. And to overcome their fears when they say no."

Emmett nodded even though he didn't really understand what Coach was talking about. He had no idea what it felt like to be a girl and thinking about it was troublesome because it gave him an instant erection. And that made him think that maybe he was gay if he was getting an erection sitting across from Coach, a guy. But it was the image of girl's bodies that made this happen so probably he wasn't gay. It was all confusing.

Coach laughed, "I'm sorry, dude. This is probably embarrassing. Too much, yeah?"

Emmett immediately rallied. "No! I mean, yeah, it's a little embarrassing, but I can handle it."

Coach nodded, "Okay. I'll spare you the details for now. We'll get to that another time. You gotta get to class anyway."

Emmett took a breath and thought about the math problem he tried to solve last night and couldn't. If he hurried, he could give it another shot, see if one of the math nerds could help him. It did the trick. His body calmed down and he was able to stand up and hitch his backpack over his shoulder in the small space. "Cool. So—see you at practice later."

"You bet. You're my man. I have high hopes for you on this team."

Emmett nodded, feeling lighter, and made his way out of the office with Coach's words chiming in his ear, making the day a better one. You're my man. High hopes. Words he'd hear often during the next six years.

Emmett finally made his way from the beach back to his father's house. Instead of leaving the tip on the kitchen counter, he went to find the women putting the house back together. Lately, he'd been thinking a lot about who counted and who didn't, who had leisure and autonomy and who didn't get paid if they didn't work. It was a small thing, and maybe it didn't matter to them, but he wanted to give the tip to each of them and he wanted to thank them, because it was hard work, and work he'd never had to do himself. And it was something he'd never considered until he'd come here with Monica.

Despite the sting of his wind-chapped skin, the grit of sand in his hair, and the ache in his bones, Emmett was relieved to be back in his car. Cranking the audio system as loud as he could, he sped away from the shore and headed north, a flash of emerald green sea grass vibrant against the gray day. He selected The Nationals from his play list and let the mesmerizing beats of "Sleep Well Beast" wash over him.

As the miles flew by beneath the belly of his car, Emmett was barraged by flashbacks of the crowded gym. He tried different music, opening the car windows, but nothing obliterated the images crowding his mind. In fact the icy wind solidified them as they pulsed and flashed to the rhythm of every song he played.

Emmett couldn't even remember making a conscious decision to slow down and jump off at exit seven instead of continuing on The Hutch toward New England. He just found himself heading across Westchester toward his hometown.

He had something he had to do. It could take a day. Or two. It meant he'd miss class tomorrow, as well as a date with Monica. But he couldn't wait another minute. They had a right to know.

CHAPTER 16

Erica's day was a busy one. Instead of doing errands direct-ly after spin class the way she usually would, she went straight home to shower because Bailey had come home to have an impacted wisdom tooth removed and Erica wanted to spend time with her.

Erica still felt horrible about how things had gone with the family dinner and the way her own father had thrown her out. She wanted a chance to make it up to Bailey as she recovered. Bailey had reluctantly agreed to mother daughter movie day (albeit reluctantly—her response was *fine Erica, I'll be on strong enough drugs to get through anything*). Erica found her comment unnecessarily rude, but she would take what she could get and Bailey even agreed to let Erica choose the movie (if saying *I don't care* was a form of agreeing.)

Erica chose an *Officer and a Gentlemen*. Although she'd been a kid when it first aired there had been a retrospective of it during the 90s when she'd been at college. Erica would venture as far as to say it had been formative. The power she'd seen in Debra Winger's portrayal of Paula, the way she'd been so sure of her own sexuality, her own beauty, even though she wasn't what people traditionally thought of as beautiful back then. And Paula was a working class girl, like Erica had been. In fact, before Erica became wealthy and could afford the most discreet and talented plastic surgeon in New York, she'd had a similar bump on her nose. And Debra Winger had made her feel like it was okay. Sexy even.

Erica had fallen in love with Richard Gere and everything about that movie. She *was* Paula! She was convinced that once Bailey saw this film she would understand everything there was to understand about her mother.

Erica planned their mother/daughter bonding experience as meticulously as she planned everything. Popcorn was out because of Bailey's wisdom tooth so she made them both delicious healthy smoothies and piled the couch with soft throws and cozy blankets even leaving her phone in the kitchen so she wouldn't get distracted.

"Thanks mom, this is nice," Bailey said and Erica's heart soared. It was the right move. It would set their relationship back on track. And then they'd started watching the movie.

Formations of officers in a straight line. A stern pacing Sgt. Foley played by Louis Gossett, Jr. berating them. Zach Mayo (Richard Gere) whispering under his breath to Syd Worley (David Keith) referring to skuzzy female types trying to trap officers into marrying them by biting tiny holes in their condoms. Casey Seeger (Lisa Eilbacher), the only female officer snickering at Zach Mayo's description of the local women. Sgt. Foley yells at them for talking and makes them do push-ups. Seeger can't do them. Foley yells at her and makes snide remarks about upper body strength and tells her to watch how it's done. Sid Worley and Zack Mayo execute many pushups. Paula (Debra Winger) and Lynette (Lisa Blount) walk by in heels and dresses. Syd Worley references their bodacious tatas. Mayo, Seeger, and Worley, snicker.

Bailey paused the remote. "What is this? A gross example of patriarchal capitalism and the capitulation to it by women?"

Erica rolled her eyes. "It was the 80's, Bailey—can't we have one night of fun without gender politics or railing against the man?"

"Sure, Erica. We can do that. But if that's what you wanted, why would you put this garbage on?"

Erica stared at Richard Gere and David Keith frozen in their pushups. Celluloid encapsulations of everything she had found sexy and masculine and desirable. She tilted her head. "Look it was the 80s—things were different—but we have to keep watching. The characters evolve. That's the point! That's what makes it so good."

So they did. They watched.

Lynette engages in a decades old tradition of her town by trapping an officer into marriage by telling him she's pregnant. Yet, Worley loves her. Even when she tells him she miscarried, he wants to marry her. She, however, does not want to marry, as she says, an Okie from Muskogee. An irate Zach Mayo calls her a bitch and a cunt. Paula, Lynette's former best friend agrees (she'd already denounced her, *God help you,* she'd said.) Righteously, Paula and Zach walk out leaving Lynette shamed for her craven manipulation of an officer whose only crime was to love her and be a farm boy.

Bailey grabbed the remote leaving Lynette frozen in 1982. "Erica, seriously?"

"What, Bailey? As a feminist do you think it's admirable that Lynette tries to trap a man into marriage? I mean—it's what she was taught to do, but Paula understands..."

"Erica. This isn't about women making poor choices or admirable choices. This is about a patriarchal capitalist system forcing these choices. How do you not understand that? I mean— I get—sort of—that when you were my age watching this you were seeing it through a different lens—but now?"

REBECCA CHIANESE

"Okay but you have to watch the whole thing—they really do evolve."

"I don't think I can do it."

"I just—I thought—maybe—I really identified with Paula in this movie! I *was* this girl! I even looked like her before you know—the nose job and boob job. She made me feel pretty!"

"Ummm, you still got the boob job and nose job so…"

"Are you judging me for that Bailey?"

"No. Actually I'm not. And I get the whole working class roots thing—but do you get that this is just a glorification of that entire system that made you feel bad about yourself for being working class? For having a slight bump in your nose? For having small breasts? Which I have too, by the way."

"And you're perfect the way you are but if you wanted—I mean we can afford…"

"Ugh! No!"

"I just want you to see the end. It's so romantic."

"Then you have to fast forward. Because I cannot watch any more of this."

"Really?" Erica gave her a sly smile. "If you do, watch it all the way through, I'll watch something with you! That "Euphoria" show which looks so horrible but you seem to like."

"No thanks."

Erica looked disappointed. "I made the wrong choice. We should have watched, "The Seventh Seal.""

Bailey rolled her eyes, "But I don't think you really get why this was the *wrong* choice. You're just upset because I don't like it. Because I don't have the same worldview as you do."

"The Seventh Seal" would have been a better choice, Ingmar Bergman. More symbolism—much more up your alley."

"Let's watch it now then."

Erica wrinkled her nose. "It's so dreary. Black and white.

Another time? Let's fast forward. I want you to see the ending of this. It's so romantic! A modern day fairytale!"

Bailey looked dubious.

"I mean—you may have to suspend some of your belief—but just—try and look at it as a modern day fairy tale."

"Erica. Modern day fairy tales still have women locked in rooms by women who are jealous of their beauty and freed by the desire of men. How can that possibly be romantic?"

"Just let's watch—the music alone!"

So they watched. The opening chords of "Love Lifts Us Up Where We Belong." Zach Mayo strutting through the factory in his dress whites. The working class men and women look up in awe. Paula is working there. She is independent and proud. She has eschewed the need to marry an officer. Richard Gere, white and crisp, in his officer uniform in relief against the drab factory colors, stands behind Paula. He kisses Paula on the back of her neck. She wheels around startled but sees it's him. She kisses him back. Lynette, also relegated to being a factory girl now that her dreams of marrying an officer have evaporated glares resentfully, then becomes swept up in the purity of their love. In a moment of female solidarity she yells, "Way to go Paula!"

Zach sweeps Paula into his arms, her cap falling off, her hair tumbling around her shoulders in a symbol of femininity. Of softness. Of capitulation. Zach strides out, carrying Paula, while all the working people clap. It's a fairy tale ending. Paula will no longer work in the factory she will be Zach's wife and live happily ever after.

Erica turned to Bailey, eyes shining. "Well?"

"Yay, Paula gets to wash Zach's underwear and be loved by him forever."

Erica laughed, "In retrospect it's kind of cheesy."

Bailey looked at her. "Is that why you think I don't like it?"

Erica laughed again, "You kids are so cool now—but it was the 80's, we were dweebs."

"I don't dislike it because it's cheesy or dweeby."

"Oh!"

"I dislike it because it makes me think you hate yourself. And by extension—since you must clearly think I am an extension of you or you never would have made us watch this, you must hate me."

Erica stared at Bailey. "I think you're being very dramatic about a silly movie."

"Maybe I just didn't like watching Richard Gere call Lynette a bitch and a cunt. Maybe I think Paula had more to offer than her sexuality. Maybe I think you do, too."

Erica sat up straighter and taller, letting her voice go cold. "Well. I guess that's that then."

The credits finished rolling and Bailey left the room. Erica hit the power button and watched the screen go black.

CHAPTER 17

"Lange!" Coach poked his head into the locker room. "My office."

Kam whipped his towel at Rory. "Go get 'em sweet cheeks."

The rest of the team laughed. It was the Monday after the big match and Rory was riding high on adrenaline from his big win, from the adulation he'd received in the halls, Isa's rejection, the emptiness of the hookup at the party, all those moments of insecurity, relegated to a lockbox in his mind.

Rory kept his eyes on Coach, trying to decipher his mood. Coach was leaning back in his chair, his fingers a steeple under his chin. The familiar grin on his face, but his eyes were cold. Rory decided Coach's mood could best be described as neutral. Rory's hopes of further accolades diminished.

"That last win's behind you now, you understand that, right?"

"Yeah, of course, onto the next."

Coach kept his gaze on Rory. "Gonna mix things up a little this week."

Rory felt his stomach drop. "Oh—but…"

"Give some of the younger guys a shot. Gotta start building the team for next year."

"Sure, Coach." Rory said, plastering a smile on his face and trying to keep the panic from showing in his eyes.

Coach locked his eyes onto Rory's. "Big weekend?"

Rory shrugged. "The usual."

A grin slid across Coach's face. "Partying?"

Rory nodded. "You know—typical."

Coach stared at him. "Guess you boys were pretty busy. I tried texting."

Rory paled, "I didn't get anything."

Coach laughed. "No action?"

 "I meant no texts."

Coach raised his eyebrows. "Oh yeah? Who's the lucky girl?"

"An 8."

Coach smiled and put his hand out.

"Oh, uh…I didn't get any footage, she's a sophomore."

"So that's why you ignored my texts?"

"Um—I didn't see them—I was distracted, you know, and um, we didn't get that far. You didn't miss anything."

"That isn't how the game works. You understand that, right?"

"It was one night—I figured with the big win—I could use a break…"

"Breaks? You think there are breaks in this life, Lange?"

"I—"

"I'm risking everything here, to make you a better man. And you thought taking a break was the way to go. Let me ask you something, Lange—do you appreciate the work we're doing together? Not just on the mat, but the making of a man? Do you want to be some weak little bitch? Or do you want to become a man that knows how to please women?"

"Obviously, I…"

"There's no obviously. Because you fell down on the biggest night of your career. You went after a sophomore. So no footage. No way to evaluate your plays. No way to improve. You know what that tells me?"

"Coach—"

"That you're a scared, selfish, little boy."

Rory felt his face flush with shame. Coach looked away from Rory, his ice blue gaze on the door. Rory stood up knowing he was dismissed.

"Oh—and Lange—send Jake in. He's going to be Captain next year, so no time like the present, yeah?"

And just like that Rory knew his place in the pecking order had been taken.

On Tuesday morning as she was putting the finishing touches to her face, Erica Lange received a panicked phone call from the high school athletic director, Cal Hadrick.

He refused to give her any details over the phone except that Rory was physically fine and asked her to meet him in his office immediately.

Erica never left the house without her eyebrows. In fact she carefully washed around them at night so she even woke up with them. The only time she was without them were the few minutes between removal and a careful reapplication. Yet, after that call Erica grabbed her handbag and keys and left without eyebrows, lips, or sunglasses. She went bald-faced into the world with horrifying images cycling through her brain, Rory was in trouble, his college acceptances at risk—had he been fighting? Drinking? Heaven forbid using drugs? She couldn't imagine why Cal would be calling her in such a panic. Yet she couldn't imagine Rory getting into this much trouble even if he had been fighting, drinking, or using drugs. Her heart felt as though it was skittering around inside her chest, like a chipmunk trying to dodge a car.

By the time Erica made her way to Cal's office, she was afraid she was going into a full-blown panic attack (something she'd never experienced but was sure would feel like this). Her eyes searched for and lighted on Rory's face, pale, with two bright red spots above his cheeks, his eyes glassy as though he were feverish. Erica immediately felt relief. Clearly he was ill. That's why she'd been called in. She stifled the urge to rush to her son. She had been well trained not to baby or humiliate him.

Erica settled herself. "Rory? Are you sick?" She looked to Cal. "Did something happen to him?"

Rory sprang up, "No! Nothing happened to me! This is all bullshit!"

Erica quickly shut the door. "Rory! Don't curse!"

Cal stood up and gestured for Erica to sit. "It's okay, Mrs. Lange. Emotions are running high."

"Can someone please tell me what's going on?"

Rory glared at her, then, at Cal. Erica searched his eyes; she knew them better than anyone's. He had that squint around the edges, signaling anger. He'd had the same look as an infant, when she waited too long to feed him, or change him, or pick him up. She felt a familiar impulse to soothe him. She forced herself to sit and say nothing, to wait for Cal to explain. For a moment Rory's gaze locked on hers, and she saw something else. Fear.

Cal sat back in his chair and placed his hands squarely on his desk. "Yesterday afternoon, a former student came in and lodged a complaint."

"Against Rory?"

Cal watched her bristle and made soothing motions with his hands. "Of course not. As I told you, Rory isn't in any trouble."

"Okaayy?" Erica looked over at her son. He looked murderous. "Then why are we sitting here?'

Cal took a breath. "The complaint was quite serious and as a district we care deeply about the welfare of our students. We need to address it head on."

"Who was the complaint against?"

"Coach Walker."

Erica laughed, "That's ridiculous! Did he hurt someone's feelings with playing time? Honestly these parents need to get a grip! They're raising a bunch of crybabies."

Cal sighed. "I wish it was as simple as that. The allegations are much more serious. They involve things of a sexual nature, and the accuser specifically named students he believes Coach Walker has perpetrated these actions against, including Rory."

Erica scoffed, "I assure you no one is sexually abusing Rory! And it's ridiculous to suggest…"

"Mom! He knows that! I told him that! And no one said anyone was—just stop talking!" Rory's entire face was red now and his eyes were filling up. He clapped his hands over his ears and bent forward, rocking slightly.

"Easy now, Buddy." Cal leaned forward and spoke in a calm voice, but there was an edge to it that made Rory's entire body still. "I know you're upset, but you need to take a minute, okay? Pull yourself together."

Rory nodded, but didn't look up.

Erica also took a breath. Rory was upset because he was defending Coach. He's a good boy, loyal, and cares about others. She felt a surge of pride, then a rapid uncoiling of fear. "Is this—" she looked at Cal, "Going to affect their season? Or—college?"

"No, no, of course not. But we do need to contain this. We don't want the reputation of our schools—and the legacy of Rory's senior year—tarnished in any way. Not to mention the reputation of Coach Walker, I mean assuming these accusations are unfounded. We can't have a man's reputation ruined because of an unstable former student."

"Who was it? Who's saying these things?"

"I'm afraid I'm not at liberty—legal and ethical constrictions—you understand."

Erica didn't understand at all. She felt as if her entire foundation had tilted, that she'd been standing on what had been a strong slab of mountainous rock, high above a glorious valley, and now she was free falling into a crumbling mass of debris. Her stomach turned and a squeezing sensation began in her chest.

Cal must have noticed because he quickly turned to the mini-fridge behind his desk and grabbed a bottle of water, twisting the cap off and thrusting it at her in one fluid movement.

Erica drank the cold water and tried to regain her composure. Rory was okay. This wasn't happening to him. It was clearly a misunderstanding. "Did you say—the person—this former student—*may* be unstable."

Cal leaned forward again, "I mean, I'm not a mental health professional. And I really shouldn't discuss this—but between you and me—and Rory—the guy, when he came in, seemed very unstable. Wild, almost."

"Was he incoherent? Drug-fueled?"

Cal hesitated, "He wasn't incoherent. But it's interesting that you mention drugs. That was my impression."

Rory was settling. Erica could feel him. She wouldn't look at him, and kept her attention on Cal. "I know you can't say a name—but, was this a recent graduate?"

Cal looked at her. Now she was speaking in a language he could engage in. "Not last year."

Erica looked at him. Speculated. "Yet, he mentioned Rory by name. So they must know each other. Even been teammates?"

Cal shrugged. "You're not wrong."

"So, the year before?"

Cal leaned back in his chair. "I can't stop you from guessing the year."

Erica nodded. Satisfied that they had found, as she was fond of saying, *their groove*. "But why now? After all this time?"

Cal shrugged again. "Who knows? If drugs are involved, and I'm not saying they are, mind you, but if they are, who knows what it does to a person. Especially cocaine. Messes with you. Makes you paranoid and manic. You try the best you can to instill this in the players, ya know? But once they graduate…." Cal looked over at Rory. "Let this be a cautionary tale for you next year—stay on the team, whether it's D1, D3, or even club. Keeps you focused."

Erica narrowed her eyes. Something was hovering around her peripheral vision, she imagined it like text on a page, swimming in and out, she actually turned her head to the left, as if it were waiting there for her to read, but the imaginary words moved with her, just out of sight. Then a memory flooded her, the last match. The roaring gym, the pride, and excitement she'd felt for Rory. The crowd was chanting for someone else too, Erica felt connected to it, imagining Rory coming back, a state champ in high school, playing D1, a homecoming game, no—a January game, when college kids typically came to cheer on their former teammates. Erica remembered a feeling of disappointment, a lessening of esteem, the thought that Rory would never do that, quit a team, especially D1. Especially Dartmouth…

"Emmett Ainsworth!" She shouted.

Rory looked at her sharply, "Mom," he angry-whispered.

"Quiet."

But Cal just looked at her knowingly.

Erica bristled at the very idea. This boy went off to college, squandered his opportunity and now he was coming back here and stirring up trouble for her son in his senior year. How dare he? "Well, Cal. What are we going to do about this?"

CHAPTER 18

Isa, Olivia, and Delaney huddled on couches around a small table at the local coffee shop, clutching lattes.

"My mom got the call from the superintendent." Delaney rolled her eyes. The other girls knew it embarrassed Delaney that her mother was frequently on campus. Margie was a familiar fixture, walking officiously through the hallways, talking into her bluetooth.

"What exactly did she tell you?"

"Nothing, of course, but I could overhear her end of the conversation, wait I taped it—here."

Olivia laughed, "You're badass."

The girls squeezed together, hunched over Delaney's phone...

"She went into the pantry to take this call—like I couldn't hear her, I was two feet away making the twins lunch." Delaney smirked.

Margie's voice sounded tinny but the girls could hear the fear and desperation in it...*Cal if word of this gets out—how much truth is there in this? I mean, I heard he had a drug problem—and he quit the team—I'm not spreading rumors! I'm just asking how reliable is this person? These accusations are serious. We need our own internal investigation—if there is any truth to this then of course we'll follow up—but if there isn't—we can't*

*ruin our reputation our BRAND because of some drug addled—
I'm just saying—we will do our own very thorough investigation
and the truth will prevail. Of course! If there is any truth to any
of it the necessary steps will be taken—yes including the authorities…but we don't need to move on this now…we will do our
own investigation and if nothing turns up then we squash it."*

"What!" Olivia shouted.

"Shhh, there's more." Delaney said.

*Okay start with the boys. Then call the mothers in—this way
we're covered…okay call me after the interviews…I'll follow up
on my end as well.*

"Hunh," Isa said. "That explains Mrs. Lange—she was unhinged this morning, cut me off in the parking lot and pulled
into a spot too small for her SUV. She had to crawl out of the
passenger side because she couldn't open her door."

Olivia looked at her. "That means Rory's involved."

"My guess is it's the wrestling team." Delaney said.

Isa nodded, "So, Hunter and Kam too."

"What the hell happened?" Olivia said.

Isa grabbed Olivia's hand. "Someone was in that closet
taking that video of you. Someone the guys trusted."

"But, it was Hunter's phone that had the snap, right?
So…"

"Maybe, whoever was in the closet had his phone?" Isa
said.

Delaney looked at Olivia, "Liv, I think we need to consider the fact that it was Walker—that he's behind all of this."

Olivia looked at Isa. "It's like these guys had personality
transplants—I've known Rory my whole life and what he's
doing—it's like he's a different person."

"What's Rory doing?" Delaney asked.

Isa grimaced, "I've deleted them and blocked him but—"

"Is that shitbag sending you dick pics!"

Isa nodded, "And as disgusting as those are, his texts are worse—what he wants to do to me, what he wants me to do to him…"

"Why didn't you tell me?" Delaney looked back and forth between Isa and Olivia.

Isa answered, "I didn't want to give it any life—but now I'm wondering if it's part of something bigger."

Delaney nodded. "You know, Walker's always been creepy, they way he has all those girls hanging on him, calling him Ice—but this…" Delaney gestured to her phone, "makes me think there's some dark shit going on."

Olivia glared at the phone then looked at Delaney, "Your mom pretty much said they're gonna cover it up."

Delaney nodded, "My mom would stab herself in the throat if it meant protecting our *brand.*

Isa stared at Delaney's phone, thinking about Margie's words: *these accusations are really serious.*

Isa felt a familiar detachment come over her. Throughout her senior year she'd been waiting for the feelings everyone else around her seemed to be exhibiting. The anxiety about college applications and admissions that consumed everyone else seemed to pass right through her. Sure the admissions process had been rigorous and intense, but Isa thrived on academic rigor and intensity. Sure she cared about where she was accepted, but as easily as she could imagine herself at her three top choices: Brown, Barnard, Vassar, she could just as easily imagine herself at NYU, a school she was already accepted to, with full tuition because of her father's tenure, tuition reciprocity being a perk in lieu of higher salaries. In fact she was leaning toward NYU even if she did get into the other schools. She knew she would thrive in any academic setting, and New

York City was familiar and comfortable. Yet she felt no anticipation, no excitement; she almost wished for the wracking anxiety her friends were experiencing, at least she would feel something, and at the culmination it would be exhilaration or disappointment. Whether she was accepted to Brown or not, she couldn't imagine feeling exhilarated or crushing disappointment. It would either be an ego bump or an ego bruise and neither of those seemed like any big deal. The only time Isa felt anything other than the lull of a holding pattern was when she thought of Rory and the pictures, and the pool of dread it created made her long for the negative space of the unknown. Isa forced herself to think about the pictures in this new light. To examine the idea of people knowing about them in the light of Coach Walker and not just the weird nocturnal longings of a creepy high school senior who went from being a childhood friend to what felt very much like a stalker. What if he'd been put up to it? Taught to do it the way he was taught to throw a long pass. What if he weren't just a creep, but someone perpetrated against? It didn't make her feel any better about Rory and the repulsion she felt for him, but it did make a little more sense, that maybe it wasn't puberty alone that took her childhood friend and made him into a pod person. Isa felt the welcome flush of anger surge through her. She looked up and caught the gaze of the other girls. "We're gonna take that fucker down."

Delaney laughed and caught her gaze. "I didn't know you could curse."

Isa stared. "I can do a lot more than curse."

CHAPTER 19

Bailey Lange, still in pain from the wisdom tooth extraction, was curled in a ball on the family room couch in a Percocet, induced sleep. She woke up to her mother shouting *there was no sexual abuse* into her phone.

Erica, sans eyebrows, pacing the kitchen, had no idea Bailey was on the couch, frozen in place, listening to every word.

"Margie, it isn't true. Rory denies anything like that— I don't know why Emmett would lie—but obviously he did! Well, who else could it be?" More pacing, her heels clacking sharply against the floor, "Margie, look at the facts. A well-regarded coach—his current athletes are saying these things never happened—and one kid, one! You're going to derail a man's life's work—not to mention the reputation of our entire district because of one disgruntled—yes, Marge, Emmett quit wrestling for Dartmouth! He's clearly going through something. Don't you remember that heinous divorce his parents went through? It clearly deranged him. And his mother never went to any meets—I remember because Rory was on the team then—I mean only doing exhibition and training, but I went to every single match—Emmett was the star! He went to States! And his mother was too busy feeling sorry for herself—I'm not being mean! It's just true. Forget about all of this, it doesn't even matter. You can't allow our district to be tarnished—think of the real estate values! Our schools are our brand! I'm not suggesting you ignore it—do the internal investigation—just keep it internal!"

Erica stabbed at her phone then tossed it onto the counter. She took five deep breaths, *in through her nose, out through her mouth, feel the air against your fulcrum, focus on your breath,* channeling the calm soothing voice of her Friday morning Yoga teacher (her day off from spin). It worked! Then she looked up and saw Bailey.

"Oh, I didn't see you there."

Bailey just stared at Erica who walked over and sat down at the end of the couch.

Bailey sat up and put her hand tentatively on her mother's knee. "Are you ok?"

Erica looked up, but not at Bailey. "I just can't—everything I've worked for—because of one unstable person...."

"Can you start from the beginning?"

"There have been accusations made...."

"About Rory?"

"No! No of course not! About his coach."

"What type of accusations?"

"That he's been—inappropriate. Giving kind of—I don't know—sexual education to his players."

"So what? All of the phys ed teachers do sex ed."

"No—not curriculum sanctioned—more graphic. And there were videos involved."

What? Like porn? Was he showing porn to his players?"

Erica snapped to attention. "He didn't do anything, Bailey!"

"Okay. Were the accusations that he was showing porn to his players?"

Erica wrinkled her nose, "Yes. And—and other things—images of girls."

"Images? What girls? Mom? What girls? Students?"

"It's all lies! Don't you think if something like this was going on it would have gotten out by now? Allegedly it's been going on for years! I don't believe a word of it."

"Okay. Then it will be disproven and that will be the end of it."

"How do you *disprove* a negative? His reputation will be tarnished forever and our district will be dragged through the mud. All those haters out there—they'd love to see us fail—have egg on our faces."

"What haters?"

"Everyone who isn't us!" Erica screamed so loud her words echoed back at them from the cathedral ceiling of the family room.

"Mom...what if they're true?"

Erica glared at Bailey with such intensity that Bailey reared back.

"Just once," Erica hissed, "I wish you would have your brother's back instead of going against him."

"Mom, I'm not—but if there is any truth to this you need to be worried about the effect on Rory."

"There isn't! Why would you wish this on him?"

"I don't wish this on him. You're acting crazy."

"I'm not the one acting crazy! The whole world has gone crazy and as usual you would rather side with the whole crazy world than with your family."

"Or...I would rather face the truth than hide from it."

Erica closed her eyes and leaned her head back against the couch. "Get out of my sight."

Bailey rose unsteadily to her feet. "You know, mom—the fact that I'm different from the rest of this family doesn't make me bad or wrong. If you weren't so busy trying to fit all of us into some ideal fantasy you concocted, maybe you could have actually lived your own life instead of living through Rory's. And maybe—just maybe—you would be able to look at this objectively."

Erica stood up. "Never mind. You stay here. I'm leaving."

Erica turned her back on Bailey and walked into the kitchen, picking up her phone from the counter, punching numbers into it as she left the room.

CHAPTER 20

Right after practice Coach called Rory, Hunter, and Kam into his office. When Coach awarded points or went over technique for The Game it was always done individually, so the boys assumed Coach was calling them in to strategize for their next match. Rory did however, hope that Emmett's disclosure made Coach realize how loyal Rory really was.

When they took their seats, Rory noticed that Coach looked pale and irritated.

"You're going to have to clean up the mess Ainsworth has made for us. Start with the phones," Coach said.

Rory knew he meant the burner. All the videos were taken on their personal iPhones. It was a simple enough plan. Whoever had the hookup left their phone in the closet and took the burner so they could send and receive texts, telling Coach when to go to the room and wait. No hookups with underage girls ever, only seniors or of-age juniors. When Coach was in place, whoever was up got a burner text and it was game time. Coach only recorded one personal video a month for each of them. The other times they recorded each other or, if it was possible, took selfies.

"We'll take care of it, Coach." Rory said.

Coach nodded. "And I'm assuming you've all deleted every video—no saving any."

"Done," Rory said.

Kam nodded, "Done."

Coach looked at Hunter, "Confirm?"

Hunter thought about the still he'd kept of him and Olivia. He'd erased the actual video as soon as he and Coach had gone over the plays, but he'd stupidly captured that one still. And Rory had sent it on his snapchat. It was possible someone had grabbed it. Should he tell Coach about it? He couldn't bring himself to. Besides, he reasoned, there was no way to prove who took that video. It could have been a selfie set up, or anyone else. It was on Hunter's own phone. Those were the rules. Nothing had ever been taken or viewed on Coach's phone. He was fully protected. It seemed all of them were. Except Olivia.

"Hunter!" Coach prodded.

"Yeah, Coach?"

"Confirm."

"Confirmed, Coach."

Coach swallowed. "Get busy. And be smart."

Rory, Hunter, and Kam piled into Hunter's Range Rover and drove north after fourth period. They had a few hours to kill before practice and didn't want to risk going to any of their houses and seeing any parents. They needed to get their stories and their heads together and they needed to be uninterrupted to do it.

Rory rode shotgun and controlled the playlist until they'd driven half an hour away and pulled off onto a deserted dirt road leading to a quarry. It was frequented in summer by kids from all over the county who were lured by the danger of jumping from the rock cliffs into the cold dark water, but in winter it was desolate.

The boys got out of the car and wordlessly made their way to Castle Rock where they stood looking over the expanse of limestone and water.

Kam looked at Rory. "Fuck Emmett Ainsworth. What a tool."

Rory just shook his head. He was still reeling. "Did the AD pull either of you in?"

Hunter shook his head and Kam breathed out, "Nah. Guess Ainsworth didn't give our names."

Hunter looked at Rory, "He might not know about us."

Rory just looked out over the cliffs. His stomach was churning, and he kept having nightmare images of all those texts he'd sent to Isa becoming public. And all those videos he'd taken. He'd skipped fourth period, spending an hour in his car deleting videos of himself that he'd sent to Isa from his phone. If any of this ever got out, Rory's college career was over before it began. Why had he sent all those pictures and texts to Isa? He wondered if she'd really deleted them. He'd begged her not to, he'd liked imagining her looking at them. Keeping it a secret, even from him. It used to drive him wild thinking about it. He used to find the thought more arousing than the actual experience of any of the girls he'd been with. But now he hoped she really had deleted them.

Rory looked at the expanse of sky. He could feel the cold, but the sky could have been any season. He wished he could fly up into it and just be…gone.

Instead he held the burner phone up. "Toss it?"

Kam and Hunter nodded and Rory wound his arm up and swung with all his might, watching the small black rectangle fly through the air descending into the dark pool of water, taking all their secrets with it.

When Indira hopped into Margie's Subaru, which smelled overwhelmingly of fake-freesia air freshener, she could tell immediately that something was off. Margie greeted Indira with her usual ebullience, yet it seemed obligatory. And although Margie was always rushing, she never appeared harried, which she did as she peeled away from the curb.

When they got to the preserve, Margie surprised Indira by taking her headset off and throwing it into the car console. "I need a break from this thing."

Indira nodded and they set off toward the trails. They walked silently for a few paces until Margie broke the silence, "Has Olivia seemed—on edge—or mentioned anything to you about anything at the high school? Any issues with boys or...."

Indira felt a lurch in her stomach. She wondered if Margie knew something and was afraid to tell her. Suddenly the changes in Olivia's behavior she'd chalked up to senioritis seemed more ominous. "Nooo—she hasn't mentioned anything. Is there —should I be—concerned?"

"Not at all. Delaney plays everything so close to the vest. I get nothing from that girl."

"Is there something to get? I mean—are you worried about something specific?"

"No."

Indira heard the hesitation. "Marge, if there's anything I need to know, you can tell me."

Margie looked at her. "I'm sorry. I didn't mean to worry you. It's nothing to do with Olivia. And I don't mean to sound so cryptic."

"What is it?" Indira tried to keep the panic from surfacing. She had noticed changes in Olivia. Irritability. Sleeping late. Lethargy. She had assumed it had to do with the pressure valve of senior year. Indira looked up at the hill in front of them, it loomed out of nowhere, and she picked up her pace so she'd be able to make it up, Margie right beside her. Their breath quickened, and for a moment Indira focused on that, and the sound of dry winter leaves crunching against the hard soil beneath their feet.

When they reached the top Margie spoke again, "I can't get into specifics. But there have been some allegations made, about a faculty member, it doesn't have anything to do with Olivia—I just thought maybe she heard something."

Indira waited for the flood of relief she expected, but the cluster of fear inside her chest and stomach remained. She purposely lightened her voice. "Olivia hasn't said anything."

Margie waited a beat, then, attempted a nonchalant air, "Are Olivia and Rory still close?"

Indira thought before answering. The kids were so much more independent now it was difficult to tell. Yet in her heart she knew there was a rift. She never heard his name mentioned anymore, couldn't remember the last time she'd seen him smiling at her kitchen table or pulling up to give Olivia a ride somewhere. "Not the way they used to be."

Margie looked sharply at her. "Was there a falling out?"

Indira shrugged, feeling uncomfortable. Was this prurient interest on Margie's part? She'd always been a gossip and seemed to enjoy being the first to know things and the first to impart information. "Not that I know of."

"So no falling out—just what—different social groups?"

Indira sighed, "I don't know. I guess. Liv seems to be going out less this year. She spends all her time with Isa and Delaney. And Bailey when she's around."

"What boys are they hanging out with?"

Indira thought about it. "I'm not sure. She did a poetry slam with Lee Aaronson."

"So… not so much the athletes?"

Indira stopped and looked at her. "Margie. What is this all about?"

Margie sighed. "I'm sorry to sound so cryptic. And I apologize if I've been giving you the third degree."

"You kind of are. And it's starting to freak me out. Do you know something about Olivia that I need to know?"

"Not at all. Not about Olivia. It pertains to some of the male athletes and I was just wondering if Olivia has said anything to you."

"She hasn't.

Indira and Margie traversed the last of the hills in silence, the wide-open field ahead of them, brown cattails swaying against the gray horizon.

When they hit the top of the wide field, Indira turned to Margie. "Will you promise to tell me if you hear anything about Olivia?"

"If I can't give specifics, I will tell you if you need to talk to her. That's the best I can do."

"Cause if you tell me you'd have to kill me?"

Margie laughed. "Something, like that."

The wind picked up, biting their cheeks and causing their eyes to water, so they bent their heads and leaned in, pretending not to worry.

Isa, and Olivia were sitting on Delaney's twin bed, their backs against the wall and their feet dangling over. Delaney was at her desk chair a few feet away. They had the house to themselves because Margie was driving Delaney's younger siblings all over Westchester for various after school events.

Delaney drummed her fingers on the desk, her green nail polish flashing in the fading light. She reached across her desk and switched the lamp on. "So. How do we lure the freak out?"

Isa frowned. "He's going to be more cautious now. I won't be able to trick Rory after the other night, he'll smell a trap."

Delaney looked at Olivia. "It's gotta be you, Liv."

Olivia looked up in alarm. "Why?"

Delaney shrugged. "You and Hunter. You're the only one who makes sense. Kam and I are so over, he'd never go for it—and Isa's right, there's no going back with Rory after the other night."

Isa looked at Olivia's panicked face. "What about you, Delaney? You can pretend you're interested in Rory."

Delaney smirked. "He'd cream his underwear in half a second."

Isa grimaced. "Disgusting.

Olivia looked sick to her stomach. Isa couldn't bear it. "Liv, you don't need to do this."

"Well, what's your suggestion?" Delaney asked.

"I don't know! But I'm not letting Liv do anything she's uncomfortable with."

Delaney got up from the desk. "Stop being so dramatic." She looked at Olivia. "You don't have to actually hook up. We'll do the set up and stop it before it goes that far."

Isa was getting angry, "This isn't an episode of *Law & Order.*"

Delaney gave Isa a disparaging look. "What's your suggestion? They get away with this fuckery?"

"No, we let the administration deal with it."

Delaney snorted. "Right. Like Erica Lange is going to let anything happen to her precious little baby."

Isa looked at Olivia with sympathy, "I don't see the Logans or Connovers letting anything happen to their sons either."

Olivia thought about the video. The sensation of Hunter's body when she'd leaned into him, the salt of his mouth when he kissed her. She was so angry with him and felt so betrayed by him. But what happened between them felt real. And she felt the pull to do it again. Which made her a hypocrite. And that thought alone made her want to dissolve, molecule by molecule, until she couldn't feel anything anymore, until she lost form and became nothing.

"Olivia" Isa said. "You don't have to do this."

Olivia heard Isa's voice, felt the delay in her own thought processes, saw Delaney's steady gaze. Olivia imagined the text exchange with Hunter, luring him in, Delaney and Isa skulking in the bushes trying to catch the set up. The performance for the camera, the knowledge of the eyes in the closet, the feeling of Hunter's lips on her neck, the moment of victory when the girls would rush into the house and reveal who was in the closet with his iPhone. The power she could snatch back from all of them. Hunter especially.

The dead space inside her chest began to open and swell. "I'll do it."

"Shit's about to get real," Delaney said and smiled her widest smile.

CHAPTER 21
Early February 2025

Dartmouth campus was gray with drizzle and the ground was sloppy with slush from the previous week's snowfall. Emmett knew this because he could see it from the window in his room, which he hadn't left since returning from his meeting with the Athletic Director. Emmett waited for a call. None came. His sleep and waking states were continually interrupted with flashes of images, as though snapshots of his life that had been tossed in the air landing haphazardly in front of him. The athletic director and school superintendent staring blankly at him while his words rushed from his mouth, the roaring gym, Coach leaning in and whispering, *Lange's the new you.* But the most intrusive and overpowering images, the ones that were coming relentlessly now, were images of sitting in Coach's office as a new player, after Coach had plucked him from the JV wrestling team when he'd been in 8th grade. The same way he'd plucked Rory Lange when he was barely thirteen.

Coach had been organized. They began slowly, but by his sophomore year, Emmett was a pro. Together he and Coach carefully compiled a list, conducted in near whispers, and Emmett kept track by putting flame emojis next to his contact for each girl. If he hooked up with a girl who had three flames next to her name he got the most points, two flames was still valuable, one flame less so. If the girl didn't have a flame next to her name, she was off limits.

Watching Coach watch the videos had become a terrible mixture of pain and pleasure for Emmett. Pleasure because of the pride he felt when Coach would look up at him with admiration in his eyes. Embarrassment at how sometimes Coach's breath would quicken and hitch, how color would flood his neck and cheeks, how he'd open his mouth as though he were having difficulty breathing, swallowing roughly, his Adam's apple bobbing in his throat. The mixture of shame and arousal was something Emmett both longed for and dreaded, carving a groove in his psyche, which grew deeper with each encounter.

Coach told Emmett that the best way to evaluate Emmett's masculinity was not only through sports, but also through sexual prowess. Coach explained throughout their many sessions that sexual prowess wasn't defined simply by how many girls you got or how hot they were, but whether or not you were pleasing them. Coach explained how easily men were sexually satisfied, but that girls were more difficult to satisfy. That their bodies were mysterious and that there were very specific techniques that even girls didn't know were necessary. If Emmett wanted to be a real man he would need to learn those techniques. And the best way to do that was the same way you became a better athlete, by taping and evaluating your skills in action. The first couple of years the training consisted of anatomy lessons. By the time Emmett was a sophomore he was bringing girls to Coach's office, the supply closet in Coach's office was big enough for Coach to stand in, the slats in front were slanted down so that nothing was visible inside the closet, but if Emmett hooked up with a girl on Coach's desk, Coach could easily see every move and he would later break it down and evaluate them with Emmett. By the end of sophomore year Emmett was hooking up with juniors who were of age and even some seniors. And that's when Coach began videoing the sessions with Emmett's iPhone. As soon as they'd evaluated the tape, Coach would delete it. Emmett had his own keys to Coach's office that he'd returned upon graduation. Coach told him he'd been special, that none of the rising junior or senior boys would be bringing girls to the office. That had been a special one-time thing for his star.

Emmett could no longer control the flood of memories from those years. He experienced each one as if it was happening again in real time. Scenes he'd long forgotten but had been embedded in the folds of his cerebrum and were now flashing continuously, rendering it impossible for him to function. He wasn't showering and was barely eating, subsisting on the power bars from a box on his desk and a Brita filter of water in his fridge, refilled from the bathroom sink. He knew eventually he had to get it together, but he couldn't imagine an end game. The air in the room grew chilly as the gray day darkened with dusk. Another day had come and gone and he still hadn't heard anything from Cal.

When Rory returned home, right before dinner, he found his mother and Bailey in the kitchen. His mother looked like herself again. Something had looked weird about her this morning; maybe he just wasn't used to seeing her without make up, but it had been startling and made the whole scene in the AD's office seem even more surreal than it had been. Yet here she was, back in full Erica Lange mode, put together, table set, dinner smelled delicious, and he marveled at himself that he could still feel hungry despite the gnawing anxiety in his stomach and the tightening of his throat and chest. He knew the only survival tool he had was to act normal and deny, deny, deny. He had seen Coach for a hot minute when he was leaving school. Coach caught him in the parking lot, a warm easy grin, but he'd spoken through clenched teeth.

"We've prepared for this, Lange. Just stay cool and deny, deny, deny."

Simple, Rory told himself when he walked in the door flashing a wide smile at his mother before turning to Bailey with a derisive snort, "What's up with your fat face?"

Bailey looked at him straight in the eye without flinching. "Wisdom tooth extraction."

"Nice. Got any good drugs?" Erica whipped around and Rory and put his hands up, laughing in what he was sure was a good natured and downright charming way, "Kidding!"

Bailey was studying him.

Rory laughed, "You're giving me the creeps. Cut it out."

"And you're trying too hard."

He turned to his mom, "That smells delicious. What's for dinner?"

Erica smiled, despite the pain behind her left eye and the knot in her shoulders. "Chicken cacciatore and apple dumplings for dessert!"

"You're the best," Rory said, and squeezed his mom, ignoring Bailey as she narrowed her eyes at him.

"Soo... " Bailey questioned, "Any truth to the accusations against Walker?"

For the greater part of the day, Rory had thought a lot about how to play things off with everyone. If he acted too incensed it may come off like that Shakespeare quote old people were always throwing around, "*methinks the lady doth protest too much*," and if he was too nonchalant it may just seem like he was naïve, and that could fuel suspicion. Rory was a skilled liar. Scoffing, a little indignation, and some well-placed deflection seemed indicated. "Nah. None of that crap is true. And anyone who believes it just wants to be a hater. Shame about Ainsfield. Kinda hurts, ya know? I looked up to the guy." Rory shook his head and waited for Erica, who came in right on cue.

"It's criminal! That's what it is. The School Board needs to shut this thing down right now. Ruining a good man's name because of a drug addict!"

"Whoa, mom. No one's saying Ainsworth is a junkie—let's not add to the rumors."

"Well, how would you explain it?"

Rory shrugged, "I seriously can't." And he couldn't. He had no idea why Emmett would do a thing like this. But he was fairly certain drugs had nothing to do with it, although any rumor that cast doubt on Emmett's credibility was fine with Rory.

Rory tried to gauge whether Bailey was buying it. He didn't think so. He wished he hadn't looked over at her because she began hammering away at him.

"Has anyone contacted any of the girls? I mean if what Emmett is saying is true, maybe the girls know about it."

Rory felt a flutter of panic and tried to disguise it, "Really, lezbo? You wanna see naked pics of girls that don't even exist?"

"Rory!" Erica shouted and swatted him with an oven mitt. "Don't call your sister a lezbo." Then with a look of horror she compounded it by saying, "Not that there's anything wrong with being a lezbo—being gay! Nothing wrong with being gay! Or lesbian! Or trans! Nothing wrong with being trans!"

Bailey rolled her eyes and went to set the table and Rory sighed with relief when the rumble of the garage door sounded. His father was home, and he was pretty sure that round one of the shit storm had ended with a decision in his favor.

Olivia was in her room finishing a history assignment when the text came from Bailey. Olivia had a feeling the request to meet up was more than a last minute desire for Rocky's Deli. She slipped quietly down the stairs and into the cold night wearing an oversized sweatshirt and fleece lined slippers and got quickly into Bailey's car. Her face must have shown her surprise at Bailey's swollen jaw.

Bailey grimaced, "Wisdom teeth."

Olivia nodded. "Milkshake run?"

Bailey smiled. "Sure."

Lorde was playing, and for a moment Olivia let herself believe there was no other purpose for this trip, but as soon as they turned off their road Bailey tore away the pretense.

"Is there any weird shit going on with Rory and that Coach?"

Olivia held still and waited too long to answer, causing Bailey to look at her sharply. Finally she shrugged, "Rory's like all the rest of the guys."

"What does that mean?"

"You know what it means."

"Hooking up with girls, dick pics, being an all-around douchebag?"

"Pretty much."

Bailey stared straight ahead. "I don't know why I'm surprised."

"Because." Olivia said, "He's your brother and he used to be my best friend."

Bailey nodded. "I guess, in spite of him being such an asshole, I hoped it was just show."

"Yeah."

"Not to minimize misogynistic fuckery—but is there anything else?"

This time Olivia was ready for her. "Not that I know for sure."

Bailey pounced on that. "For sure?"

"I'm assuming you're talking about Emmett Ainsworth—and what he said."

"So it is out there?"

"Seriously, B? You know this town."

"And?"

"They're just rumors. What does Rory say?"

"He denies all of it."

"There ya go."

Olivia pressed her lips together. She wanted to purge all of it to Bailey. The way Rory stalked Isa. The pictures Hunter circulated of her. The way she felt when he held her, the way she wanted to close her eyes and taste him again without knowing who he was. She wanted to ask Bailey if she understood what was happening inside of her. If she were a traitor to all women, if there was something wrong with her that she could feel this way about a guy who had done something so terrible to her. If she hated herself because she was attracted to a guy she had zero respect for or if she was attracted to a guy she had zero respect for *because* she hated herself. She wanted to not care about guys or sex or socializing. She wanted to be the kind of person that only cared about school and dance class and friends like she used to. She wanted to focus on important things like combating hunger and finding a cure for cancer. She wanted to make a difference in the world, not fall asleep thinking about the way Hunter's eyes seemed to penetrate hers even when they were on opposite ends of the cafeteria. They had every single class together. She wanted not to care when he gave answers in comparative literature. Especially when he argued vehemently that Juliet's words *But I a maid, die maiden-widowed* were the most poetic words Shakespeare ever wrote, and that if Romeo had listened to Juliet and not killed Tybalt the tragedy could have been averted. It was a surprising argument, Olivia thought, because the other guys in the class were adamant that Romeo had to kill Tybalt or he would have lost all respect and may as well have killed himself in the moment. That it was indeed Juliet's beauty that *made me effeminate And in my temper softened valor's steel.* When Hunter said, *if Romeo had truly been influenced by Juliet, they would both have lived and been together,* he'd looked right at her, his eyes caught hers and it was impossible to look away. He turned away first and Olivia nervously scanned the room, relieved that no one had seemed to notice what had felt like an eternal moment to her. Olivia thought it was a brave argument because all the guys in the room laughed at him and the teacher took his side, which made it even worse. But Hunter just shrugged at the guys taunting him and laughed. He didn't care what they thought. Later Isa and Delaney said he was just trying to get in all the girls' pants with his pseudo-feminist bullshit, but Olivia had believed him. And then the picture circulated.

Olivia wanted to tell Bailey all of those things. But they were jumbled in her mind like a tangled ball of yarn and she couldn't find the thread to pull, so she just stayed silent and listened to Lorde sing about bloodstains, ball gowns, and trashing hotel rooms instead.

A week went by while people whispered about the rumors. The players rallied hard around Coach without ever explicitly addressing the rumors. The cheerleading squad made batches of brownies and cookies, and left them in Coach's office, packaged in shiny green paper with sparkly gold cheerleading bows on top to represent the school colors and their allegiance.

"Where are we, Cal?" Margie leaned forward as Cal leaned back into his seat.

Taking a deep breath, Cal launched into what sounded like a very practiced recitation. "The Superintendent launched an internal investigation. He spoke with Coach Walker, interviewed him in my presence extensively..."

"And?"

"He was shocked. Distraught not only that these accusations were alleged against him but that Emmett Ainsworth may be in trouble of some kind."

"Trouble?"

"Mental health, substance abuse..."

"Did he have reason to think..."

"No, no, it just—seemed so out of character and I was the one who asked because quite frankly he seemed really out of it when he came to talk to me. My secretary thought so too, I got the Superintendent in and he thought the same thing."

Margie leaned back, the air pushing through her lips. "Trauma responses can seem like—"

"But that makes no sense, these allegations go back years, how is there a sudden trauma response?"

"Look, I'm not saying there is, I'm just saying these are serious accusations and we need to consider everything."

"Agreed. I'm just telling you what Coach said. I asked if Ainsworth had a history of substance abuse or mental illness as far as he knew. He said he didn't know of any substances but that he was a depressed kid and had family problems and that wrestling was the one thing that made him feel better. He floated the idea that quitting the Dartmouth team may be an indication that he was spiraling. Walker seemed more concerned for Ainsworth than he did about himself to be frank."

Margie nodded. "Who else was interviewed?"

"Well, a few things came out."

"Let's hear it." Margie planted her feet, sat up a little straighter.

"Walker admitted that he's had players here after hours. That he has keys and he has locked up at night and the custodians were interviewed extensively. They said they were told to steer clear at night or on the weekends when Coach was here with players because he wanted them to focus."

"What players?"

"The elite wrestling players, Rory Lange, Hunter Logan, and Kam Connover. There were also some outings—Applebee's."

"Well? Did you interview the boys?"

"Extensively."

"And?"

Cal shrugged. "Nothing. They all said the same thing, they go over plays and discuss strategy. Nothing irregular or out of the ordinary."

"Did you interview them together or separately?"

"Separately, of course. Hunter and Kam weren't even implicated in anything Ainsworth said. But they have been here after hours so…"

"Wait, was Rory implicated?"

"Yes, I told you this."

"By Ainsworth—he just said he thought Coach had moved onto him, whatever that means."

"Yeah, but we take it seriously. I had Erica up here. That was some scene."

"Oh, I know, she called me."

"You can't discuss any of this with her, Margie."

"Obviously, Cal." They stared at each other for a while before Margie took a breath and let it out. "What now?"

"There doesn't seem to be much else. We interviewed teachers, assistant coaches, a few other players on a variety of Walker's teams. Everyone says the same thing, great guy, dedicated, tough but caring. Nothing out of the ordinary. Nothing unusual. There just doesn't seem to be much to go on."

"Do we need to alert the authorities?"

"And say what?"

"Tell them allegations have been made."

"Ainsworth isn't a student here and our students haven't made any allegations. If anyone is going to the authorities it would have to be Ainsworth."

"Is he going to?"

"I have no idea."

"How many people know about the after hours thing and the key and all that."

"The custodial staff. Walker. The three boys."

"That's it?"

"As far as I know."

"Does that need to be made public?"

Cal shrugged. "To what end? I've put a stop to it. Seems like it would just add gas to a fire that isn't even sparking."

Margie nodded. "So back to business as usual?"

"Let's hope."

"The Superintendent thinks the internal investigation was thorough enough?"

"He does. And so do I. Look, this is a man's career. Did he make an error in judgment keeping the kids here after hours and on weekends, yeah. But we handled it. As you know we are not at liberty to discuss any personnel matters outside of the executive board. I'll give a full report during executive session. And I don't think there is anything else we can do—without running the risk of Walker suing us—or Ainsworth for that matter."

"I've briefed all of the BOE members. We're all on the same page."

"Then I think we've said all we need to, I'll give my final report at the executive session and this whole sordid thing will be behind us."

Margie nodded, picked up her purse and strode out of Cal's office and immediately texted Delaney

where are you i can drive you home

thanks but i have a ride

thought we could have a chat

Margie waited as bubbles appeared and disappeared and appeared again.

when i get home? going to study at isas

Margie sighed and responded with thumbs up. She felt relieved and hopeful, maybe some of Isa's brain power would rub off on Delaney. Maybe this incredibly shitty day was turning around. Not that she didn't trust Cal, but Margie thought perhaps she could have a personal chat with Walker. This way no one could ever say she hadn't done her own due diligence.

Delaney was waiting on the curb her gold-red curls and colorful outfit bright against the pale winter day.

Isa pulled up and Delaney climbed into the car complaining. "Margie runs a complete freak show in there. I saw her marching out of Cal's office so I ran out the side door. She wants to *chat.*"

Isa thought it was hilarious how Delaney and Bailey both referred to their parents by their proper names. She also thought it showed a profound dislike of them and wondered if her friends truly didn't like their parents. Isa didn't like Margie or Erica. They were overbearing and annoying in different ways. But she assumed their children felt differently. She loved her own parents, and every time she spent any time at anyone else's home she felt lucky to have them. Olivia got along well with her parents. Isa loved Indira and thought Jimmy was the coolest of all their dads. But their house was always kind of chaotic and Indira was a little too flaky for Isa; she needed the order and harmony she was used to from home. Sometimes Isa wondered what it would be like if her parents socialized more with the other couples in their neighborhood. It seemed like the other parents were always getting together. She asked her mother once and her mother just smiled and showed Isa her calendar packed with obligations. "Our social life is directly tied to our professions. When we have an empty space in it, we just want to be home with each other and the two of you." Isa nodded, satisfied, but sometimes she couldn't help wondering if it would have made her feel more a part of things.

Delaney was still talking about her mother and Isa tried to focus.

"Seriously, Margie and her little board of flunkies are working overtime to cover this whole thing up. Did you know that Walker has keys to the building? Someone gave them to him on the down low. And Walker was meeting with students late at night and on Sundays. And, during the evening when he held *captain's meetings.*" Delaney made giant sarcastic air quotes. "He told the custodial staff not to enter that part of the building because it was disruptive. What in the fuck is that?"

Isa felt every muscle in her body begin to ache, heaviness in her arms, making it painful to turn the wheel onto school grounds, a dull throb in the back of her neck and head.

"Isa? Do you hear what I'm saying? The fucker is going to get away with it."

Isa turned to Delaney, "No, he isn't. We're going to catch all of them in the act and that perv is going to jail where he'll get his ass kicked every damn day."

Delaney laughed. "I love when you get fired up." Then she unbuckled and jumped out before Isa even got her seatbelt off. Isa felt like she was moving through molasses, but Delaney was right, She was fired up. She felt a heat of anger from deep inside her for what that coach had done. She believed every word of Emmett's accusations and she was sure he did every one of those things to Rory too. He'd stolen her friend and turned him into something else. Something sludgy and filthy like him. Isa wanted to end that cycle. Stop him before he did it to someone else. She wanted revenge. But the thing she wanted more than anything she knew she'd never get back. She wanted the before.

Margie marched into Coach's office while there were still students milling around and shooed them all away, waving her hands at them, her thick acrylic nails flashing in the fluorescent light of his office.

"Madame President, to what do I owe this pleasure?"

Margie smiled and sat down, "Oh, just a chat."

Coach dipped his head, looked up at her, and smiled. "I'm all yours."

"So, I spoke with Cal. About the Emmett situation."

Coach's face turned serious. His eyes filled with concern. "Terrible what that poor kid is going through. I blame myself."

Margie leaned forward. "Why is that?"

"I just don't know how I could have missed the signs."

"Signs?"

"Well, something has to be wrong. For him to be this upset, to make things up like that. I just—I've been wracking my brain and I can't think of any hint of mental illness or drug use—I mean he was certainly depressed but—"

"Clinically?"

"I'm not a doctor—I don't know if he was clinically depressed."

"But you wondered?"

"I worried about him. When he was practicing or competing he was a machine. Focused. Tight. There was no one like him. But off the field—"

"Go on."

"He seemed kind of sad. That's all. I know there were problems at home."

"That divorce was notorious."

"I think it was tough on him. And as a coach I try to be there, but we also have boundaries we can't cross you know?"

"I understand. But what about the accusations? Some kind of weird contest involving girls— students?"

Coach shrugged, "I honestly have no idea. None of my players would have been involved in anything like that. I'd vouch for every one of them."

"Maybe you didn't know.

"I can't imagine I wouldn't have gleaned something, you know? High school boys aren't known for their discretion."

Margie nodded. "True."

"I just can't help wondering if there was more I could have done for him. I just never saw anything like this coming—a complete break with reality."

"Well, he hasn't been your student in two years, Coach. You don't know what could have happened in college."

"I hate to think of all his talent—wasted. I guess you heard he quit the Dartmouth team." Coach shook his head. "Tragic."

"Coach." Margie tried for delicacy but it wasn't her strong suit. "What is this I'm hearing about after hour meetings in your office? Keys to the building?"

Coach laughed, "Of course we have after hour meetings, these kids practice late—but no different than the theater kids or band kids. And I do have keys, but so does the drama teacher, I never thought it was a big deal. I don't even remember where I got them. Maybe your predecessor?"

Margie made a mental note to check. It was highly likely. Her predecessor had a thirst for her son who had only middling talent, she could imagine a little quid pro quo attempt there. It hadn't worked; her son rode the bench all through high school, but maybe once the keys were given she didn't want to ask for them back. Margie also made a note to follow up with the drama teacher and get those keys back. In this day and age teachers couldn't be in the building with students after hours. Honestly, did these people still think it was the 90s? Which reminded her…

"Emmett said you met off campus—at Applebees?"

"Sure we did! There were celebrations. Parents were invited. Also I'm there quite a bit, a coach's salary doesn't let me go to all those fancy places you and your friends frequent." He winked. "And yeah, kids have bumped into me once in a while, too. They say hello, and if I'm at the bar they keep going. The bartenders are strict about no one underage bellying up—they have to go straight to their tables. Makes it less awkward when I'm on a date." He winked again.

"You're stipulating that you've had players to dinner as a reward at Applebee's, but the parents knew and were even invited."

"Absolutely."

"And that there may have been chance meetings when you were frequenting Applebees and students showed up but just greeted you in passing."

"Exactly."

Margie nodded, "None of this seems so terrible."

Coach turned his palms up. "Obviously I didn't think so, or I wouldn't have done it. But I understand optics matter. The key has been returned and my players and I can meet on the field or in my office during regular practices, when custodial staff are there."

"Thank you. I'm glad you understand."

"Of course. I told Cal the same thing. When something like this happens we have to delve into it as much as possible. Leave no stone unturned, so to speak."

"Thank you for understanding. And for being so forthcoming."

Coach beamed his widest smile at her and when Margie left his office and made her way to the nearest exit, her relief so great she half expected to be levitating through the halls.

Indira sat down at her computer. She intended to go straight to her work emails but found herself clicking a link on facebook because she'd gotten an unusual number of notifications from a local moms group filled with rancor and an inordinate number of judgy mcjudgers. From the copious amount of notifications she'd gotten, it was proving to be a very rancorous day indeed. Indira hesitated, she knew the time-sucking rabbit hole she was about to enter, but it also seemed that whenever she ignored these kinds of things, it resulted in missing information that every other person seemed to have. Indira promised herself that if it didn't directly affect the schools or her family in some way she wouldn't read the— *Oh my*, she exclaimed, *326 comments.*

> **Moms of varsity athletes and parents who care about the stellar rep of our schools!**
> **Have your child proudly wear green and gold to show we believe in our coach, our kids, and our community!!**
> **Don't let the false accusations of one sad ex-athlete bring us down!!!!**

Indira's initial reaction (besides rolling her eyes at the excessive exclamation marks) was confusion. There wasn't much clarity gleaned from reading the top comments. Who made the original post? Most were a demand to take the post down primarily because the post itself had lit a match and fanned the wildfires of gossip. Several comments berated the original poster for being too vague and not spelling out the accusations. Indira remembered the cryptic conversation she'd had with Margie and with a growing sense of alarm wondered if Olivia was mixed up in any of this. Yet Olivia wasn't an athlete or on the cheer squad so she wasn't sure how it would directly affect her. Still the feeling gnawed at her. The paleness of Olivia's face, the perpetual half moons of bruised skin beneath her eyes, the uncharacteristic late mornings, the overall dimming of Olivia, as Indira had begun to think of it.

Indira's coffee cooled as she followed an exchange among four moms. As was often the case, most of the 326 comments had been made by fewer than ten people. There was the requisite name calling, one woman called someone a Karen, a woman who was actually named Karen told a woman named Jenny to move back to Brooklyn and Jenny retorted that she should fuck off because she came from the Upper West not Brooklyn and she moved here in 2006 long enough to be sick and tired of snobby suburban shitheads! Someone else reported her for cursing. That comment caused at least four or five tags to the administrator of the page and Indira still hadn't gleaned any information other than a former student had accused a beloved varsity coach of inappropriate behavior, the school board had investigated, and found there to be absolutely no wrongdoing.

And then just as Indira was reading the end of the comments she saw bubbles appear. It was an administrator! And it read…

What a thread to come home to! I've been alerted via messenger by many of you and after reading through this I recognize it violates many of our standards. Specifically spreading gossip. It is not enough to turn off comments. I'm deleting the post and notifying the OP.

And right before Indira's eyes the post disappeared. She sat numbly for a moment, trying to make sense of all of it. She a sip of her tea, which had gone cold, grimaced, then felt a cold hard ball of worry form deep inside of her.

CHAPTER 22

Initially, Monica believed Emmett when he said he was sick. After a week, when he hadn't emerged from his room, and she hadn't heard a word from him, she stood outside his dorm suite, texting, then eventually banging on his door and yelling, "Let me in or I'm calling the RA!"

Emmett believed her, and the fear of the extra drama was enough to get him to crawl from beneath the covers and unlock the door.

Before he could get back into bed, Monica manhandled him into the shower and threatened him until he picked up the bar of soap and began washing. Monica took in the lack of a mess that would have meant illness tissues, over-the-counter medicine, ramen noodles, mugs of tea. She saw instead a half-eaten power bar, several crumpled wrappers, an empty Brita, and a single smudged glass.

Emmett's eyes were dull, his speech lethargic, the room smelled of stale bedclothes and unwashed body. She recognized the signs of depression. She'd grown up with them. Her family wasn't as perfect and easy as Emmett liked to think. She slipped into the familiar role with an ease that was more comfortable than it should be. She knew what to do.

While Emmett showered, she stripped his mattress, found his spare sheets, and quickly remade the bed. Shoving his sheets and dirty clothes into a mesh laundry bag, she debated whether they should go directly to the laundry room or take a walk in the fresh air first. When he emerged from the shower, pale and thin, with black circles under his eyes, she decided on the fresh air.

"Bundle up. We're going for a walk."

Emmett looked longingly at the clean sheets.

"Get dressed."

Slowly, Emmett went to the wardrobe next to his bed and opened it, pulling out his clothes piece by piece and putting them on with the movements of a man four times his age. But at least he was complying. Fifteen minutes later, Emmett registered the air on his skin. As they trudged across campus toward the trails, he registered the warming of his bones, the loosening of his joints. A feeling broke through the gray haze he'd been in. He struggled to identify it. Appreciation maybe. He looked over at Monica. She turned her gaze up to his. He felt his lips crack as they lifted, the muscle memory resulting in a slight smile.

"Feels good to be outside," he said.

She smiled at him, and it was too much, too bright. So he turned away. But he was able to reach for her hand, and take note of how light and small and smooth it felt in his, he held it as they walked silently into the shadows of the trails. Eventually they paused at the top of a remote trail where there was a large rock, flat and wide enough for both of them. Monica pulled Emmett down next to her. The view of the woods below even in the dead of winter was expansive and inspired awe in anyone lucky enough to find it. But Emmett had his head cradled in his hands.

"You can tell me anything. It won't change how I feel about you."

It was the challenge that made him tell her, the certainty that he would prove her wrong. The chance to bare all he had done. Her disgust, the repudiation that would have to follow, would be his punishment. And then maybe, he could get it all to stop. Maybe if he was rightly punished, this spinning hellhole would slow, and he could climb off, stand on steady ground, until he could see straight.

Emmett heard his own voice as if he were somewhere else far away. "I was almost thirteen when Coach pulled me up from modified to join the varsity team. I was—flattered. That he saw something in me. And I was—I don't know—relieved I guess. To have someone take an interest. Things were bad, my mom was falling apart. My dad was just—gone, I guess—I mean his stuff was still there and the bills were paid—but he wasn't. And Coach kind of—stepped in. I felt lucky. At first it was all sports. And grades. He took an interest. Became a mentor. And I don't know when the other stuff started…"

Emmett fell silent, his eyes focused on something Monica couldn't see. She waited.

"It was about fishing at first. He talked to me about fishing. And how it was a metaphor for—I don't know—life, I guess. He called it luring and unbuttoning. He said it was a fishing term, and it was an exquisite analogy because fishing is something expected of men, that women expect it of us. They also want to be lured they also want to be unbuttoned. And somehow, I believed him—at the time—he was looked up to by everyone—students, parents, teachers. And it made a weird kind of sense back then—but saying it out loud now—it just…" He took in a breath. "Depraved. It sounds depraved."

Emmett nodded and spoke again, rapidly, as though he needed to purge the thoughts in his brain. "All the girls— friends—classmates I knew from the time we were little—all these girls I brought to him—they never knew of course, but I captured images of us and brought them to him. My friend Sophie—we were in our junior year but she was eighteen already—Coach had an elaborate system where they had to be 18 if I wanted points for hooking up.

He'd say, *Pics or it didn't happen.*

I wasn't to capture any images unless the girl was 18. So he told me to practice on the younger ones and only get pics of 18-year-olds. He would leave lists on his desk of girls and their dates of birth. I had almost every phone number, because of the grade group chat so I'd simply go into my contacts and put a star next to the ones who were 18. Then he'd have me read from my contacts and together we would rate the girls—"

"Rate them?"

"Yeah. We would decide together—with the flame emoji—three being the hottest."

"I get it."

"So if I hooked up with a younger girl it would never be as many points as an 18-year-old, but I was still awarded points for flames. Then images from the 18-year-olds had the most points and—it was just so fucked up—and when I pushed back about it at all he would tell me I needed to be realistic. That we lived in a world where people valued looks and maybe it was superficial but that it was no different from a football draft. He would say, we rate men on their athletic prowess like they're slabs of meat—there are entire industries based off of it. He said it was sexist of us not to reward women for the same type of prowess, whether it was athleticism or how well they took care of themselves. And I—believed it. The first time it happened I was thirteen. I hooked up with an older girl, a sophomore. And I—I didn't get pictures that night. But eventually—we um—Coach taught me what to do—how to unhook a bra—where to kiss her to get a smile—how to you know—touch her so she'd like it—how to touch her to make her orgasm—he said it was really hard for women to you know—anyway—her name was Ashleigh—she was—a nice person and I really liked her and I shouldn't have done it—gotten the pictures and brought them to him—it was so—twisted."

Emmett thought about Coach sitting across from him. Watching the images on the phone. The way his cheeks would flush, the hitch in his breath, the way his eyelids became hoods over his eyes. Emmett knew what he was watching and the idea of it caused a painful erection and it was humiliating and confusing to sit across from Coach with one, and watch as Coach was obviously also aroused, and that was arousing and confusing and Emmett found himself thinking about it obsessively but also trying not to. He didn't know how to put that into words for Monica. So he didn't.

Monica saw the shame and confusion and desperation on Emmett's face, the way he placed his head in both hands.

"Emmett…" She moved to place a hand on his shoulder but he moved away and began talking robotically.

"Coach said as men it was our job to empower women. That I was lucky to be growing up in the two thousands because in the nineties when he was in high school girls were still being slut shamed. That guys like me could take part in the feminist sexual revolution as allies by helping girls explore freedom of sexual expression.

Coach said not to listen to the feminazis, they're secret dykes who hate men and that they would call me a player or a misogynist but that was bullshit and it was my job not to give into it. He said true feminists were the girls who knew what they liked and went for it.

Coach said what the girls didn't know about the videos wouldn't hurt them. He always deleted them from my phone as soon as he watched them. He said it was the best way for him to assess my skills and teach me how to be—better. That it was no different than assessing the practice matches on video which the team did regularly. That the best ways to strengthen your weaknesses and exploit your strengths was by analyzing yourself on tape, whether it was on the mat or during the unbuttoning."

Emmett stopped speaking. He sat still, eyes tightly shut, chest heaving, head hanging. Monica knelt in front of him. She took his hand, began massaging his palm. "Emmett..." Her voice was soft, "Emmett I need you to look at me."

She waited until he opened his eyes.

He forced himself to hold her gaze with his. He was confused by the kindness he saw there. His eyes burned, and filled, and spilled onto his cheeks. He tasted the salt before it dripped away.

"Emmett, you know I'm a psyche major right? You know I lead the Take Back the Night program on campus. So I need you to understand that what I'm about to say—I don't say it lightly."

Emmett waited.

"What you've just described is sexual abuse."

He closed his eyes against the truth and nodded.

"You need to go to the police."

He nodded again. He was ready. The expulsion from school, the possibility of jail time, the eternal stamp of sexual predator. When he spoke his voice was stronger than he'd thought it would be. "I'll accept any punishment that comes my way, I can't live with this anymore."

Monica took a step back before grabbing hold of his hands.

"No, no. You don't understand. He abused you! He sexually abused all of you, he's a predator. I've read about this…I know about this from my coursework.

Emmett let those words settle into him. He'd never considered that. He thought about Rory, how young he'd been when Coach started bringing him around. How seeing Rory at the match in January and recognizing that swagger, that puffiness, made him want to punch him in the face, but it also made him want to drag him out of there, away from Coach, away from all of it, the tsunami of despair that washed through him when he recognized he was too late. Coach had already corrupted Rory and there was nothing Emmett could do about it now. Emmett never felt like a victim. That's what fed his shame. He'd felt powerful. He'd exploited all of those girls, harmed them worse than they even knew, and he'd done it to feel powerful. And to compound his shame, he'd watched it perpetuate, he'd been the poster child for it.

"Emmett," Monica said again. "We have to go to the police. We have to stop him."

Emmett looked up from the ground and nodded.

CHAPTER 23

Olivia lifted her face to the sky as she walked, listening to the rattle of a nearby woodpecker. She was so immersed in trying to identify the Woodpecker's location that she didn't hear the car pull up beside her. When Hunter rolled down his window and said "Hey, weirdo," in a normal voice, she startled, jumped, and let out a tiny mortifying shriek. Which made him laugh.

Olivia looked at him, her face burning with a residual adrenaline and deep humiliation.

"Want a ride?"

"No."

"Come on. I'll let you pick the playlist."

"No, thank you."

Hunter laughed. "Come on, we'll make a detour to Rocky's, get one of those cappuccino things you like."

Olivia narrowed her eyes, wondering how he knew that.

He shrugged. "I pay attention."

"I said, no thank you."

Hunter looked at her and she saw a settling come over his features. It was the same look she saw when he concentrated on a math problem. "Please? I need to talk to you."

Olivia was intrigued. Maybe he was going to spill the beans about his creepy coach. Or maybe he was going to try and manipulate her into covering for him. Either way it could be an opportunity.

He must have seen the acquiescence in her thinking because he stopped rolling alongside her and waited for her to walk behind his jeep and climb in. "Rocky's?"

Olivia thought about missing first period and decided it was worth it for a cappuccino. She nodded.

"As promised." He handed her his phone. She quickly scanned his playlist and threw him the most withering glance in her arsenal of deeply withering glances, and typed Beach House into the search bar. He winced when the first strains of "Myth" began to play, but she caught him listening, and saw his fingers lightly tapping.

They drove for a while, the landscape flashing past them. She'd known Hunter in one fashion or another for as long as she could remember. He was both familiar and unfamiliar. They were never close the way she and Rory had been. Their families had never socialized and barely knew one another. They'd orbited through the same nursery school, but in different sessions, and so never played together. It wasn't until middle school that they ever had class together and it wasn't until high school that they hung out together. And with the exception of those two brief hookups they had never been alone together. Although, Olivia realized, this was *actually* the first time they were alone together. The betrayal bloomed in the prefrontal cortex of her brain, shortening her breath, causing her eyes to narrow into slits. Her anger froze her in place and stopped her from what she wanted to do, which was to scream at him to pull over and let her out of his car. As though he sensed the shift in her mood, Hunter looked over at her. Something about her body language caused him to hesitate and kept him from speaking. Olivia sat looking rigidly ahead, lamenting her song choice. It was one of her favorite songs and she'd ruined it, tainted it with the scent of Hunter's shampoo and the vision of his hands on the wheel, his tapping fingers.

The last of the lyrics were sounding as Hunter pulled over half a mile before they'd reached Rocky's.

Olivia resented the way his eyes penetrated hers, how fascinating she found them, like river rocks turning from gray to green depending on shadow and light. Olivia felt her body sprint into action on its own volition, like it could obey the part of her brain she wanted it to, instead of the frozen bewitched part that wanted to make sense of things that weren't worth discovering, and she found herself unbuckling the safety belt, opening the door, and sliding out in one volatile but fluid motion.

Hunter was equally quick and had gotten out on his side and rushed around to meet her, "Please, Liv, get back in."

But she was already trudging away from him.

"Liv. Please. Give me a chance to explain."

She hesitated in spite of herself and he saw it. He stayed where he was, as if he knew approaching her would make her take off again. He raised his voice and let the wind carry it to her. "Just give me a chance to explain, and then if you never want to speak to me again, I'll understand."

Olivia was torn. The need to get away from him was palpable, but the adrenaline surge was ebbing and the practical notion of having to walk the side of the road with nothing but traffic whizzing by was suddenly daunting, and the knowledge that maybe she would get answers from him, and be able to report back to the other girls, was tempting. Enough so that she stood still for a while until her heartbeat slowed. Then she turned abruptly and marched past him and climbed back into his jeep. He waited until she settled in then looked questioningly at her. "Rocky's?"

She shook her head.

"Okay, but I don't want to talk here on the side of the road."

She glared at him.

"What if we go somewhere in town? This way if you get mad and leave at least I'll know you're somewhere safe."

She rolled her eyes. "I can take care of myself."

"Yeah, but I don't want you walking along the highway—okay? Let's just head back to town. We'll go to the rocks, OK? It's quiet there but you can walk to school in ten minutes if you can't stand the sight of me."

She nodded and stared straight ahead. He started the car and the Beach House playlist was still on. Mitsky's clear high notes filled the car. *My God I'm so lonely...*

Hunter looked over. Olivia was torn. She didn't want to ruin one of her favorite songs ever recorded and yet she couldn't bear to turn it off.

"I love this song," Hunter said and she stared at him in disbelief. She knew Mitsky wasn't on his playlist. Then he began to sing, in perfect keeping with Mitsky, which Olivia knew from trying was not easy to do.

And in that moment Olivia hated Hunter more than she'd ever hated anyone. Betrayal was almost a taste in her mouth. Because it would have been so easy to fall in love with him, and he'd ruined it.

Olivia sat rigidly next to him in her seat listening to him sing. When the song finished, she didn't even register what came on next. They finished the ride in silence and as soon as they pulled over she got out of the car and walked away from him.

"Liv, wait." This time he rushed up to her and placed his hand on her arm.

She shook him off with such violence she almost catapulted onto the ground, then kept walking as he ran alongside her. There was no explanation that would matter. No apology that would make it better.

"Please, Liv, I never meant to hurt you—I was wrong—I'm sorry."

"Get. Away. From. Me."

He watched her storm away. Olivia didn't see the way his eyes filled, turning them the color of sea glass, staring after her as she grew further and further away, until she was gone.

By the time Isa left school, between the yearbook meeting and a student government meeting, it was five o'clock and the sky was violet. A wave of nostalgia hit her as she stood at the crest of the parking lot. From here she could see the campus spread before her. The high school against the darkening sky, football field stretching away from her, the sheen of the empty bleachers against a backdrop of trees. In a few short months the stands would be packed with parents and siblings and she would be walking onto a makeshift stage in her mustard yellow cap and gown (boys wore green, girls wore gold), retrieving her diploma and leaving this place behind. She still hadn't written her valedictorian speech because she had no idea what to say. Thank you to the teachers who inspired me to learn, thank you to my two best friends. And to all the boys and their pervy coach, there isn't a hell I can conjure for you, so I wish you instead an existential hell right here on earth, one that comes out of your own filthy minds and I hope that for every moment you spend in it, the girls you perpetrated against are released in light years, until the memory of what you did is fully erased from our minds and bodies and you are left in your own perpetual filth with no respite. Isa realized that for the first time since Rory had sent her a picture of his swollen penis, she was able to shrug it off. It had nothing to do with her. It was separate and far away from her and she was done seeing it as anything other than what it was, a narcissistic image of some random guy's body part. It couldn't hurt her and had no more influence on her than a picture of an old chicken bone. With that realization, Isa got into her car, selected Lizzo from the top of her playlist, and drove off campus singing along in perfect accord, *Bling bling, then I solve 'em that's the Goddess in me.....*

The high school was quiet. After-school activities were finished, late buses were long gone, as were the lines of parents in cars picking up students. An occasional straggler carrying a flute case, or pairs of students in athletic gear, dotted the campus, but the halls had an empty echo to them and the athletic department was quiet. Coach Walker leaned back from his desk, his body language suggesting ease, and openness. His eyes lively and engaged, his smile wide. Rory settled himself in the chair across from Coach, trying to stretch his legs, but finding it impossible to do without touching him. He settled for leaning his chair back against the locked door and attempting a smile, which felt more like he was contorting the lower half of his face.]

"Soooo...party tonight at Kam's huh?" Coach asked.

"Gonna be bangin'."

"Sweet."

"So, you, planning on—."

Coach shook his head. "I've got a thing tonight."

"Cool, cool—you want us to..."

"I'm thinking you boys need to take it easy. Don't party too hard. No shenanigans, ya got me?"

Rory watched him carefully, waiting for the wink.

Finally Coach leaned forward, the ease dissipating from his eyes he spoke in a harsh whisper. "Do I need to spell it out for you, Lange?"

Rory looked at him.

"I'll be keeping a low profile from here on out. And so should all of you."

Rory nodded.

"And the rotation's back to normal. That rookie had his shot—and I'm not impressed. You're my guy."

"Thanks Coach—I—"

Coach waved him off, "You earned it, Lange. We've got a big match Tuesday. Go have a boring weekend."

Rory left Coach's office and headed into the blue light of early evening. The cold air loosened his sweat-dampened hair from his neck. He thought about the party tonight and what it would be like to just attend, without the incentive of points or a specific mission to accomplish. He expected to feel disappointed. Instead he felt lightness, as if a weight had eased away, and he was suddenly free.

By Friday evening the week of storms had cleared and the air had softened. Isa, Olivia, and Delaney were piled on Delaney's bed, trying to figure out the best strategy to catch Coach Walker in the act. Delaney wanted Olivia to reach out to Hunter and suggest a hook up at Kam's house.

Isa couldn't keep the impatience out of her voice, "Have you met Olivia? She'd never do that!"

Olivia nodded, "He'd know it was a trap."

Delaney took a minute to study her manicure, then popped her head up. "I know! Let's just tell Kam we need a party!"

Isa shrugged, "He'd be down."

Olivia tilted her head to one side, "I don't hate it."

Delaney smirked. "I'll text Kam." Then she looked at Olivia, "Girl, we need to get you fixed up. You look like hell."

"Wait—when are we doing this?"

Delaney held up the phone with Kam's text *fuck yeah* and laughed, "Tonight, bitches!"

Isa left Olivia alone with Delaney while she ran home to get dressed. A fateful error, Olivia decided, because it gave Delaney ample time to bully Olivia into a "makeover" which Delaney had been trying to do to her since seventh grade.

Without Isa there to protect her, Delaney curled Olivia's hair, and applied so much makeup (including tiny lashes glued to the outer corners of her upper-eyelids and a thick sparkling eyeliner) that Olivia kept thinking there was a fly on her left eye, and had to stop herself from swatting at her own face. Then she let Delaney shove her into a slinky black dress that looked suspiciously like a piece from her OnlyFans wardrobe. There was a brief tussle as Delaney tried to force her into a pair of heels. Olivia had to threaten to kick her in the vagina and punch her in a boob if she didn't get off of her.

Delaney backed off breathing hard enough to show that her determination had been real, and said, "Fine! Wear your filthy garbage Vans and ruin the outfit!"

"I'll go home and get cute shoes, I do have cute shoes, you psycho bitch."

"No fucking way you're going home. I know you, you'll ruin the look."

They glared at each other.

Delaney broke first, "Fine. You don't have to wear these awesome fuckme shoes. But we're the same size—so you don't need to go home—choose whichever ones you want."

Olivia glared and pushed Delaney out of the way and surveyed the ridiculous amounts of shoes lining a rack taking up an entire wall of Delaney's small room. She found a pair of chunky heeled black suede shoes that looked comfortable.

"Huh." Delaney bit her lip a sure sign she was concentrating. "That could work—different vibe but cute."

Olivia pulled them on, torn between fury and the fact that she'd always admired these boots of Delaney's.

Delaney eyed her up and down. "Those look better on you. They're yours."

"I accept."

Delaney laughed and looked at her phone. "Isa's out front— let's bounce."

Bowie's "Oh! You Pretty Things" was blasting from Isa's car, Olivia rode shotgun and Delaney pushed her head between them singing with Bowie, *the earth is a bitch we finished our news homo sapiens have outgrown their use...*

When they arrived at Kam's house, the party was in full swing and their mood had shifted from nihilistic to dangerous.

Delaney led the way in, pushing past the LAX players who had commandeered the wide front porch, twenty ounce solo cups of warm beer in their hands. One of them raised his eyebrows at her in a way he'd been told was hot often enough that he believed it. When Delaney looked past him, he showed her his tongue piercing, when she looked past that, he slid his arm out and snaked it around her waist in an almost balletic movement, gripping her obliques with his fingers. She pried them away and gave him the flapper, a backhanded punch to the balls typically delivered as a sneaky foul on a soccer field. Without looking back, she heard the satisfying *oof* as she kept walking.

Isa surveyed the room and took note of who was there. Pretty much everyone she knew. She saw a group of four senior girls who had never been invited to one of Kam Logan's parties and made a vow to keep an eye on the whereabouts of each one of them. The girls were strong students, each played a musical instrument at the all-county level, their mothers were overly involved in school activities, and the boys they tended to date were nice. Isa realized they'd been invited as targets.

As bad as Isa had thought Rory's behavior was, she'd believed it was just Rory being an asshole. She'd never have guessed it was an actual organized hunting of girls. She'd never have guessed that the boy she'd known and in her own way loved since kindergarten was in fact, a predator. And so were Hunter and Kam.

Isa turned to Olivia, who was standing close to her. She looked at Olivia's heavily made up eyes. "Liv, you don't need to go through with this."

Olivia pressed closer, her arm touching Isa's. "I'll be fine."

Isa nodded slightly toward the girls she was worried about. "I'm gonna hang with them. Cockblock those pencil dicks."

Olivia laughed in spite of herself. "I love the new you."

"Don't drink anything here, unless it's water from the tap and you get it yourself."

Isa moved away and Olivia watched the girls turn toward Isa, their eyes shining as Isa turned the power of her smile on them.

Olivia pulled her shoulders back and down, away from her ears, moved her wing bones toward each other, feeling her back straighten. She scanned the room. When her eyes landed on Hunter Connover, his eyes were already on hers.

She moved toward him. When she reached him, he lifted his hand to her face and brushed his thumb across her cheek, sending a current into her skin and through her body. Her lips parted to take in air. The room receded, until it was only the two of them standing there, the noise of the room hushing to a hum, then only the thumping of her own heart. He dropped his hand from her face letting it brush her shoulder, the inside of her elbow, until he found her hand. He held his hand against hers, palm to palm, causing sensation to surge through her. He kept his hand there until she threaded her fingers through his.

He smiled at her. Not the thinning of his lips when he was about to say something challenging or cruel, but the full one. The one that seemed just for her, not during their brief and heated hookups, but the few times they'd found themselves having actual conversations.

He began to walk backward. She didn't feel her feet against the floor as she moved with him; she only felt the place where her skin touched him.

Hunter led Olivia through the sliding doors onto the patio, down the steps and across the pool. The heat of their movement caught the sensors and the area flooded with light. Hunter moved quickly down the patio steps and off into the trees on the side of the house. There was no moon that night and the darkness was complete. She couldn't see him for a moment while her eyes adjusted, but she felt the hardness of his chest and stomach as he circled his arm around her back and leaned toward her, she felt the warmth of his breath against the side of his neck, and her knees almost collapsed at the sensation of his voice near her ear.

"I'm so sorry, Liv. About all of it. The camera. The pictures. It's unforgivable."

Olivia closed her eyes and whispered back, "I don't forgive you. I don't think I ever can."

She felt his stillness. Heard him swallow. He rested his forehead against hers. "I get it," he whispered. "Is there anything I can do? Not for forgiveness—but to—make things right?"

Olivia pulled her head away and looked at him, her gaze adjusting to the light, she saw the gleam and shape of his eyes. "You can tell the truth."

"That I wished it never happened? That I'm an asshole? That I love you? I'll shout it from the rooftops."

"What?"

"I do. I've loved you since sixth grade."

Olivia shook her head. She couldn't focus on that statement and the questions it raised. "Okay, not relevant."

He laughed.

When she didn't, he stopped. "Then what truth? Everyone knows you didn't know about the camera. Everyone knows I'm an asshole."

"The real truth, Hunter. About your pervy fucked up coach."

Hunter dropped his arms away and took a step away from her, "The Ainsworth thing."

"Yeah."

Hunter lifted his hands to his head. Elbows out. A move she'd seen him do a thousand times, on football fields, during wrestling tournaments, whenever he was losing.

"Is that why you came tonight?"

She nodded. "Come with me."

"Where?"

"Just come."

"Okay."

Her eyes were adjusted to the darkness now and she could see the path clearly through the trees. She led the way, Hunter close behind her.

When they got to the back door, she heard him give a slight groan, but she punched the code in and held her breath, the handle turned immediately and they were in. He followed her silently through the shed, to the other door and up the stairs. When they got to the door of the bedroom he placed his hand on her shoulder, "Liv—"

She shook him off and opened the door slowly. It was empty, he followed her in, and she closed the door tight.

"Liv what are you doing?" She turned and faced him. He went to speak but she placed a finger against his lips. She watched as his eyes softened. She let him draw closer. She moved her hand from his face and curled her fingers against the nape of his neck, surprised by the softness of his hair. She kissed him gently. Then again, feeling his mouth open against hers, the familiar salt and beer taste of him. She drew back slowly, still kissing him. She wanted the element of surprise. She lifted his shirt from the bottom, the heat of his skin burning hers. He craned his neck forward and down, kissing the side of her neck, creating that melting feeling inside her. When he brought his lips back to hers, she allowed herself one more, deep kiss, before she broke abruptly away. Noting the glazed look in his eye she acted quickly, turned her back on him, and pulled the closet doors wide open in a sudden movement.

"Gotcha, Perv!" she yelled, coming face to face with the white terrycloth robe, hanging just as it had weeks ago, the same expensive jars of lotions and shampoos and perfumes lined neatly on a neighboring shelf.

"Olivia." He put his hand on her arm.

"Don't!" She shook him off.

"There's no one here. I wouldn't do that to you again."

She turned and glared at him.

"Olivia, you can't pretend what's happening between us doesn't matter."

"It doesn't!"

"I don't believe you."

"Fuck you, you fuckin' fuck!" Olivia saw the corner of his mouth lift and his eyes crinkle. "Don't you dare laugh!"

"You're cute when you curse—"

"Shut. Up."

"Okay—but just hear me out—you wanted the truth, I'll give it to you."

She stopped moving. She'd come here for the truth. She couldn't let her temper get in the way.

"Liv, I'll tell you the truth but you've got to hear me out, okay?"

She felt the uncertainty on her face, and she knew he could see it, because he backed away, and sat down on the floor, his back against the bed, his hands up behind his head again, elbows up. "Please. Just hear me out, then you can leave."

Without speaking she went and sat across from him. Close enough to talk but not close enough to touch.

"Liv, I get that you came here to catch us out. But I meant what I said. I would never do that again. I'm sorry I ever did it."

"Sorry you did it or sorry you got caught?"

"Sorry I did it."

"So where's the perv?"

"It's over. We'll never do anything like that again."

"Even if I believe that you won't do anything like that again —" She saw hope flare in his eyes, "I said IF, Hunter, and it's a big if." She waited for his nod of understanding, "I don't trust that perv coach of yours. He'll do it again as soon as he gets the chance. Predators like him don't just stop."

"What makes you so sure—."

"Do not lie to me."

"I'm not! I'm asking you a question."

"Why would Ainsworth lie?"

"A million reasons."

"Is he lying?"

Hunter wouldn't look at her.

"I'll take that as a no."

"Olivia—it's complicated."

"Really? Cause I think it's pretty simple. Your pervy coach got a bunch of his players to let him watch you hook up with girls so he could get his rocks off."

"It's not like that."

"Okay. Explain it to me."

He shook his head. "I can't." It was barely a whisper.

"Then fuck you straight to hell."

"Olivia —."

"If you can't tell me the truth then don't fucking come near me. We are going to take that motherfucker down. Stand in our way and we'll take you down too."

As if on cue, or maybe because she heard Olivia's raised voice, Isa burst through the door. Hunter jumped to his feet.

Olivia looked at her. "Nothing."

Isa nodded, "You ok?"

"I'm fine."

Isa glared at Hunter and whipped out her phone, showing him a selfie of her and the four senior girls she'd taken a few minutes ago, in flagrant disregard of the Kam Connover no-selfie rules at his parties. The girls had been quick to pose, they were experts, Isa had memorialized them quickly with their forward thrusting hips and pouting lips. "Look carefully."

Hunter glared at her, but he let his gaze rest on the image. "What am I looking at?"

"Any pics of these girls show up, I'm coming for you."

Hunter sighed, "I guess I deserve that."

"You guess?"

"Ok, I do deserve it, But I can't control—"

"Figure it out."

"I—"

"And while you're at it, tell your sad little horny friend Rory that if any of these girls get unsolicited dick pics sent to them, I'll kick his balls so far up he'll be spitting them back out."

"Wait—what?"

But Isa and Olivia knew how to make an exit. They were down the stairs and sauntering through the party. Delaney was standing at the patio doors looking bored. Without a word the three girls walked out, creating a small ripple of disappointment.

Kam was doing a keg-stand in the kitchen and never saw them leave, but Rory followed Isa with his eyes, caught the determined look on Olivia's face, and saw Hunter come down the stairs red faced with his hair sticking up, which meant he'd been raking it with his hands, a tell that he was upset. Rory's stomach wobbled and the calm feeling that had settled over him at Coach's proclamation earlier that day fizzled and disappeared, leaving a familiar gnawing feeling in its wake. Mistaking it for hunger, and knowing he had to make weight, he slipped his hand into his pocket and felt for the smooth capsule. In one swift comforting movement he popped the Vyvanse into his mouth and waited for it to hit his bloodstream.

CHAPTER 24

Erica went down into the kitchen in a pair of yoga pants and an oversized sweater even though she wasn't scheduled to work out. She left her master suite with minimal makeup, no jewelry, her hair flattened with sleep sweat against her head, wearing bedroom slippers. She stood blinking at the coffee machine where she waited as it brewed. It was a departure for Erica to come downstairs without being fully dressed. She had inadvertently forgotten to sign up for her Monday morning spin class, an unprecedented failure on her part, and no manner of cajoling or threatening was going to allow her in. It felt odd to walk around the kitchen without her heels or running shoes, the slippers making a depressing scuffing sound.

The coffee finished brewing. Erica inhaled the rich scent of it and she looked longingly at the thick crema the expensive machine spouted. She defiantly pressed the espresso button on the machine, letting her coffee cup fill with another four ounces. She took it black and unsweetened and savored her first sip.

She looked around at the spotless quiet kitchen, relieved to have the house to herself. She ignored the hunger pains in her stomach, picked up her phone, and walked into the solarium in the front of the house, a seldom-used room, but it had a lovely view, a comfortable sofa, and it was far away from the refrigerator. No spin class, therefore no smoothie for her.

Erica curled into a corner of the couch, happy to be alone, watching the shadow of her magnolia tree on the other side of the window project patterns across the soothing whisper-gray walls. Just as she began to relax, Erica's phone buzzed a frantic alert. Erica fumbled for it and saw three texts from Margie. *Call me. Now. Urgent.* Erica's hand shook as she pressed Margie's number and put it on speaker.

"Margie here."

"Everything okay?"

"Ainsworth went to the local PD."

"What!"

"You heard correctly."

"What do you mean he went to the local PD? What did he say?"

"He filed a formal complaint against Coach Walker. The Superintendent called me early this morning."

"Well, he should be arrested for making a false report."

"This is serious."

"You can't believe it's true!"

"Of course I don't believe it." Margie yelled.

"So what are you going to do about this? Sue him for defamation? Keith has a shark of an attorney, your school attorney isn't up for the task."

"Erica, has Rory mentioned anything to you?"

"Keep Rory's name out of this, Margie. He has nothing to do with it. He doesn't even know this Emmett character, they're two grades apart. Rory was an underclassman when he was a senior!"

"Have you had a conversation with Rory? What does he say about it?"

"Nothing! He says nothing because there's nothing to say. Rory doesn't hang out with that—that—person—and he doesn't do drugs!"

"Erica, no one is accusing Rory of anything."

"Then why are you asking about him?"

"These allegations are serious. And they are very specific."

"So what? All that proves is that Emmett Ainsworth is an imaginative liar!"

"They are very specific, they include names, dates, and details."

"What does that have to do with Rory?"

"Emmett was concerned that Coach Walker may be continuing the behavior with Rory."

"ALLEGED! ALLEGED BEHAVIOR!"

"Erica, calm down. We can't have a discussion about this if —."

"Fine. Just—say alleged."

"Of course it's alleged. We aren't on camera, Erica!"

"I know Margie, I'm sorry. It's just—this is so distressing."

"I understand. But things are going to move quickly now. We have to focus."

"What exactly is Emmett accusing Coach of?"

As Margie spoke, Erica listened with her hand over her mouth and the other wrapped around her stomach. She felt herself grow sick.

"Erica?" Margie asked after the litany of words had slowed, then stopped, and there was only the sound of Erica breathing and Bailey holding her breath.

"If any of this had happened to Rory, I would know."

"Talk to him."

"None of these things are true. Coach Walker is a good man." Anger was making it difficult for Erica to speak. "The

211

only pervert here is Emmett Ainsworth. You need to shut this down now."

"We're handling it."

"If Emmett and these girls were doing anything filthy with each other, that has nothing to do with Rory! Or Coach Walker for that matter."

"In that case we have nothing to worry about."

"And if you don't care about my son, and the other boys on the team, then you should be worried about your property values, Margie, like you're always saying our schools are our brand. And our brand is what drives our home values."

"How about you let me worry about the School Board and you worry about what's going on in your house."

"What's that supposed to mean?"

"Talk to Rory, Erica. And find out if there is any truth to this."

"There isn't!"

"Whether we like it or not, there is now an external investigation. If Rory is somehow involved, you need to prepare yourself."

Erica disconnected and threw the phone down. It made a muffled *thunk* as it hit the thick carpet. Erica whispered a soothing mantra to herself *none of this is true none of this is true none of this is true....*

CHAPTER 25

Isa pulled her favorite sweater over her head. It was the perfect weight for a chill in the air but not too bulky, and the bright yellow cheered her. Her phone dinged and she picked it up. Rory. How did he always manage to get past her blocks? The words *this song makes me think of you* seared her. She didn't want to know which song made him think of her. It was a concert video.

Isa saw a bunch of pale arms waving in the air. Then, a skinny Mick Jagger strutting awkwardly around the stage, shouting his lyrics, *gold coast slave ship bound for cotton fields/ sold in the market down in New Orleans....brown sugar how come you taste so good...*

Isa pressed the stop button. "Oh, hell no." Her thumbs flew across the tiny keyboard, anger radiating through her. **Don't send me this racist shit.**

Bubbles appeared almost immediately. He must have been waiting for her response.

Racist? WTF

Isa blocked him *again* and stood breathing heavily in the middle of the room. There. She'd done it. Called out the racist fuckery she'd been dancing around every day of her life at that school.

The anger shimmered inside her, until it was euphoric, despite her hammering heart, the tightness in her throat. She had spoken out. She would never swallow her words again. She felt the power of speaking truth. She was done giving it away.

Rory felt stung by what he determined to be an extremely unreasonable response from Isa. Racist! Him! He caught sight of himself in the mirror. His face showed the injury he'd felt at her words and made him look weak, like a sulky baby. He watched a flush of anger spread up his neck and into his cheeks. *She had no right.*

He pulled up the YouTube video of Mick Jagger strutting around like a boss. Without thinking he sent it to Coach Walker with the caption, *Gonna have to find me some new brown sugar, my last booty call don't love me no more*

His phone jumped in his hand.

"Hey Coach, pretty fu—."

"Are you this stupid? You can't send stuff like this to me!"

"What? It's a song?"

"Lange, you can't be this thick. Don't text me. Don't call me."

Rory stared at the phone. He tried to call Coach back, it went straight to voicemail, Rory tried texting and watched for the word delivered to appear, but his text just sat hovering, unanswered.

The day was going from bad to worse. Rory had woken in a great mood, reached out to the people he cared the most about, and suddenly he was in a vortex of shame and rejection. He dressed quickly. He needed a mood pick me up, something to help him focus on the good shit and not all this stupid drama with a girl and his temperamental coach. Rory found the orange and white capsule, which was quickly becoming synonymous with happy, and popped it into his mouth, letting it slide easily down his throat. The Vyvanse would hit his blood stream soon, making everything shimmer with possibility. *Fuck them all,* he thought to himself. In a few short months he'd be leaving this all behind him. He had a bold, beautiful future waiting for him at Duke, and he'd show them all.

He went down the back stairs, looking forward to the breakfast his mom would be making. It was Monday, so it would be a four-egg-white omelet, with spinach and tomato. And a hot steaming cup of black coffee.

But when he got to the kitchen there was no food and no sign of Erica. "Mom?"

He looked around, startled, when he saw a figure in the doorway of the kitchen. Erica had materialized from the front of the house. She looked—messy—was the only way he could describe it. Her face was slack and she spoke in a flat monotone, as though she were sleepwalking. "Rory. We need to talk."

"Okaaay? But can we talk while you make breakfast?"

Erica was wearing slippers and they made a weird scuffing sound as she shuffled slowly to the pantry. Once inside she came out with a box of raisin bran, then she shuffled over to the gleaming giant fridge, pulled with what seemed to be an inordinate amount of effort, and retrieved a quart of skim milk. She placed it on the counter next to the cereal, pulled a bowl from the cabinet, a spoon from the drawer, and slid it toward him.

"Cold cereal? I have practice this morning."

"If there is any practice."

"What are you talking about?" Rory felt a moment of panic. Had Coach been so angry about that stupid song that he'd kicked him off the team? Had he called his mom and barred him from practice? Nothing was making sense.

"Mom!"

Erica looked up at him. "Emmett Ainsworth went to the police. There's going to be a full investigation."

Rory paled.

Erica walked closer to him. "Rory, is there anything you need to tell me?" Even Erica's voice sounded different. As if she were on the other end of a long tunnel.

Rory shook his head.

"Rory. You can tell me. If any of those girls threw themselves at you—I understand that a boy your age has—."

The two of them stood in the kitchen. The early morning sunshine had dissipated, and no one had bothered to turn the lights on, so it was cold and gray with the lingering smell of coffee.

"Where are you getting this? Isa and Olivia? They have it in for me for some reason."

"But —." Erica almost wailed, "They're your friends."

"They're feminazis. They hate dudes."

"The allegations are that Coach is a sexual predator. That he's manipulated his wrestlers into abusing these girls." He heard her swallow. "Are you a part of this, Rory?"

He couldn't answer, the words stuck in his throat.

"Tell me it isn't true!" Erica screamed.

Rory saw her face change and it scared him.

"You're ashamed," she whispered.

"I'm not—I didn't do anything—I'm just—this sucks! It's so unfair!"

Erica drew herself up and spoke with what seemed to Rory to be newfound calm. "I spoke with Margie. They're squashing this. Just keep your mouth shut and focus on what you need to do. We're in the home stretch—focus on wrestling and your studies. You're a Lange. So act like it."

Jimmy Irizzary took the stairs down to the kitchen two at a time. He found Indira at the coffee maker. He walked behind her, wrapped his arms around her waist, bent his head, and found the place on her neck that made her weak kneed when he kissed her.

She shivered, then turned to press her body against him, and lifted her face, kissing his lips, lightly, then again.

They broke apart when Olivia walked into the room and whistled. "Hi, love birds. Can I have some of that coffee?"

Indira smiled. She untangled herself from Jimmy and poured three cups of coffee. "Blueberry pancakes?"

"Yeeeeesssss!" Olivia pumped her fist.

Jimmy smiled at her. She looked like her ten-year-old self when she did that. A melancholy feeling rolled through him.

Olivia looked at her phone and frowned, "Actually—I'm good with just coffee." As suddenly as she'd appeared, she was gone.

Indira looked at Jimmy and rolled her eyes, which made him laugh because she looked like Olivia.

Moments later the front door opened and closed. Indira walked to the window in time to see Olivia leave. "Hunh."

Indira walked back to the kitchen and tried her best to smile at Jimmy. "Blueberry pancakes for you?"

He shook his head, "I'll just grab a banana. I've got work to do, I'll be in my office."

Indira moved absent-mindedly to the dishwasher and began unloading it. No need to make breakfast if Olivia was gone already. She fought her disappointment, Olivia didn't have class until 10:00 on Mondays and it was the one morning she was able to see her for a bit. It was one of the reasons she chose this day to work from home. Indira wondered where she could possibly be going this early. Maybe, she decided, it was a good sign. Olivia had seemed so sad lately. Getting up early had to be positive. The whole thing going on with the athletes was upsetting, but Indira couldn't see how it would involve Olivia.

Emmett and Monica sat in Beth's kitchen across the table from her. They'd arrived after dinner the evening before and Emmett knew Beth couldn't figure out why they were there.

Beth slid cups of black coffee in front of Emmett and Monica and placed a bowl filled with blue packets of artificial sweetener in front of them.

"Oh…" Emmett said, "Monica takes cream and sugar."

"I'm so sorry, dear." Beth said taking a sip of her lemon water, "I don't have either of those things here—if I'd know you were coming—" She looked pointedly at Emmett, "I'd have gone to the grocery store."

"Oh, this is fine, thank you!" As if to prove it Monica sipped the hot bitter coffee.

Emmett noticed how thin his mother was. She'd begun coloring her dark hair platinum blonde and cut her formerly shoulder length hair into a pixie. Emmett found it startling and wondered if he'd even recognize her if he passed her randomly on the street. She'd also done things to her face, he'd noticed. Her forehead was as taut and unlined as a doll's, her lips smooth and puffy as though she was enduring a painful case of sun poisoning. She seemed even more vulnerable than usual and it increased his anxiety about what he was about to tell her, this wasn't a conversation he ever thought he would be having.

Emmett looked at Monica who nodded, almost impercep-tibly, and that gave him the courage he needed. "So, mom— there's something I need to talk to you about. I've asked Monica to come today because—she's—really helped me through this—and...."

Beth had placed her glass down and was wringing her hands. "Are you dropping out of school?"

"No—I...."

"Are you in trouble?" She glanced over at Monica and let her eyes wander pointedly to her stomach.

"No! Mom, let me get this out my way."

Beth's hands untangled themselves and fluttered up, hovering around her face.

As Emmett spoke, his words came out broken and halting. This would now be the fourth time he had told the story, and to spare his mother, he left out the more graphic details. He focused on the coffee mug in his hands as he spoke, the dark swirl, the heat between his palms. He looked up once and Beth's hand was covering her mouth, the thumb and pointer squeezing the tip of her nose so hard that he was concerned she would hyperventilate and pass out.

When Emmett finished, Beth's body straightened. Her arms lowered until she was gripping the sides of her chair. Her eyes, red-rimmed and glittering, focused on Emmett's.

"Why didn't you tell me?"

"I don't know—it was a secret. Coach said not to. That he'd lose his job —."

"And that didn't give you a hint that what he was doing was wrong?"

"It's hard to explain."

"Please try. I want to understand."

"He made it seem like people would say it was wrong—but that it really wasn't."

"This makes no sense to me," Beth said. "Didn't we teach you right from wrong? You were always a principled boy, a

good sport. Strong student. Helped around the house—"
Beth stopped. "Am I sounding judgy? I don't mean to—"

Emmett looked at her and saw the confusion on her face.
He understood it. He had felt similarly confused. "I don't
know if there is any way to understand if you weren't there.
It was like—he just made it seem like it was the right thing
to do, a rite of passage. And that we had to keep it a secret
because the administration and our parents would freak out—
but that they were the ones who were wrong—and what we
were doing was actually right."

"How? How could a grown man asking for sexual details
and— and—naked pictures of high school students be right?"

"I don't know—it's not right! He just made it seem—like
it was part of my education—part of coaching."

"But the girls!"

"I know. He said it was good for them too. That girls have
the same opportunity as guys do to explore sex and that he was
helping me help them—that it was a new brand of feminism."

"What!"

"I—I know."

"Tell me again—when all of this started?"

"In the beginning—when he first recruited me."

"But—you were barely 13!"

"Yeah."

"And there were others?"

"I think so."

"But you don't know?"

"I was never there for any of it—but I think so."

"I don't understand. This doesn't—doesn't make any
sense."

"Mrs. Ainsworth?"

Beth looked at Monica, who spoke softly. "It's what guys

like Coach do, they gain the trust of someone when they're in a vulnerable state. Emmett's age made him vulnerable. Coach was an authority figure, and a benevolent one, right? He made it seem like an honor that he'd chosen Emmett, any one in Emmett's position would have been grateful. Then he used Emmett's trust and the vulnerability to coerce him—to trick him. Convincing him that what he was telling them to do was right but needed to be secret because the rest of the world didn't understand, assuring secrecy by eliciting fear responses. Classic tools of the predator."

Beth looked at Emmett. "Did he hurt you?"

"Not in the way you mean—but it messed me up. Somewhere deep inside I knew the things he was getting me to do were wrong—and I didn't want to be part of it—but I was. When I went to the match, during winter break—and I realized how young Rory Lange was when Coach recruited him—and I realized how young I'd been—I just knew I couldn't stay quiet anymore."

"So now what?"

"We," he looked at Monica and she nodded encouragingly, "We went to the police yesterday. That's why we came home."

"What! Why didn't you tell me—you went there without a lawyer? Does your father know?"

Emmett leaned forward. "I didn't want you or dad talking me out of it. And I didn't need a lawyer. I needed to tell the truth."

Beth looked at him, "We need to tell your father."

Emmett shrugged, "Yeah. He's going to hear about it one way or another."

"And you need a lawyer."

"I have money saved, I'll get a lawyer."

Beth glared at him, "Your father will get you one."

"I don't want —."

"This is going to cost thousands of dollars."

"I have five thousand dollars in my account—from working —."

"Don't be a fool, that's what a retainer costs. A lawyer will eat that up in no time. Your father has an army of attorneys." Beth glared at Monica who was slumped in her seat. "Emmett should have come to us before going to the police."

Emmett's lips thinned, "Yeah, well, I wanted to tell the truth before it all got swept under the rug. I'm going back to school today. The police have my number. If they need me they know where to find me."

Beth's eyes filled again, "I'm just worried about you."

Emmett got up and hugged her. "I know, Mama, but I'm better than I've been in a very long time."

His use of his childhood name for her made Beth cry harder. Monica watched, torn between empathy and a horrid fascination. Beth's face crumpled oddly, the lower half of her jaw quivering, eyes squeezing into slits, but her forehead and lips didn't move, as though she were a candle melting from the wick out.

"I'm so sorry." Beth wept and Monica instinctively reached out a hand only to pull it quickly back in. She was an unwelcome spectator to Beth's grief. There was no space to offer comfort.

"Don't be, Mama."

Emmett stepped back and took Monica's hand. "We're heading back to school now. Don't worry, I'm okay, everything's going to be alright."

And for the first time since Emmett was propelled out of childhood, he believed that everything would be all right.

Isa had a rare morning of sleeping in; when she woke up and reached for her phone she was surprised to see it lit up with texts from Olivia and Delaney.

She heard a car in the driveway. Isa hurried to the window in time to see Olivia and Delaney. Isa knocked loudly on her window. Olivia looked up then pointed to the screened porch on the side of the house.

Isa pulled a sweatshirt over her T-shirt, and went down in her pajama pants and slippers.

The porch wasn't heated, and the morning air was chilly. Olivia set a cardboard tray of hot drinks on the small coffee table.

Isa sipped gratefully at her cappuccino and pulled her sweatshirt closer to her throat.

Olivia looked at Isa. "We tried calling you."

"Oh, I was sleeping—I didn't get up until you texted me just now."

"My mom called Erica Lange this morning and I heard the whole conversation. Emmett Ainsworth went to the police about Walker. Emmett had a list of girls that Walker targeted, he had an entire system, he groomed Emmett, coached him on how to get girls to have sex with him, coached him to video them so he could give him *pointers*. He said it made them feminists because he was helping the girls realize their full sexual potential by treating them as sexual equals. But that it had to be secret because adults didn't understand and they were all hung up in old ways of thinking. He's a sociopath." Delaney took a breath, "He thinks Walker is doing the same thing to Rory, and maybe others. And I guess that would make us—the girls."

Isa's phone lit up in her hand chiming with a Facetime. She looked at Olivia. "It's Bailey!"

"Answer it."

Bailey's face appeared "Isa, did my brother do anything to you?"

"Not really... not in the way you mean...." She caught Olivia's eye. "We don't talk anymore——he hasn't touched me or anything."

"But...."

"I block him. Constantly. But he finds ways around my blocks."

"Why are you blocking him?"

Isa took a breath. "He sends me dick pics constantly—and as disgusting as that is—it's what he writes—the things he wants to do to me—the way he begs me to send pics of myself—yesterday he sent me lyrics from "Brown Sugar"."

"That little asshole." Bailey's face flushed with fury.

"I don't want my parents to know—it will upset them."

Bailey looked at her, "They should be upset. He's sexually harassing you."

"I can handle it on my own."

Olivia looked worried. "Isa, the whole thing is going to come out. The police are involved."

Isa looked down. "Can we leave my name out of it?"

Bailey looked skeptical. "If that's what you want."

Isa nodded. "I do."

"I won't say anything."

"But it may not be up to us." Olivia said. " If they search Rory's phone...."

"If that happens, I'll deal with it."

"I'm sorry my asshole brother put you through this."

"You have nothing to apologize for. None of this is your fault."

Bailey looked uncertain,."My family has a lot to answer for."

Isa shrugged, "Maybe so. But you don't. You didn't do anything wrong."

Bailey seemed uncomfortable, "Isa, I know you and Rory had a thing for a while...."

Isa nodded, "I mean—nothing really happened back then. We made out a few times——but I just wasn't feeling it. We could have stayed friends but then he started being disgusting." She shook her head. "And I didn't know how to stop it."

"Isa, don't feel like you have to protect my family."

"I just don't want the drama. I can't wait to graduate and get as far from this hellhole as possible."

Olivia nodded. "Same."

Bailey grinned. "Ha. Don't come back. That's been my downfall."

Isa laughed. "I'm getting a job in the city so I never have to come back. And I'm renting an apartment. It's cheaper than NYU dorms. You can visit!"

Bailey smiled. "Be careful, I'll take you up on that."

"You better." Isa smiled back and let her gaze linger on Bailey and wondered how Bailey and Rory could be related. Isa thought Bailey was everything Rory wasn't, thoughtful, a profound thinker, funny when she wanted to be, and beautiful. Isa knew Bailey was considered plain by high school standards but Isa thought Bailey had the most beautiful eyes she'd ever seen, wide and gray the color of glistening stone, a dark double fringe of lash. Her lips were wide and smooth. Kids made fun of her unibrow but Isa loved that she was confident enough not to care about it, or the light fuzz above her lip. All the girls at their school had such a weird phobia about body hair. Even Olivia went insane if she noticed an errant eyebrow hair. Yet Bailey just allowed herself to be unadorned and unplucked. Her light brown hair, unprocessed, fine, and silky, was usually pulled away from her broad face, showing off her high cheekbones. Her skin was alabaster, clear, shimmering, and pale, with translucent blue lines. The only DNA Bailey and Rory seemed to share was their athleticism. Bailey was tall, five foot ten, with a rangy build, and the easy graceful lope of an athlete.

Bailey lifted the corner of her mouth. "Bard is boring as fuck so you may see more of me than you want to."

Isa laughed, "Okay, then."

As suddenly as she'd appeared, Bailey was gone. Isa's gaze lingered a moment more at the blank screen then looked up and found Olivia smirking at her.

"What?"

"Oh nothing." Olivia said, but she smiled her wide brilliant teasing smile. It was one Isa hadn't seen in a long time and she realized then how much she'd missed it.

Isa took another sip of her coffee and let her shoulders relax. Well, she'd told Bailey the truth and the world hadn't ended. In fact it seemed a tiny bit brighter despite the gray late-winter light.

The axiom 'bad news travels fast' exists for a reason, Margie thought to herself as she closed her laptop in disgust. As hard as she and the Superintendent had tried to contain this thing, it had taken off with a life of its own. The local social media pages were blowing up with wild accusations and rumors. On one particularly angry MOM page, her own head had been called for in detailed ways that made it difficult not to take it all personally. Blaming her for not nipping this in the bud sooner! Meanwhile the social media pages were spreading the word faster than she could shut it down! Margie felt a burst of acid in her stomach, shooting up through her chest and into her throat. Her job was thankless; no matter how much she accomplished someone was always displeased and complaining. Margie had countless moments when she considered giving it up. Let someone else do the hard work required to keep their district number one, allowing their home values to soar with a robust market despite the high property taxes. You couldn't have one without the other, and if they cut even a smidgen of the school budget their district would simply have high taxes with a subpar school system, and all her critics could blame those fat defined benefit pensions which were completely beyond her control. Still, she'd never give it up. She loved her power. It was so unlike anything she experienced at home or in her previous job. Yet this was a crisis of a proportion she had yet to encounter in all of her years as School Board President. In fact it may be the worst crisis the district faced for as far back as institutional memory served. There had been a science teacher who impregnated one of their senior students, but that had been back in the 90's when scandals of that nature could be dealt with quietly and a well-timed retirement and the resulting shame of the girl's family could be relied on to put an end to it.

Her approach had to be four-pronged at this point. First they needed to deal with Coach Walker. Next they needed to control the message to members of the school district. Cooperating with the local police investigation was taking up much of her time. The fourth prong was the one she had the most anxiety about, contending with the public at the Board of Education meeting that was happening in approximately ten hours.

Margie felt a prickling along her upper lip and a gathering of sweat at her fulcrum. She took a deep breath and made the first call. It was time to deal with Walker. And she needed a foolproof plan.

"Cal, Margie here."

"What a shit show."

"Have you heard from Coach?"

"He was brought in for questioning. Called a high priced criminal defense attorney, a friend of Walker's father apparently. According to Walker they didn't have enough evidence to hold him. Without any corroborating witnesses, they don't seem to think they have a case. But the cat's out of the bag and now we have a PR crisis."

"We can't fire him for cause if there are no charges, and public opinion is very much for him."

"Either way, this won't play well for any of his athletes."

"What do you think, Cal? Any fire behind the smoke?"

"Nah. If I thought that—I'd—I don't believe a word of it. I think Ainsworth went off to school and had some kind of a breakdown. It happens."

"Do you think there's anything we need to worry about with Walker?"

"I mean—yeah. How much time he spent alone with kids in the building, he may have joked around in ways that if it became public—you know the climate today —can't tell an off-color joke—can't rest your hand on a kid's shoulder. I mean any kind of scrutiny in today's world would turn something up. But nothing like what Ainsworth is alleging, I'd bet my year's salary."

"Well let's hope it isn't going to come to that, Cal, because it won't be good for anyone."

"You want Walker at the meeting?"

"No!" Margie shouted. Realizing how she sounded, she took a deep breath and tried for a better, more modulated tone. "It's going to be heated as it is. Tell him to stay home. And for God's sake, to keep his head down."

"You don't think it will make him look guilty?

"If he's not guilty nothing will make him look guilty."

"You know that isn't how it works, Margie."

"I think we need to hold this meeting, keep it as short and sweet as possible and wait for the next imminent controversy to get these parents' panties in a bunch."

"Agreed. See you at the meeting tonight."

"Hope for the best, Cal. Hope for the best."

CHAPTER 26

The Center for Education was packed. The vaulted glass ceiling provided views of scudding clouds and sunlight during the day, but at 7:30 in the evening, the starless sky loomed dark and empty above the crowded auditorium, a cacophony of angry voices and shouted recriminations echoing in the large space.

Margie was doing her best to keep order. She was seated in the middle of the long table flanked by the Athletic Director and Superintendent of Schools, the remaining board members fanned out on either side of the table each with their own microphone and gleaming nameplate, they sat stoically and faced the rambunctious crowd.

"The meeting will come to order, please take a seat and stop talking." Margie was on her individual mic but no one was listening. The audio-visual tech was manning the standing mic at the front of the aisle below the stage with a removable feature that allowed people to come up and speak at the mic stand, or if they were close by the tech would simply remove the mic from the stand and pass it around. It was supremely organized and efficient with all of the latest gear any school district could want. Margie prided herself on the technology budget she had worked so diligently on. The fact that her constituents were not responding as requested was definitely raising her blood pressure. The lack of gratitude from these people, she thought for the gazzilionth time, was astounding.

A large group of student athletes, wearing school colors, congregated in the first row holding signs in green and gold stating things like SUPPORT OUR COACH, WALKER IS THE MAN, COACH WALKER HOOT HOOT because their mascot was an owl.

"Please settle down!" Margie finally shouted into the mic and it reverberated off the sleek wooden walls and into the room, startling the crowd into silence.

The Langes, Connovers, and Logans were seated together right behind the student athletes. They were chatting with one another. Erica's color high with indignation, CeCe Logan looked concerned, and Ginnifer Connover was attempting to lighten things up as if they were merely poolside at the club instead of sitting in an overheated school auditorium. Keith was bragging to Don Connover about a recent wine acquisition, and Hal Logan was staring at his phone trying to keep up with emails from the West Coast. He was furious that Cece had insisted he be present during this circus. He'd told her so angrily in the car on the way over, reminding her that he was in the middle of an important deal, school matters were *her* domain, not his. He was happy to attend games or award nights, but this kind of petty nonsense was not worth his time or effort.

Isa and Olivia's parents were sitting together, directly behind Rory, Hunter, and Kam's parents.

Isa, Olivia, and Delaney were sitting off to the side. They had an unobstructed view of the student athletes and the Board of Education members.

Beth Ainsworth stood at the back of the large room. She was wearing a silver puffer jacket even though the room was overheated, a beanie, which covered her platinum hair, and oversized Celine sunglasses, which set her back $1200 and would allow her to listen without being scrutinized.

The person notably missing from the event was Coach Walker. There had been much discussion of it by everyone in the auditorium, but there were enough parents *in the know* and news quickly circulated that he'd been asked not to come.

Margie was speaking commandingly into her microphone. "I'd like to remind everyone that by law we are not able to discuss any personnel matters so please be respectful of that."

There was a loud grumble from the audience.

Erica Lange jumped to her feet. She was wearing a Saint Laurent winter white suit, her hair straight and sleek hung midway down her back. "This is a witch hunt! What is the Board doing to mitigate this situation?"

The room erupted with applause and cheers.

Margie spoke calmly, "There is an ongoing investigation by the local police department which we are cooperating with."

Indira raised her hand and Margie pretended not to see her but someone on the Board panel pointed to Indira.

"Oh I'm sorry, yes, Indira? Do you have a question?"

Indira stood up. She was wearing the same faded jeans she usually wore and a black pullover. Her brown-gold curls glinted in the auditorium lights and her glasses perched on top of her head were slightly askew. When she pulled her hand down in the quiet of the room, her silver bangles jangled against one another. "Is it true that the Board of Education conducted their own internal investigation into these allegations earlier this month? And if so, what was the result of that investigation?"

Margie colored. "Obviously, any kind of internal investigation is confidential and cannot be discussed in a public hearing."

Erica turned around and glared at Indira who stared defiantly back.

Joyce Davies raised her hand. Isa groaned and Delaney laughed. "My mom looks like she's shitting a brick."

Joyce was still dressed from her workday, a navy blue Theory suit, pale blue silk top, and diamond studs that winked in the light. Her hair was pulled tightly into a bun at the nape of her neck and she wore little if any make up. Her voice was measured. "It would seem that if the Board of Education felt an investigation was warranted, there is no reason that in the interest of full transparency we shouldn't be told why it was warranted and what the results are. I'm sure you can tell us that without compromising any sensitive personnel matters."

Margie sighed, "Generally speaking, when allegations are made against a faculty or staff member, we of course take it very seriously and conduct an investigation. When we investigated, we didn't find any corroborating witnesses, no evidence that anything…untoward, had occurred. In order to protect the confidentiality of the parties involved we laid the matter to rest. Obviously, if we had found anything we would have taken the appropriate action."

Thomas Davies was on his feet now, "And yet there is involvement from local law enforcement, so clearly there was more to investigate. Meanwhile, none of the parents have been notified about what risks our children may be facing. All we've heard is rumor and innuendo and nothing at all from the administration. We need to know if our children have been harmed in any way."

The Langes, Connovers, and Logans all looked angry. Kam Connover's father Dan stood up, "I have confidence that the Board members will not allow any harm to come to our students. As Dr. Davies stated,"

Don Connover stood up and shouted, "Gossip and innuendo aren't helpful. Let the administrators do their jobs. Let's trust them to watch out for the best interests of our students. There isn't any reason to believe there is a cover up going on…"

With that people began shouting again. Ginnifer Connover pulled him sharply by the elbow, causing him to sit unceremoniously in his seat.

Margie struggled to be heard over the room, "I assure you there is not a cover up. Yet we do need to be careful about ruining the reputation of a well-regarded upstanding teacher."

Applause and cheers of HOOT HOOT thundered through the auditorium. Erica turned around and hissed at Indira, "What are you doing? Trying to ruin the reputation of our schools?"

"We have a right to know what the charges are."

"No, you don't!" Erica shouted, "They are false allegations! They don't concern you!"

The auditorium had grown quiet allowing Erica's words to ring out.

Margie was speaking into the microphone. "As you know we cannot discuss an ongoing police investigation other than to say we are cooperating fully…." She put her hand up to quiet the instant rumble of complaints. "As I stated earlier, the Board of Education did conduct an internal investigation and concluded there was nothing to be concerned about, the allegations were unfounded, and while we did put some extra security measures in place, we are going to get on with the very important business of continuing the school year, go class of twenty twenty-five! HOOT, HOOT!"

The auditorium erupted and Isa's mother once again stood at the audience mic. "What type of security measures were needed that didn't already exist?"

Margie swallowed and forced her features into a semblance of openness. This was the question she was hoping to avoid. The Board of Education needed to contain the truth about how much unfettered access Coach Walker had to students in the school building after hours. "Thank you for your question, Joyce. In an abundance of caution we reminded all staff members of our existing policies for safety."

More yelling, more hands shot up in the air. This time Keith Lange had the mic. "So all of this fuss because some drug-addled former student decided to throw around a bunch of baseless accusations?" Applause and cheers of HOOT, HOOT rang out. "I say we call it a night and let these hard working people get back to running our district!" Then he turned over the mic to the beleaguered tech director who fumbled to put it back on the stand.

Margie noticed Beth Ainsworth lean against the back wall of the auditorium, as if she were cowering, as if she'd been struck. Margie knew that the applause of what seemed to be the entire community was overwhelming to Beth. Beth's son had gone from a State Athlete to a pariah, being jeered in his own alma mater. It would be too much for any mother to bear.

Suddenly Beth pushed her Celine glasses on top of her cashmere beanie, revealing her face, slid off her winter puffer jacket and marched down to the microphone. Several parents who were standing in line to ask questions at the mic saw her coming and stepped out of her way.

Beth's hands trembled as she pulled the mic off its stand and turned to face the crowd.

Beth faced Keith Lange, "You're calling my boy drug-addled because you're sick with fear. And you know what? You should be! Everyone in this room should be. We've been so caught up with our success, our lifestyle, our self-congratulatory narrative about our home values, and our excellent schools that we threw our own children to the wolves."

The large room was silent. Slowly, surreptitiously, people began lifting their phones up to film. If Beth registered it, she didn't seem to care. She turned toward the School Board. "My son came to you last week. Did any one of you think to call me? Did any of you report this? Not one of you followed up to see how he was doing? You were under no legal obligation, but what about an ethical one? Either you care about your community members or you don't! You loved bragging about Emmett Ainsworth. He put this athletic department on the map." She pointed at Cal, "He put you on the map! You got to go to your conferences in Albany and strut around as though you were personally responsible for his success, you leveraged that success for yourself, didn't you, *Mr. President*? Correct me if I'm wrong, but wasn't it the state win that led you to be voted in as President of the New York State Athletic Council?" Cal had the grace to look away from Beth. It was true and everyone in the room knew it.

"And yet, when my boy was in trouble, when he came to you, instead of trying to help him, you all rushed to cover it up. What kind of internal investigation could you have possibly done if you didn't even reach out to Emmett's father or myself? I'll tell you what kind—a Cover Your Own ASS INVESTIGATION!" Beth took a breath, and still the room stayed silent, the Board members frozen in place.

"You have a predator in your school. He groomed my son," Beth looked right at the Langes, Connovers, and Logans, "and he groomed yours too." She looked over at the large crowd of slack faced student athletes. "He harmed all of the students. He preyed on our sons and taught them to help him prey on our daughters." She swept the room. "If you don't believe me, ask them!"

And with that she handed the mic to the tech director, turned, and walked back up the aisle.

Erica Lange jumped up, "That's a pack of lies! Get your son the help he needs and leave our children out of it!"

A chorus of cheers went up. Calls of HOOT HOOT once again filled the room. Beth kept walking, and without missing a step, shot her arms straight up in the air, giving the entire auditorium two stiff middle fingers. The students went crazy and people jostled to capture her on their phones. The student athletes in the front of the room began their most jeering of cheers, the one saved for their worst rivals, *Na Na Na Naa Na Na Na Naa Hey Hey Hey Goodbye… Biiiiissssssshhhhhhh.*

Margie watched Beth pump her arms and waggled her stiff middle fingers in time with the chant, stopping to scoop up her jacket right where she'd left it, and push her way out, through the auditorium doors.

By this point the school superintendent had replaced Margie at the head microphone and was trying to restore order, to no avail.

The student athletes were now cycling through all their cheers as though they were at a state championship and it was a pivotal point in the game.

Parents were stomping and cheering along as though they were on the sidelines. Isa and Olivia's parents as well as a smattering of parents throughout the room were gathering their things to leave.

The auditorium suddenly quieted, which caused the few parents making an exodus to stop, turn around, and pay attention.

The Superintendent had given up any semblance of control and Margie was sitting back in her seat with a stunned expression, so when Hunter came and pulled her microphone out of its stand and walked to the front of the stage, she barely looked up.

"Emmett Ainsworth accused Coach Walker of taking him under his wing at a young age. Of noticing the vulnerabilities of a thirteen-year-old freshman athlete and using those vulnerabilities to coach him on and off the field not only in athleticism and sportsmanship, but in the pursuit of sex. I say sex even though Coach presented it as romance, as feminism, and as empowerment of girls to have a positive sexual initiation by the boys he was tutoring."

A murmur went throughout the crowd. Cece Logan had her hand over her mouth as if she could stop her son from saying the words she didn't want to hear.

"Hunter, son, get off the stage," Hal Logan pleaded.

"No, Dad, this needs to be said."

Hal gave up and sat down.

"I've never spoken with Emmett Ainsworth beyond a superficial greeting here and there. He was two years older and I was still on JV when he was a senior. I had watched him compete over the years and he was a hero of mine. When I heard that Emmett had come forward with these allegations about Coach Walker, I was sick to my stomach. Not because I was offended on Coach's behalf, but because I recognized the truth in them."

The entire room was silent, a sea of phones in the air.

There was a strangling sound from Rory, and Kam Connover looked like he was going to throw up. Margie bet they were watching their college acceptances, their wrestling careers, their promised chance of a golden future evaporate on the stage with every word Hunter spoke. More than that, she knew that the code of silence, the oath they had taken, the belief system they had constructed, the illusion of safety was crumbling in front of them and they were powerless to stop it.

"I am not speaking for any other student here," Hunter continued, "but I am speaking for myself."

His voice grew softer which had the effect of mesmerizing the audience. The Board of Education members, the Athletic Director, and the Superintendent were, frozen in their seats.

"I wasn't Coach Walker's top pick for wrestling or football. He had other stand-out players. But I was consistent and reliable and a strong enough contender to join the team in my junior year and was off the bench as soon as pre-season ended. I was never his star, but I was his go to. His confidant. He would bring me into his office to 'coach' me about life events and as he called it 'romance.' He'd show me his dating apps, and he'd have me swipe for him. Right for the 'hotties' and left for the 'uglies .'"

A murmur went throughout the auditorium.

"I felt privileged, taken into his confidence. He told me not to tell the other guys because they'd be jealous."

Margie looked out at the boys in the audience. Rory's cheeks were flushed, and Kam's expression toggled between stupefied and indignant. So no one was the only one, Margie thought. No one was special.

"He told me I had a 'good eye' for the ladies. And that if I wanted to be respected I needed to be a true feminist."

"A true feminist ally, Coach told me, required us as real men, to initiate girls into sexual acts in ways that pleasured them, taught them to pleasure us, and threw off all the old sexist values of slut shaming and sexual repression. He told us that our techniques as real men needed to be carefully honed and cultivated and the only way to do it was to obtain video, especially live and in real time." He paused and exhaled. "Coach Walker told me to take girls into a room, while he hid in a closet and used my phone to record us together."

Rory Lange stood up and left the room. Kam Connover ran onto the stage, tackling Hunter Logan.

The Langes, Connovers, and Logans rushed the stage.

Erica Lange grabbed Cece Logan screaming *your son is a fucking liar* in her face, when suddenly Cece pulled her arm back and smacked Erica in the face. Margie and two other board members rushed to separate the women, who were now locked together and fighting.

Keith Lange and Cal Hednick, the Athletic Director, were trying to untangle Don Connover and Hal Logan, who were grappling in the middle of the stage. The four of them engaged in an awkward dance, red faced, stumbling first one way, then the other, until they crashed into the 6-foot folding table where only moments ago Board members had been sitting. Hunter and Kam had been successfully separated by their teammates and were now being held apart on opposite sides of the stage. Hunter's eye was already swelling and Kam's nose was bleeding.

Delaney rushed up on stage to pull her mother out of harm's way right before the dads crashed the table.

Rory had two thoughts as he left the auditorium to call Walker. One was *oh shit oh shit oh shit.* And the other was an almost irrational fury of betrayal because Hunter made it

240

sound as though he was as close to Walker as Rory was. Rory had believed he and Coach were close and that Hunter and Kam were firmly relegated to, if not bit players exactly, less important ones. They weren't stars. Hadn't Coach had told Rory over and over again *you're my star.*

Rory was outside when Coach answered. The winter air cool against his burning face, a strong breeze came in from the west, lifting the hair sticking to his neck. It was quiet on the walkway to the parking lot, away from the bedlam going on inside. There was a waning crescent moon and a thin cottony cloud cover over the starlight. The motion detectors hadn't picked him up yet so it was dark and Rory felt an illusion of intimacy when Coach answered.

"What's up, kid?"

"They know everything. Hunter's on the stage with a mic telling it all."

"Who knows you're on the phone with me?"

"No one."

Rory listened to Coach breathing for a moment.

"Hunter's been acting erratically lately. I've had to write him up a few times."

"What?"

"I should have handed it in to guidance, or Vice Principal Herbert, but I felt bad for the kid. It's in my file."

"Oh. I didn't know that there was anything off. He seemed the same to me."

"Did he? That's not what you told me...."

"Huh?"

"Are you forgetting? The concerns you came to me about? I started paying careful attention—his Vyvanse use? For grades?"

Rory gulped. Coach was the one to tell him about Vyvanse, ostensibly to help him study, so he could keep his grades up to the standards of a scholar athlete, and it had worked. He said it was their secret. Had he also told Hunter? Hunter hated drugs. He wouldn't even vape. He drank beer like a Viking but Rory had never seen him on anything else. Was Coach confusing Rory and Hunter? Had he meant so little to him?

"Rory? You there?"

"Yeah, Coach…"

"You get where I'm coming from, right? I wanted to protect Hunter. But I see now, in retrospect, that it was the wrong move, the kid clearly has problems."

Then Rory understood. Coach hadn't written Hunter up. He was lying and he wanted Rory to confirm it. Hunter had betrayed Coach. Had betrayed all of them. And yet Hunter had taken all the blame, leaving Rory and Kam's name out of it. Rory wasn't ready to let it all go—the Duke acceptance, wrestling for the Blue Devils. He was angry with Hunter for blowing it all up, but was he ready to betray him like this? Rory felt his head swimming, he was having difficulty focusing.

"Rory! You there?"

"Yeah. I'm here. I understand."

"Good. Listen, Lange, I need to fly out to Arizona in the morning, a family emergency."

"Oh. Okay. What kind of emergency?"

"My parents retired there this year, they're getting older and need some assistance. I'll check in with you in a few days."

"Okay. What should I do?"

"Sit tight, Lange. Remember everything I've taught you about loyalty. I'm sorry Hunter's imploding. I know he's your friend. Mental illness and substance abuse don't mix. This district, ya know? So much pressure. Thank God you've got a good head on your shoulders. Starting Duke in the fall, Blue Devils, yeah? You've got the whole world in front of you.

Don't let the weak ones hold you back, kid. You gotta look out for number one. You're a star. You know that, right? Don't let anyone mess this up for you. In a few short months you'll be out of this place for good."

"Okay, Coach."

The line went silent. Rory stood in the dark chilly night and tried to think. But his mind kept flashing back to Hunter's words. Rory's mind was stuck in a terrible loop. Hunter on the stage, *Coach Walker told me to take girls into a room while he hid in a closet and used my phone to record us doing things together,* Coach Walker's flushed face, the way his mouth opened in a slight pant, the narrowing at the bridge of his nose, the heaviness of his eyelids, as he watched the images Rory had handed over to him. Coach's obvious desire linked to the painful exhilaration of Rory's own erection in that small close office looking at Coach watch Rory and whatever girl he'd gotten that weekend. Coach's words in Rory's ear a few minutes ago *you're a star...don't let anyone mess this up for you... you're a star....*

Rory stood in the cold dark night, took deep breaths, and noted the silence, as though the large auditorium doors had sealed off the mayhem inside, keeping him safe. He didn't know what to do or where to go. He slid his hand into his pocket, his fingers searching for the familiar capsule, but all he touched were specks of lint. His pocket was empty. He thought about the stash in his underwear drawer, the power and magic once the contents of those pills hit his blood stream, rendering him invincible. He thought about the relief it would be to feel that power in a state of perpetuity. Would that happen if he took all the pills at once, or better yet, first one, so he could feel that surge, then a handful so he could feel nothing? He imagined having the stash in his palm right now. Walking up the slight incline behind the school and into the woods. Where he could take one and feel his own strength bloom inside him, climbing higher and higher up the incline into the woods, taking pill after pill after pill, swallowing them easily, letting them slide one by one down his throat until he stood at the top of the crest deep in the woods, where he would be closer to the starless sky, and he could lie down, and make it all stop, make it all go away. He calculated that he could walk to his Range Rover, drive the seven minutes to his home, get the pills, and be back in less than twenty minutes. He knew by then the parking lot would be overrun. Maybe he could go home, take the pills right then and there, and lie down in his bed, but he couldn't do that to his mother, letting her find him. Maybe he could get home and take the pills up to the quarry. Maybe the pills would give him the courage to soar off the highest place on the cliff side, like a bird of prey, or a superhero. And instead of crashing into the rock below, his mind would take him higher and higher and by the time gravity pulled, he'd be gone, and the smashing of his body on the rock wouldn't matter. He wouldn't feel it. He wouldn't feel anything ever again. It was a plan, an easily executed plan.

Rory turned toward the parking lot and took three steps when the sensor went on and he found himself blinking into the light.

"Rory."

He turned around and saw her coming toward him. Her familiar walk, a face he couldn't remember not knowing. From the small round cheeks of babyhood, to the awkward seven-year-old, with adult teeth too big for her face, her tangled dark hair, dirty scabbed knees and a mean kick when he pushed her too far, to the shiny beautiful girl she'd become, the friend he'd lost, who hated him, who knew all his filthy secrets, his shame.

Olivia was walking out of the shadow and into the light. He stood transfixed as if he were in an interrogation room. And she didn't need to question him, because she already knew.

"Rory. Where are you going?"

"Nowhere."

"Was that Walker on the phone?"

"Yes."

"What did he say?"

"He's leaving."

"Where?"

"Another state, I forget, Arizona maybe?"

"He's running."

"He said his parents are there, they need his help."

"You need to call the police."

That's when they heard it. Sirens.

"They're on the way."

Olivia looked out into the distance. Still dark. No lights flashing. The sirens were still far enough away that they couldn't be seen. "Someone inside must have called."

"Okay."

"They're coming because of the brawl," she said.

"Brawl?"

Olivia thrust her chin toward the auditorium. "In there."

He nodded, not really understanding but too tired to ask.

Olivia put her hand on his jacket sleeve and tugged gently. "Come on. We'll go to the precinct. We'll find someone to tell."

He followed her deeper into the circle of lamplight and toward her car, the sirens drawing closer, the starless sky receding and falling away.

They drove to the police station and stood in front of it for a while before walking in and standing before the officer seated behind plexiglass. It seemed to Olivia that everything in her life had pointed to the moment when that image of her exposed would surface, and she would be forever held in that space, of having to pretend not to care, of swallowing the humiliation of her pleasure, of holding it inside herself forever, of being complicit in the illicit secrets of sex in the age of perpetual cameras and information technology. There was no way out. She was trapped by her own decisions, her own desire. They all were.

Unless... She thought... *The images themselves were unimportant. Catching the man who'd carefully curated it without her knowledge or consent was what mattered. If telling the truth could stop Walker from ever doing it again, maybe that was what mattered. Maybe that was a way back to the essence of her true self. Maybe this wouldn't define her after all.*

"Do you need something?" the officer asked.

Olivia looked at Rory and he nodded.

CHAPTER 27

"Isa?" Her mother waited until Isa's father had placed the hot chocolate in front of them. She waited while Isa held the mug, the temperature perfect for warming her hands without burning. Isa met her mother's gaze.

"Rory has been your friend since kindergarten. You had to have been affected by all of this."

Isa looked away. "I handled it."

"Handled what?"

Isa looked over at her father who was humming and washing.

"The pictures."

She saw her mother swallow. Heard the hitch in her breath as she went to speak, then faltered, then recovered herself.

"Pictures of you?"

"No—not of me—there aren't any of me."

"Okay—then—pictures of him? Did Rory send you pictures of himself?"

Isa caught her mother's eye and nodded. Understanding pulsed between them like an electric current.

"Are you—how are you?"

Isa shrugged. Then began to cry.

Her mother was there in a flash. Hugging her. Isa was surprised by how much she needed that hug.

"You know this isn't your fault right? You didn't do anything to bring this on."

Isa let her fingertips rest against her forehead. "I know it here." Then she placed that hand over her heart, her other hand against her stomach. "But not here."

Isa's mother nodded. "You will. You will know it there, because it's the truth. These were decisions made by other people and they were perpetrated against you."

"I didn't know how to stop it."

"You didn't feel you could come to us?" her mother asked.

Isa cried harder. "You would have freaked out."

"We would have put a stop to it."

"There isn't any stopping this. It's what happens now."

"It's always been this way and it's never been okay," her mother said. Then she told her about her time in law school. The catalog of male voices she'd heard and dismissed, telling her it was the way of the world. Complimenting herself for taking it in stride, not letting it stop her, not making a big deal out of it. Even now the voices sounded in her head as loud and as clear as they'd been in 1988, as though the words had been spoken moments ago.

You're pretty for such a dark-skinned girl.

You can sit closer, I don't bite. But I'd like to. His laughter. His gaze on her breasts, craning his head to take in her backside.

Is it true what they say about Black chicks? Insatiable?

Can I touch your hair? Do you ever let it go native?

Smart and pretty, my favorite combination. If you're good in bed you're a trifecta.

Is it true about Black guys? Wanna do a little comparison shopping?

She'd handled it by deflecting. Ignoring. Staying focused on whatever point she was making. Not smiling but not looking aggressive. Not cowering but looking unfazed. Like she'd heard it all before, she'd hear it again, and she didn't care. Did she think she brought it on herself? Sometimes. She wondered if she'd stood too close. Smiled too broadly. Acted too friendly. Wore a blouse with one too many buttons undone. Wore pants too tight across her backside. Wore a skirt that showed too much thigh. She was too Black. She was too female. She was too smart, pissed off the white guys in her class. Had she taught her daughters to do the same? She thought she'd taught them confidence. Strength. Power.

"I thought if I ignored it—he'd just go away." Isa said.

Her mother nodded, "I get that."

"But he just kept at it."

"You may not have been able to make him stop. But you don't have to take this inside yourself. You understand?"

Isa looked at her and nodded. She did understand. She may not have been able to control Rory. But she could control the way she thought about it.

"You didn't engage with him," Isa's mom said. "That was an interruption to the ease of flow. When enough interruptions happen the system breaks down. That's what happened tonight. Enough girls pushed back at the boys, enough boys felt an interruption of the systemic flow, enough boys challenged the direction of the flow, and the system has broken down. You'll see. It's happened already."

The second he hung up on Rory, Coach called his mother in Arizona.

"Darling," Coach's mother exclaimed when he'd called to tell her he was considering a change. "There is so much to do in Paradise Valley, you'll love it! Stay in the guest house for as long as you like until you decide if you want to make it a permanent move."

"I'll have to see what kind of jobs are available."

"With your accomplishments, I should think they are lucky to get you."

As Coach packed his personal belongings and finalized the arrangements for his upcoming trip, he thought about what he was leaving behind.

He'd worked hard to gain the professional reputation he had, he'd earned it by developing a winning team, by gaining the trust and respect of students, parents, and colleagues. He was smart enough to know that it would be unlikely that he'd obtain another teaching job in the state of New York with the scandal following him. The HR department wouldn't be allowed to disclose the arrest or allegations, but word of mouth would take care of that. Arizona, however, was a different state, and his public record of wins spoke for itself. His likability quotient was extremely high and gaining trust and admiration from school district members was a transferable skill. Coach Walker congratulated himself that he was humble enough to know that he'd learned from his mistakes. He would need to take a more subtle approach in the future.

Coach poured himself a generous glass of WhistlePig 15-year Estate Oak Rye Whiskey, a gift from Dan Connover the previous season. He couldn't bring it with him and he still had a quarter of a bottle left.

Settling himself in front of his laptop, the whiskey at his side, he began to search school districts within an hour and a half drive from his parent's home. Perhaps, he thought, his mistake this time around had been teaching in a highly visible wealthy community. While the parents showed their gratitude, there was a sense of entitlement the kids had that while easy to manipulate grew tiresome after a while. The parents held too much sway. He was tired of having to work that hard to gain their approval. He didn't need Dan Connover's expensive Christmas gifts slash bribes. Coach's father had a whiskey collection that would put Dan's to shame. The more Coach thought about it the more his plan took shape. He needed a poor district, where they would be grateful to have him, and he could be the hero that brought scholarship opportunities to impoverished scholar athletes instead of wealthy ones. He'd find the more vulnerable kids, the hungry ones that wanted out; it would be a host of new challenges. He wouldn't be able to manipulate them with the same psychological tactics, they would be more wary, less trusting, but he prided himself on being good at figuring out people's strengths and weaknesses. They would be equally pliable, with a less likely chance of running to their mommies and daddies. He would take it slow. No sexualizing any of them until he was tenured, until he'd figured out the school dynamics. He was patient. He could wait. And while he was waiting there were other places he could go to get his needs met.

Coach's fingers flew across the keyboard as he searched census data for Phoenix, Arizona. He smiled as his screen filled with possibilities. He took a sip of whiskey and savored it. He'd taught himself to enjoy every moment of the pleasures he sought in life, because while he was confident in his abilities to get more, he knew that each and every time might be his last. It was part of the thrill for him, how illicit his appetites were. He thought being discovered would have removed some of the pleasure. Instead, it made them even sweeter.

CHAPTER 28

Margie went into Cal's office and complied with his motions to shut the door. *The New York Post* was splayed open on his desk and Margie winced at the headline, "Moms Maul and Dads Brawl." She sat at the edge of the chair and looked at Cal, trying not to register how shocked she was by his appearance. His face had a sickly gray tinge to it, there were heavy purple pouches under his eyes, the skin around his jowls seemed to be hanging, was it possible he'd dropped significant weight in a few days, he seemed almost...Margie sought for the word while trying to keep her face neutral...frail.

Margie attempted a smile, trying to steady herself. "Any updates?"

Cal nodded. "The DA has declined to prosecute."

Margie felt herself slump with relief. "So there was nothing to this? Just false statements?"

Cal stared at her for a moment. "You think Emmett, Rory, and Hunter got together and blew up their lives to smear Walker for no reason?"

"No—I mean—you said he wasn't being prosecuted—I thought —."

"You thought what, Margie? That prosecutions are—an indication of guilt or innocence?"

"Well—yes."

"They're a function of how much evidence there is to bring a case to trial."

"Okay. So there's no evidence that any of this even happened."

Cal stared at her. "You mean besides the testimony from three of our students?"

Cal sighed. "There won't be a trial or any criminal charges against him. He denies it and there isn't any actual proof other than the word of these three students. Even the girls he perpetrated these acts against never saw him say or do anything."

Margie leaned back. No charges meant no trial, which meant no more news coverage. She wondered if the intense relief she felt made her a bad person. "So what does this mean?"

"It means...." Cal shut his eyes for a minute and Margie wondered why he seemed so angry, "he gets away with it."

Margie leaned forward, "Well, surely he'll lose his job! They'll force him to resign."

Cal blinked. "Yes, Margie. He'll lose his job. And somewhere somehow he will get another job. Probably not in New York. Maybe not even in a school, but he will live and work somewhere. And have access to kids."

"Well, surely he will have learned his lesson."

"Right Margie. Because sexual predators always learn their lesson."

Margie swallowed. "I didn't think—I mean—he didn't touch anyone. And it was just kids—messing around with each other."

"Tell yourself whatever you need to Margie. But I'm done with this. All of it. I'm retiring this year."

"Oh!" For the second time in a span of ten minutes Margie wondered if she was a terrible person for being relieved. "We will throw you the best retirement dinner this town has ever seen! I'll put Erica Lange on it! She's the queen of parties."

Cal just stared at her. "My guess is she's got other things to think about. And I don't want a party."

"Nonsense!" Margie stood up. "Try and get some rest Cal. You look tired!" she shouted over her shoulder as she left his office.

CHAPTER 29
College Spring Break March 2025

Isa and Bailey sat side by side in the corner booth of their favorite diner, forgotten milkshakes in front of them. Their thighs touching, leaning in, sharing Isa's earbuds. Isa didn't use wireless ones—she complained they fell out when she ran. Bailey didn't mind because the cord kept them close.

"Listen to this," Isa said. It was Sarah Vaughn's rendition of "Summertime."

"Better than Mahalia Jackson?"

"Not better. Just—it's Sarah Vaughn!"

"How about "Summertime" by Mahalia and "Whatever Lola Wants" by Sarah?"

"Hmmm, acceptable," Isa agreed and watched as Bailey added it to her list.

When the song ended they pulled their earbuds out and Bailey turned to face Isa creating space between them. Isa missed the warmth of Bailey against her side.

"I'm glad you came home." Isa said. "I thought maybe you were going away for Spring Break."

Bailey shrugged, "After everything that went on—I wanted to see how you were doing."

Isa nodded slowly, wishing they could go back to sitting closely together, sharing a song.

"So how are you doing?" Bailey reached out and brushed Isa's cheek lightly, causing their eyes to meet.

Isa wanted to lean into Bailey's hand. Instead she forced herself to answer. "It's a relief to finally have it all out in the open."

"I get that."

"But…the thing I can't let go of…" Isa whispered the last part, "Is the rage…that he's getting away with it. That he can do it again."

Bailey was quiet for a while. "You know…there are things we could do…so that he wouldn't get away with it."

"Like what?"

"You do know I have skills."

"I mean yeah…but next level hacking skills?"

"Not to brag, but yeah."

"Is this…I mean…could we really do something?" Isa thought about the empty closet, how they'd hoped to catch him, and how impossible it all seemed now.

"Here's the thing…I don't want you to let him take over your life…but I also understand wanting to do anything we can to stop him."

"This isn't your responsibility, Bailey, I don't want you to think just because…" Isa let her gaze drift to the window. The wind was picking up and the branches of baby cherry trees swayed. "I don't want to drag you into this whole mess."

"Knock it off. I'd do anything for you. And for Liv. You're like sisters to me."

Isa whipped her head around to look at Bailey. "Sisters?"

"And friends."

Isa narrowed her eyes. "Hmm." She wanted to change the subject. And she had other questions she wanted answers to. "So," she braved, "what's new with you? Seeing anyone at school?"

"Ha. Not a chance. I'm starting to think something's wrong with me. I just–I'm not feeling anyone."

Isa picked up Bailey's hand, which was lying on the table, palm up. "Let's check your love line." Isa used her index finger to gently trace the ridges lining Bailey's palm.

Isa felt Bailey shudder at the sensation, she looked up for a moment and saw Bailey's lips part. Isa's heart raced and she wondered if Bailey could hear it thumping behind her breast.

Isa quickly dropped her gaze to Bailey's palm. "Your wisdom line is here." Her voice was low, barely above a whisper. "See how curved it is?" Isa trailed the tip of her index finger across Bailey's palm. "That indicates a romantic, creative, nature. It can mean idealism, someone open to new ideas. It can also indicate strong intuition."

Bailey swallowed. "Let me see yours."

She turned Isa's palm over and smoothed her finger over the deep crease running horizontally across her palm sending a shooting thrill through her body. "It's so deep."

Isa grinned mischievously. "That means an excellent memory."

"You're lying."

"Swear."

Bailey traced it again. "Well, that's true in your case. Obviously."

Isa turned Bailey's hand over once more. "Yours reads true as well. This right here?" Isa traced the top line on Bailey's palm, resulting in a sharp intake of breath. Isa smiled and talked so softly Bailey had to lean closer to hear, "See how it curves upward? That indicates that you're emotionally and physically responsive."

"You're making that up." Bailey whispered.

"I'm not."

Bailey took Isa's palm in hers and traced the top line. It was long and slanted slightly upward. "What does yours mean?"

Isa smiled. "Openness. And warmth."

Bailey looked directly into Isa's eyes, "That's true about you."

Isa found the courage not to look away. She saw, reflected in Bailey's gaze, all of the sensations and emotions she'd been running away from. With Bailey's palm still in her hand, Isa leaned against Bailey.

They stayed pressed together, the late afternoon light fading, the bright busy hum of the diner comforting.

Bailey reached over, binding them together once more with her ear buds and pressed play. "This one. This is my favorite."

Isa listened to "I'd Rather Go Blind" by Etta James, trancy sweet notes, the drum beat, *something deep down in my soul said cry girl…I would rather, I would rather go blind now than to see you walk away from me….*Isa wished the song would never end.

It was nearly five when Isa dropped Bailey off. "Ugh," Isa said. "I wish I didn't have to go, but Addie needs a ride home from practice and I'm already late."

"That's okay. We've got all week to hang out."

"Promise?"

Bailey smiled. "Promise. Thanks for the palm reading."

"Any time."

Bailey reached the steps then turned back. Isa was still parked, her window open, watching her. Bailey waved. Instead of waving, Isa blew her a kiss, then watched, as Bailey seemed suspended in time her body pivoting slowly. The next thing Isa knew, Bailey was at the car window, leaning in and kissing her. Isa melted into the kiss, five heartbeats went by. Bailey smiled against Isa's lips, her hands cupping Isa's face, "Your lips…" Bailey whispered. "They're so soft."

Isa kissed Bailey again, tasting the salt of her mouth, her heart hammering so hard she thought she might die.

Isa's phone chimed "Just a lil Bit." 50 Cent's refrain breaking the spell.

Isa pulled back, "Shit! That's Addie."

Bailey laughed, "You gave her that ring tone?"

Isa shrugged, "It was my mom's favorite song the year Addie was born."

"You're so ironic."

Isa smirked, "I wasn't trying to be."

"Even better." Bailey leaned in and kissed her firmly. "Later tonight?"

"I'll be done by eight."

"It's a date?"

Isa nodded. This time she forced herself to pull away from the curb before Bailey got to her porch, the promise of seeing her again in a few hours making it bearable to leave.

Bailey went into the house humming the refrain from "Just a Lil Bit" she felt dazed and jazzed and sedated and buzzed all at the same time. She felt better than she ever had and slightly nauseous from the beating of something in her stomach. Butterfly wings. She'd heard it described, she'd read about in books, and now she knew what it meant.

She was lost in her thoughts and the new sensations flooding her body when she passed the basement door and heard a loud bang and her mother shout, "Fudge, Fudge, FUCKITY FUCK!"

Bailey ran downstairs. Erica stood among a pile of containers, neatly labeled, the one marked RIBBONS had fallen sideways, the lid popped off and streams of ribbons cascaded out.

"Did you get hurt?" Bailey asked.

"Only my pride."

Bailey laughed, "I'll help you."

As they worked to right the boxes Erica gave a shout, "Here you are!" she said to the box marked SPRING WREATHS.

Erica busied herself finding the exact spring wreath she had in mind, and Bailey found herself wandering over to the long forgotten file cabinet in the corner.

Bailey pulled out a drawer, flipping through the files. Erica, distracted by the array of wreath possibilities, didn't seem to notice. Bailey found the paper and pulled it out with a flourish, then waved it at Erica.

Erica squinted at her, then huffed in irritation. "I thought I told you to get rid of those."

Bailey looked down at it. "I like this version of you."

Erica looked up from the sprigs of silk forsythia she was gathering. "Don't be ridiculous. There aren't *versions* of me."

Bailey waved the paper. "I want to know about the girl who wrote this."

"You're looking at her, B! I'm the same person who wrote that, except I'm 23 years older and fifteen pounds thinner."

"I want to know about the woman who had the ideas in this paper." Bailey rattled the pages aggressively.

Erica threw the silk flowers back into the box, "Look I was a scholarship student in a prestigious wealthy school when I wrote that paper, I spent every day alternating between overcompensating and hitting people in the face with the gigantic chip on my shoulder."

"Oh—I never—I didn't know…"

"That I was a scholarship student?"

"No, I knew that—I didn't think it bothered you—I mean you should be proud…"

"I was grateful to be there and resentful that I didn't fit in—people didn't mean it, but they were really condescending and I handled it by biting back."

"I just never thought about it like that—for you, I mean."

"Because I tried to shield you kids from that! I didn't want you to feel what I felt—and now look—Rory's a mess because I couldn't face anything—and the two of you hate each other, and it's all my fault."

"Don't be so hard on yourself, Mom. Rory and I are perfectly capable of fucking up our own lives."

"Aww, you called me Mom."

Bailey laughed then surprised Erica with a quick hug. "Do you still need me to pick Rory up?"

"I thought you couldn't—"

"Turns out I can."

"Okay, yeah, thanks B." Erica smiled and picked the silk Forsythia flowers up again and fanned them out. "Pretty, right?"

"So pretty." Bailey walked back up the stairs, Erica's college paper rolled carefully in her hand.

It was Rory's third therapy visit now, and he was surprised that he wasn't dreading it.

"At first I was really mad at mom for making me go. I thought it meant—you know—that I was a freak. But you're kind of cool, and…"

"And?"

"You don't act like you hate me."

"Well, that's a start."

"I was wondering…" Rory looked over at Melanie and tried to gauge her reaction.

Melanie dipped her chin in encouragement.

"Do you think I should apologize to Isa?"

"What would the apology be for?"

"Well. What I did was wrong."

"Can you tell me about it?"

"Don't you know?"

"I know what other people told me. I don't know in your words."

"You know about the pictures?"

"The pictures of yourself you sent to a girl in your class?"

Rory's face flushed and his eyes swam. He nodded.

"From what I gather, the pictures were unwanted and you kept sending them anyway. They were pictures of your erect penis."

Rory shut his eyes and nodded.

Melanie said, "You seem upset."

He nodded again. Eyes still shut.

Melanie spoke softly, "What specifically upsets you about it?"

His eyes still shut, his face bright red, Rory whispered.

Melanie waited. He whispered again, and this time she heard it. "Shame."

"You're ashamed."

He nodded, his eyes still shut, tears leaking from the corners, "Ashamed I sent them to her."

Melanie spoke again, "Because she didn't want you to?"

He nodded.

"You're ashamed because you sent her pictures that she didn't want."

"Yes. I just…" His voice broke and Melanie waited until he could speak again, "I couldn't stop."

"Did you want to stop?"

He nodded vigorously.

"But you couldn't?"

He nodded again.

"Can you tell me a little more about that?"

She waited. Eventually he opened his eyes. He looked at her. Searched for the signs. The disgust. The hatred. The superiority. The expectation. The hope. The need. All the things he'd come to expect that people thought of him, wanted from him. She just looked like she was interested in what he was saying, why he couldn't stop. He wished he knew.

"I just couldn't—I wanted to—but every time I tried—I just—couldn't help it."

"What was it like right before you sent them—when you told yourself not to—but that moment when you couldn't help it—can you identify that moment?"

Rory thought about it. Remembered the tightening in his belly, the way it felt like his head was filling up like a giant balloon and if he didn't do something it would explode. "It was—this tension—like if I didn't send it I would…" He looked at her. "Like I'd die."

She nodded. "And after?'

Rory stared out the window, the wind was picking up, and the tree branches had a desperate quality to them. "Relieved. Like I could breathe again. But then…"

"Then?"

"It was worse in a way."

"What was?"

"The shame."

"It sounds like you were trapped in a terrible cycle."

Rory looked at her. "That's exactly it."

Melanie leaned forward. "That must have been scary."

He swallowed, "It felt like I was out of control."

Melanie nodded.

"Like someone else was controlling me."

"Can you tell me more about that?"

Rory shifted in his seat. "What have you heard about Coach Walker?"

"That he's been accused of manipulating young boys, sexualizing them and teaching them to become predatory toward girls. That he instructed his players to videotape sexual encounters with girls without their knowledge and then show him."

Rory nodded. "It's all true. And worse. There was a closet...we would leave our phones in there...and he'd use this secret entrance to get in...then he'd hide in the closet, and use our phones... to record. Then we'd go over what he'd refer to as our *technique* in his office."

"Rory, in my profession, we consider what your coach did to be sexual abuse."

"What I did. Sending the pictures to Isa."

"Yes. What you did was sexually abusive. What your coach did to you and the other boys was also sexual abuse."

Rory frowned. "He never touched us."

"He groomed you. And instructed you to sexually harass and exploit your classmates. He abused all of you."

Rory shook his head. "I was a part of it. No one forced me."

"Coercion is a common tool of sexual predators. And it doesn't make it less of an offense."

"I'm not the victim here."

"Who is?"

"The girls!"

"Yes. They were victimized. We also use the word survivors. Because they survived the abuse."

"Okay."

"Would you consider yourself a survivor?"

"Of sexual abuse?"

She nodded.

"No. I mean, I survived, but not … it's confusing."

"How so?"

"I feel like you're letting me off the hook."

"How am I letting you off the hook?"

"By saying what I did wasn't my fault."

"Do you think I'm saying that?"

Rory threw a frustrated look at her. "Sounds like it."

"I'm not. You're fully responsible for sending those unwanted pictures over and over again. And you're fully responsible for videotaping any of the girls without their consent. And you're fully responsible for sharing those videos with your friends. And it harmed those girls. It harmed them terribly, and you were also harmed."

Rory looked at her and nodded.

"Can you describe how you're feeling right now?"

He thought for a moment. "Relieved, I guess."

She nodded.

"Because—that's the truth. I did those things. And I did hurt the girls. And for a long time I felt bad about it—and the worse I felt the angrier I got."

"At who?"

"At them."

"And now?"

"I'm not mad at them—I'm mad at myself."

"Why were you mad at them before?"

"Because. They hated me. We were such close friends, Olivia was like my sister. I was closer to her than my own sister. And Isa. I liked her. And I thought she liked me. And then all of a sudden they hated me."

"Why did they hate you?"

"I think—well, the pictures."

"Anything else?"

"I was an asshole a lot of the time."

Melanie shrugged. "I have lots of friends that are assholes. I don't hate them."

Rory laughed. Melanie looked at him like she was waiting for another answer.

"I guess… I thought they hated me because they knew."

"Knew what?"

"How disgusting I am."

"You felt disgusting. And you believed they hated you because you were disgusting."

He nodded.

"And now?"

"I feel relieved that the truth is out. But…"

"But?"

"I feel guilty—especially about Isa."

"Is that the girl you sent the pictures to?"

"I want to apologize to her."

"You haven't done that yet?"

"No."

"What's stopped you?"

"She blocked me—and I haven't seen her."

"What do you hope to gain from apologizing to Isa?"

"I want her forgiveness."

"You want to apologize to her so she'll forgive you?"

He nodded. He looked hopeful.

"I want to say something to you, and it may not be what you want to hear. Okay?"

"Okay."

"It isn't Isa's job to forgive you."

He glared at her.

"You would feel better if you apologized, and Isa understood how sorry you are, and she forgave you."

Rory felt lighter just thinking about it. "Yes."

Melanie waited.

Melanie leaned forward. "Rory, what are the reasons for saying you're sorry to someone?"

"Didn't we just go over this?"

"Humor me."

"Then can I go?"

She just looked at him.

"You apologize when you hurt someone. To show that it was wrong. To let them know you shouldn't have done it."

"I'm suggesting that your apology is necessary whether Isa forgives you or not. That your apology is to Isa because she deserves one, and not for you so that you can be forgiven."

"I have to apologize for doing the wrong thing—for hurting her—and she doesn't have to forgive me unless she's ready to—and maybe she'll never be."

"Yes."

"Ha, I'm not the center of the universe after all."

Melanie smiled. "Nope."

Rory was quiet for a minute.

Melanie's smile stayed on her face, but it softened and her tone was serious. "What's it like to find out you're not the center of the universe."

Rory sighed, "If someone had told me two weeks ago that I wouldn't be accepting at Duke or anywhere else, that I'd be walking away from wrestling, and that I'd be applying for minimum wage jobs over the next year, I would never have believed them."

Melanie smiled. "And that's our time."

"Finally!" But he smiled back.

Rory left the office, walked down the eerie silent corridor, took the stairs two at a time down four flights, and pushed the building doors wide against the wind. The air was howling, a garbage can lid clattered as it was tossed against the chain link fence bordering the parking lot. Rory looked up at the sky, heavy and opaque with a thick cloud cover. Icy wind chapped his face as he lifted his arms and stretched. He needed to get some paper, write a letter, and get it to Isa. He wasn't sure when he would do it, or where he would be when he sent it, the only thing he knew was that he needed to do things differently from now on, and that he was getting a chance to try.

CHAPTER 30

When Olivia got out of her lit class, Hunter was waiting for her. "What are you doing here?" she said flatly.

"We need to talk. About us."

"There *is* no us! And if you're expecting me to thank you for..."

"No! I don't want thanks!"

"You want a pat on the back?"

"For what? Telling the truth about something I never should never have participated in? That I should have told the truth about two years ago when I first found out about it? You think I want thanks for that?"

"What do you want?"

"To say I'm sorry."

"You already did that."

"And to ask you a question?"

"Okay."

"Okay, I can ask?"

She nodded.

He looked nervous all of a sudden, pulling his gaze from hers.

"Well?" Olivia was aware of how irritable she sounded, which was preferable to thinking about how much she wanted him to look at her again.

"Liv, do you think—if none of this had happened—do you think we could have been together?"

Olivia wanted more than anything to lay her head against his shoulder. Inhale the scent of his shampoo. Feel his lips against her throat, hear his breath in her ear. Instead she whispered the thought that circled in her head, every night before she fell asleep and every morning when she woke up. "But it did happen. And there's no way to undo it."

"I know—I just—I know how I feel about you."

Olivia wanted two things at once. She wanted not to care how he felt about her. And she wanted to know. She wanted to walk away. And she wanted to step to him.

"How?" She couldn't look at him, but she couldn't walk away either.

He sighed. She felt rather than saw him take a breath. "I think about you all the time. I look forward every day to English class, because I get to see you—but more than that— I get to listen to you, hear your ideas. Your thoughts about the book we're reading and how it makes me see the world in a different way. The way you make me think about things. The way you move your hands around when you're explaining something, or the way your hair slides into your face and you do that cute thing and you tuck it—here."

He reached out, placed her hair behind her ear, his fingertip like a feather brushing her cheek. She felt a pull in her stomach, and lost her breath.

He let his hand drop, and she missed it. She wanted his hands in her hair, on her skin. She wasn't confused about it. She wanted his touch, his gaze, she wanted him to listen to her, and she wanted to listen to him. She wanted to hear his thoughts too. They always surprised her, they were never what she expected, and she wanted to listen to him so often that she would know what to expect. And she wanted to argue with him about things they didn't agree on and delve into the things they did.

So she did it. She let go of all the things she thought she should do. Walk away from him. Spurn him. Hate him. Punish him. Instead she stepped in, to him. The circle of his arms closed around her and she tilted her face to his. He kissed her lips, cheeks, eyes, he moved to the exposed hollow of her throat where her jacket was unzipped. His mouth moved to her lips again, she opened, tasting salt and mint. She was dissolving inside, losing all sense of time and place, until she was part of him, and he was part of her, and nothing else mattered.

She thought that she chose him and he chose her, and because of that a part of them would always belong to each other. His jacket was open and she was pressed against his chest, covered only by his T-shirt, and even through the puffiness of her jacket, she felt the thud of his heartbeat, heard the rush of his breath in her ear, as if he were whispering secrets to her.

All the ugliness Coach Walker perpetrated against them couldn't wipe this moment away, Olivia thought. He'd taken more than he had a right too, but not the part that mattered.

She would keep this moment as a pure one. Something she and Hunter chose together. And she would let go of the past and eschew the possibility of anything more.

Hunter loosened his arms and gazed after her when she slipped away from him. She felt a pain behind the bone and muscle of her chest. A tightening in her airways made it hard to breathe. She took shallow breaths until it eased. Then a deeper one until the pain dissipated. She even missed the pain. She needed to get used to this feeling—of what could have been. And accept the loss.

She looked at Hunter, and saw all of that loss reflected in his eyes. She kissed his lips gently, one last time, then turned towards the road, knowing she was taking the best part of him with her. That she'd have it always.

CHAPTER 31
April 2025

The wind was picking up and the sky was darkening, as Delaney waited for Margie to finish whatever she was doing at the school and pick her up. She raised the volume on her ear buds and sang along with Cardi B.

Kam ran up behind her and grabbed her around her waist. Delaney snatched her ear buds off and tried to pull away but he held her tighter until she tried to stomp on his foot (she missed), but her actions worked because he let go of her.

"Hey, now."

"What the fuck, Kam."

"You were singing our song."

"Fuck off."

Kam gave her a hurt look. "Boo, you know I never did you dirty, right?

"Don't say boo."

"What, you're not my boo now?"

Delaney rolled her eyes. "You're such a poser and I was never your boo."

"Oh it's like that, huh?"

Delaney's back was now against the stonewall and Kam moved closer to her, so she put her hand against his chest to back him up. He grabbed it and held it. She snatched it away and pushed him. "Your bullshit doesn't fly with me, Kam. We had a little thing, it's over, you're a coward and a douchebag and I've got nothing else to say to you."

"Hunh, I seem to remember some moaning, but now you've got nothing to say."

"Yeah, you're disgusting, move." Delaney slid past him.

He grabbed her and turned her toward him.

"Get your fucking hands off me, Kam."

"Why are you acting like such a bitch?"

Delaney tried pulling her arm away and he held tighter.

"Get your fucking hands off me."

"Or what?"

She stared at him until he backed up.

A horn beeped, startling both of them. Margie pulled up, "Everything all right?"

Delaney glared at him before turning and walking over to the car. "Yeah, Mom, fine."

Kam moved angrily toward his car whispering a refrain with every stomp *I hope you die you fucking hole, you cunt-bitch, cuntbitchcuntbitchcuntbitch* repeating it over and over sometimes yelling it as he raced around the narrow tree lined roads toward home, sometimes whispering it, white spittle collecting in the corners of his mouth. He never missed a beat, never took an extra breath, until he was alone in the guest house and calmed by the pop and fizz of a beer can, the cold liquid putting out the fire in his gullet as he swallowed, the words silenced while can after can of beer was opened and guzzled, and all that was left was his prone body asleep on the couch, the dimming light outside leaving him in darkness, the smell of beer mixing with the sterile scent of organic lavender cleaning solution.

Margie was halfway home before she found the courage to ask Delaney what was going on. And when she did, Delaney shuddered.

"Was something going on between you and Kam?"

"We were hooking up for a while."

"Was it consensual?"

"The hooking up was."

"Okaaay."

"But…"

"But?"

"He took a video of us."

"That little shitbag!" Margie exclaimed.

"He showed it to Coach Walker. And Walker rated him on his—performance."

"So it's all true?" Margie whispered.

"Yes, mom."

Margie shook her head. "I just—couldn't believe it." She began to cry. "I thought I was protecting the school…"

"You were protecting a predator."

"I didn't know—and I didn't think you were involved."

"It shouldn't matter if I'm involved or not."

"Well, we've seen the last of him. He's gone now."

"Yeah, mom, free to go do it someplace else."

"Delaney, what am I supposed to do about that? There was a police investigation. Wait…is that video still circulating? Has it been deleted?"

"I don't care about the video—I care about that piece of shit Walker getting away with it."

"Delaney! You should care that there's a video of you out there!"

"But I don't, mom! And you shouldn't care more about that than the fact that the coach is a predator and will do this again!"

"Delaney. If I could right now, I'd run that man over with my car."

Margie looked wild. Her face was flushed. She ran her hand through her heavily sprayed hair until it stood straight up. "I'm not kidding Delaney. I'd run him right over with this station wagon. Then I'd back up and run over him again."

"Yeah?" Delaney added, "Well if you did, I'd make Kam Connover eat his guts for dinner."

"Yeah? Well I'd force feed Kam Connover Walker's filthy guts myself."

"Ha!" Delaney cheered, "I'd love to see it."

"Maybe you will!" Margie said and stepped harder on the gas.

CHAPTER 32

"You doing Okay Buddy?" Jimmy asked.

"Yeah, yeah, thanks for…" Keith waved at the bar, "this."

"Sure."

"After everything…I wasn't sure you'd want to…" Keith wiped his palm across his face and sipped at his Manhattan.

Jimmy pointed at Keith's drink, "Thought you were a gin guy."

Keith grimaced, "She makes the best Manhattans."

She was the bartender. And as if by magic, despite the three deep at the bar, she made her way over to Jimmy and Keith who were in the far corner.

"What can I get you?" She was young (mid-thirties), efficient, and professional.

Keith lifted his glass and looked at Jimmy with bleary eyes, his face florid. "You want one of these?"

"What kind of beer is on tap?"

The bartender went to answer but Keith interrupted her. "She makes the best Manhattan in all of the city. Have one."

The bartender shrugged. "It's true. I do."

Jimmy laughed. "Ok, sold."

Jimmy watched her work behind the bar while Keith stared at his drink. The space was dimly lit, but opulent, the lighting strategic for ambience rather than to hide filth or shabbiness.

Keith looked sideways at Jimmy. "Any trips lately?"

"Just got back from Germany."

"Must be a grind. The constant travel."

Jimmy gave Keith a surprised look. "It is actually."

"We're not as young as we used to be, huh?" Keith moved his mouth in a quick approximation of a smile.

"Guess not."

The bartender slid Jimmy his drink.

"Put it on my tab," Keith said.

She nodded and wiped the bar while he took his first sip. "Wow. This really is good."

The bartender laughed as if she knew he hadn't believed there was a way to make the best Manhattan in all of the city.

"Don't ask her how she does it, she won't tell you."

"Or you'd have to kill me." Jimmy deadpanned.

She laughed as though she hadn't heard that joke a gazillion times and left.

Jimmy sipped his drink. "How are you doing, Keith? Really."

Keith though about the shame he'd felt when he woke up at midnight. Still at the kitchen table, his face smashed against the polished wood, his palm in the remnants of his uneaten dinner. It was his own snoring that woke him. He thought he was having a heart attack. He'd wiped his hand on his shirt, smearing it with cold gravy and mashed potatoes. His pants were wet with urine. He'd wiped away the wet from the chair with paper towels and Windex, stumbled around the dark kitchen, his balance off, his head pounding. He showered in the guest room, borrowed the robe Erica always kept there, and pulled it as far as he could around his middle. He rolled his expensive shirt and suit pants into a ball and went downstairs, shoved them into a garbage bag, then buried it deep in the trash can in the garage. He'd felt shaky, so he took a swallow or three of gin to right himself, then staggered up the stairs, back to the guest room and got under the covers sick with shame and booze. But he couldn't tell Jimmy any of that. "Guess you heard about Rory?"

Jimmy nodded.

"He didn't accept Duke. Or anywhere else. Planning to backpack around the country like some filthy hippy."

Jimmy didn't answer.

"Thinks he'll earn money at odd jobs." Keith continued, "Like there's some nobility in being a working stiff."

"These kids—they've been through a lot..."

"That's not an excuse. They need to toughen up. Imagine if we had just given up when things got tough? They wouldn't be living the life they have now..." Keith heard himself and stopped. Drained his drink and signaled to the bartender. "Just the bourbon. Straight."

"Dude..."

"I'm fine." Keith swirled his empty glass while waiting for his next drink, fiddled with the artisanal marinated cherry. No bright medicinal-red cherry for this place. "Fuck it. Maybe that's where we went wrong. Trying to give them everything. Making sure they were the best in a town full of bests. Maybe we should have moved to Montana somewhere. I always wanted to live in Montana."

Jimmy shrugged. "The thing I can't get out of my head... is that fucking guy."

Keith nodded. "Yeah, that fucking guy."

"I think about finding him. And what I'd do if I did."

It's all Jimmy thought about. And it scared him. That video of Olivia. His baby. His eyes swam. Not with actual water but with that feeling of not being able to see when you're underwater. It was rage. It affected his vision. His breath. Jimmy exhaled. Took another small sip of his drink. Tried to refocus on the taste. What were the notes? He couldn't tell. He could never tell.

Keith looked over at him. "It's gotta be tough. For you, I mean. Erica told me about the videos—and I'm sorry, man."

Jimmy shook his head. "There's nothing for you to be sorry about. But Walker... if I ever find him."

Keith nodded slowly. "I'd stick a fucking gun to his head."

Jimmy had thought about it. It kept him up at night. The violence. It wouldn't be a gun, or a knife it would be his bare hands. He'd smash that pervert's face until there was nothing left of him. He imagined every blow, the feeling against his hand reverberating through his arm across his chest, the blood pumping from his heart as he smashed again and again obliterating Walker. "Do you ever think about finding him?"

Keith nodded. I've thought about it. How he fucked with our kids. Ruined their lives. The thing is. There's always gonna be a guy like Walker. Our kids need to know how to protect themselves. How to bounce back. They can't just give up.

Jimmy thought about it. "I don't think Rory's giving up."

Keith snorted.

"I don't man." Jimmy leaned forward. "I've known Rory forever, right?"

Keith nodded. Listening.

"He's a good kid. He was always kind. And a hard worker. A little cocky, right? A golden boy?

Keith nodded. "Pretty fair assessment."

"So maybe this isn't him giving up. Maybe you're just taking it that way."

"Then what the hell is it?"

"Maybe it's just a way for him to figure it out. Do things his way. He's barely 18 years old! So what if he works his ass off doing menial jobs for a year. Could be good for him—you said it yourself—he's had a cushy life."

"What if—it isn't a year? What if he becomes a drug addict? That fucker had him on Vyvanse! Gave my kid fucking drugs! To help him concentrate."

"Why didn't they get him on that?"

"Because. He didn't really *give it to him give it to him.* Just told him to do it. These kids find the drugs themselves. It's easy. I don't think Rory's taking them anymore. The kid's been eating like a horse. Gained weight. Sleeps regularly. Plus…" Keith stopped. As though he couldn't bring himself to say it. "Erica's got him seeing a shrink. Apparently half the fucking town is seeing a shrink."

Keith thought about the one time he'd actually spoken to Rory in the last two weeks. He'd come through the family room while Keith was watching ESPN. Keith hadn't looked up. He wasn't speaking to his son until he'd retracted his plan to travel the country like a bum. But Rory had stopped. Asked about the score. And he'd had to answer. Then as cheerful as a kid going to a candy store he'd twirled his car keys and said *see ya later dad going to see Melanie.* Melanie. Keith thought he had a girlfriend! But when he'd asked him who Melanie was he said she was his therapist! A shrink is what she was. Keith had been so worked up. It had started a drinking binge that—well—he swirled the double pour the bartender had given him, it started a drinking binge that was ongoing. In retrospect, sitting here telling Jimmy about it, it didn't sound so terrible. He took another sip and tightened his lips around his teeth to swallow. Then looked at Jimmy when he said it,

"He actually seems to like it. He calls her Melanie, they're on a first name basis," Keith laughed.

A real laugh, Jimmy noticed.

"Okay. That sounds positive right?"

Keith stared into his drink for a while. "I guess it does."

"Maybe I should see a shrink."

Keith guffawed. "You? You've got a perfect life."

Jimmy looked at Keith. "I don't know man. I can't sleep. I just have these images—of punching Walker in the face. Just…battering him."

"That's understandable. After what he did. To Olivia…"

"But I can't control it. I'll just be walking, like on my way to work, and I just—that video of Liv…" Jimmy finds it hard to talk. Keith waits. "It just pops into my head—and then I think of her as a little girl, you know? And then the rage cycle starts and I can't get it out of my head."

"Jimmy. That's understandable. Hell, I'd kick his ass if I had the chance. Fuck him up so he could never do this again. And then there'd be another one. And I'd fuck him up too. It would never end man. Just tell yourself you would if you could and think about something else."

"What?"

"Yeah. It's called compartmentalizing. I do it at work all the time. Tell yourself it's okay to bash his fucking face in and if you ever get the chance you will and in the meantime think about something else."

Jimmy laughed. "You think it's that simple?"

"Yeah, man. I do it all the time."

Jimmy knew it wouldn't be that simple. But there was something else Keith had said. There would be another one. There were so many reasons to feel rage. Maybe his rage had become so accessible to him now because Olivia had been hurt. But Olivia was going to be okay. In fact, she seemed to be thriving. She was strong and capable and had Indira's natural optimism. She was excited about college and she was tight with Isa, Bailey, and Delaney, she had lifelong friendships already and more to come. She was fine. Maybe his rage was acceptable because the world was filled with reasons to have it. And maybe his love for Olivia was what was really important in all of this. Maybe it was the choice he made from one moment to the next that mattered. Walker *was* still out there waiting to do to another person what he'd done to Olivia. And to Rory. But it wasn't Jimmy who could stop him. Because he couldn't figure out a way to stop him short of killing him and that wasn't a choice he was willing to make. Maybe Keith was right. He just had to accept that and move on.

"I'm glad you asked me for a drink."

Keith nodded. "Glad you came out."

They sipped quietly for a while. "Those other assholes..."

"Who?"

"Connover and Logan."

"Oh, them. What about them?"

"They were never my friends. Not like you and me. Erica just wanted—you know."

Jimmy shrugged. "Happens. Life gets busy. People change."

Keith nodded. "Maybe change is a good thing. Like you said. About Rory."

"I think it is."

Keith lifted his drink. "To change. And to our kids."

Jimmy lifted his drink. "To our kids." He took another sip. It really was delicious.

It was a wet chilly spring with brief bursts of sun. So when Saturday morning dawned bright and clear with temperatures in the seventies, Indira felt her spirits lift. She'd ignored a case of plantar fasciitis long enough long that loading up on ibuprofen and running through the pain was no longer an option and she was now forced to rest. She went out to the yard and diligently did her foot exercises and decided to be grateful for the first sustained moments of sunshine in what felt like months, instead of being bitter and angry that she couldn't run. She was in the middle of rolling her foot on a frozen water bottle when her phone chirped. *Ugh,* she thought, forgetting about her positivity talk to herself only a moment ago *who is texting and what do they want.* She continued rolling her foot back on forth and gave a desultory tap of her screen to see what was required of her. For the second time that day, Indira's spirits soared in spite of herself—it was Joyce asking if she wanted to meet for coffee at the Farmer's Market in half an hour. Indira's response was immediate and she realized in that moment just how desperate she was for that connection.

"I just can't shake the feeling that I should have known." Joyce pushed her sunglasses onto her head.

Indira recognized the pain in her friend's eyes. She recognized the self-doubt and regret she saw every time she looked in the mirror. "Same."

"I know we can't go back in time."

"But if we could?"

Joyce shook her head, "We can't. Thinking about woulda, shoulda, coulda drove me insane for weeks—but that isn't what's worrying me anymore."

Indira took a sip of her coffee without tasting it. "It's the lasting effects on our girls."

Joyce nodded. "Isa told me the thing she longs for the most is the *before.*"

"I get that."

Maybe, Indira thought, Isa was too young to know how prophetic her knowledge was. How the before and after of what happened to Rory and the other boys, and in turn what they did to the girls, would linger for the rest of their lives, and how much it had already shaped all of them. How they felt about themselves, their sexuality, their ability to engage in intimacy with others, how it would play out in their relationships and marriages and friendships and parenting.

"Olivia keeps complaining that she feels like she's getting the flu. It was so pervasive that I took her for blood tests, but her white cell count was normal."

"What do you think it is?"

Indira thought about the way she'd felt every morning since that board meeting. It wasn't until this moment that she recognized the heaviness in her limbs, the pain in her neck and head for what it actually was. "Grief."

Joyce nodded slowly. "For the before."

Indira nodded. "And I don't know what to do for them."

"I guess...just this...stay connected. Listen to them, be there for them."

"It's hard not to beat myself up for not being there...before."

"I hear you. But that won't help them. In fact it will make it worse. This guilt isn't ours. It's his. We need to leave it there. With him."

Indira thought about that. Leaving the guilt where it belonged. Instead, becoming strong for Olivia. Staying connected to her. She looked up at Joyce and this time, she saw the resolve in her friend's eyes, and met it with her own.

Joyce put her hand on Indira's. "We've got this."

And Indira believed her.

CHAPTER 33

Isa and Olivia hovered over Bailey as her fingers flew over the keyboard. Delaney sat a few feet away painting her nails a vibrant shade of chartreuse. Olivia tried to watch the screen, but it made her dizzy.

Bailey didn't take her eyes off the screen. "Do I need to keep this strictly white hat?"

"What does that mean?" Isa asked.

Delaney answered, "Strictly legal."

"Yeah you do!" Isa was one octave away from shouting.

Bailey stopped typing, looked up at Isa and grinned, "Don't worry. I'm too good to get caught."

"Now I'm worried." Isa said.

Olivia rushed to reassure her, "She's not breaking any laws...."

"Well...." Bailey said.

Isa and Olivia exchanged glances.

Bailey looked up and saw their worried faces. "Relax. Walker's easy, I won't have to resort to anything criminal... and... here we are!"

Olivia and Isa leaned over. There it was. The name and address of the afterschool program Walker had already obtained a position in. A forty-five minute drive from his parent's home in a community where more than half the population lived below the poverty line.

Isa looked at the time. "We'll have to wait until tomorrow."

Bailey tapped the keyboard. "I have the director's home number."

"No!" Isa shouted.

Bailey laughed. "It was a Google search."

"Okay, but still we can't call him at home. It's creepy."

Olivia nodded. "We'll call tomorrow."

Bailey looked at them. "There's no guarantee our call makes a difference. The guy may not believe you. He may not even care."

"True." Olivia said. "But it will make him pay more attention. And it will make it more difficult for Walker."

"Any obstacle we throw in front of him is better than none," Isa said.

Olivia thought of the endless years stretching in front of them. Where they threw up obstacles and Walker skirted them. It would have to go on for the remainder of his life, because she was certain he would never stop.

"We can't let up."

Bailey shrugged. "He may learn to tighten his settings, but I'll always be able to get to him."

Isa looked at her, "Which is why you can't cross the line, B. We need you."

Bailey laughed, "Just a toe."

"Seriously, B."

"You worry too much."

Olivia placed her hand on Isa's arm. "We could let the police handle it."

Isa shook her head. "He's not even on their radar anymore. Any more than he was when he was here. We need to warn people."

Olivia looked worried. "What if no one believes us?"

Bailey looked at them, "We could dox him."

Olivia frowned, "I thought that was illegal."

Bailey shrugged, "Not if we obtain his whereabouts through public information, which I did. And not if we're careful about what we say."

Isa rubbed the back of her neck. "I don't understand."

Olivia looked at her, "Maybe... if we just... stick to the facts...these allegations were made...Walker was accused of... no indictment... no conviction... not enough evidence... that kind of thing."

"How will that help? We have the same problem, he's still free to do it again."

Bailey leaned forward. "Yeah, but, predators like Walker depend on secrecy and coercion. It will be a lot more difficult to get away with it if people know."

Olivia slammed her hand on the desk. "Let's do both. Call his director and dox his ass."

Bailey smiled. "You two handle the director. I'll start working on the rest of it. We'll kick his ass."

Isa leaned over and kissed Bailey. Right on the lips.

"Whoa," Delaney said. "I didn't know you had it in you, Isa. You hottie."

Bailey's fingers were still flying but she lifted one hand to pull Isa onto her lap.

Isa kissed Bailey again. "Get that fucker! He'll never rest again."

Olivia looked worried. "Neither will we."

Isa shook her head. "We will. Because he is not getting away with this, there are many ways to rest. And I'm very happy resting like a shark."

Bailey laughed and sang the lyrics from the *Oh Wonder* song.

The song had nothing to do with vengeance and everything to do with love. But maybe that was the point. Maybe that was what mattered more than anything. There were many ways to rest and many ways to love and maybe they'd figure it out....

Olivia draped her arms around Bailey and Isa and sang. Delaney tightened her nail polish bottle, held it like a mic and joined in, singing about love and sharks and landslides.

CHAPTER 34

Coach Walker finished his morning green drink and walked onto the guest cottage patio just as color streaked the sky. The morning was cool and the day promised sunshine and a temperate 75 degrees. Perfect for teaching tennis, a run along the trails, swimming in the crystal waters of his parent's swimming pool.

He stretched his arms above his head. He'd never felt as fit. This move was the best thing that ever happened to him. He dropped alongside the pool and executed 75 pushups in perfect form and staccato rhythm, an uneven infinitesimal hitch for a hold at the most challenging point. The endorphins rushing through him provided a feeling of well being combined with invincibility. He flipped over onto his back and began a series of crunches. Perhaps all the glory he'd sought as a winning coach was overrated. Maybe a low-key work life was the way to go and he could get the head rush of glory some other way. He'd always wanted to do an Iron Man and never had the time he needed to train properly. People were woefully ignorant about how many hours went into coaching year round athletics; games and practice schedules led to twelve-hour days, six days a week. He'd devoted himself so fully that he really hadn't had much *me* time. But this lifestyle was something he could get used to. His folks were so happy to have him nearby that they would welcome his presence for as long as he wanted to stay. He could live well on his trust and whatever income came in from tennis lessons and fly under the radar. He closed his eyes as he pushed through his last 100 crunches, the rising sun bright against his eyelids.

He thought about the boys and girls he'd be coaching. The slow burn of getting to know them, gaining their admiration, their trust. In some ways that had been the best part. The way he'd walk down the halls of the school as if it were his own personal kingdom and those kids, those bright, beautiful, malleable kids were his. They loved him, maybe even worshiped him. The boys wanted to be him and the girls wanted to have him. It was enough. Knowing that every touch those girls came alive under, were because of him. His expertise, his command. Those boys would be fumbling idiots without him. They were the beneficiaries of the time he'd put in, all the ways he'd tried so hard to please so many women and all of them always wanting more from him. More more more. His time, his attention. A night in the sack no matter how much he pleased them meant they wanted brunch, and cuddles, and talking, and they wanted to control him. Get a better paying job, more free time, put a ring on their finger, have fucking babies. Why would he want to have a mewling useless baby? He had all these boys! Better than actual sons, he could leave his mark on them, find the diamonds in the rough and make them champions. Walker felt himself escalating. He needed to calm down. He took deep breaths to slow his heart rate. He couldn't go down this path. Just like he couldn't think about the betrayal of those boys. And those little slutty holes, the way they glared at him like he was dirt. And their bitch-hag mothers and their dickless fathers. He couldn't let his rage overtake him. He was in a better place now. Far away. With a

whole new world of untarnished girls and eager boys waiting
for him. He didn't mind having to start over. He relished it.
He had a clean slate. And he learned from his mistakes. He
was golden. Powerful. In the best shape of his life. Hell, even
his own high school years, when he was the golden boy, the
cream of the crop, even then he wasn't in the shape he was
in now. He felt himself swelling with pride and excitement.
Today was the first day of his new life.

His watch jangled in his ear, shattering the zone he'd created. At first he looked at it perfunctorily, with irritation, then
with a sense of growing alarm. His new boss had texted a curt
missive... *need an explanation* followed by a barrage of images.

Walker jumped up and ran into the cottage, a roar in his
ears, heat flushing his body. His breath jagged and his eyes
bulging he ran over to his laptop and brought up screen after
screen. All of them social media pages, one for the school district where he'd begun working in the after school program,
one for his mother's local facebook page, four surrounding
local facebook neighborhood groups, the local nextdoor page,
and a slew of nextdoor pages in the vicinity. Page after page
with his smiling image, page after page of him with his team
members crowded around him, holding trophies. And with
every photo of his smiling face was text. Paragraph after paragraph describing what had happened:

Rory's story.
Emmett's story.
Hunter's story.
Olivia's story.
Isa's story.
His parents' address was listed.

The afterschool program where he was working was listed. Every single piece of public information was listed.

Newspaper articles about his arrest and subsequent release were prominently displayed.

Was this even legal? He roared inside his own head. And soon the roar became a sound outside of his head and it was so loud and so desperate that his mother heard it from her sun drenched kitchen. She dropped her coffee cup, oblivious of the splintering porcelain or the seeping stain across her white tile floor. She ran with her heart fluttering up into her throat, her arms outstretched. She found her son sweeping his desk clear, his computer crashing to the floor, his face twisted, his mouth a gaping screaming thing.

*****

2,451 miles away, four girls sat on a blanket in the park, a cardboard carrier containing an assortment of frothy iced coffee drinks in front of them and a bag of muffins next to it. Isa and Bailey sat shoulder to shoulder, their fingers entwined. Delaney's legs were tucked sideways, enormous Prada sunglasses, her latest thrift store find, perched on the tip of her nose. Olivia's legs were stretched out in front of her and her hands were planted firmly on the ground, her bare shoulders warmed by the April sun. The schools were closed for the holidays, and the girls had a few more days together before Bailey returned to the dorms and the other three began the end of their senior year.

Bailey looked at the time on her phone, "Huh, eight a.m. Mountain Standard Time."

There was a tremor in the air and the girls looked to the sky in time to see a flock of large black birds.

"A murder of crows," Olivia said.

The girls smiled at each other, Delaney took a sip of her drink, Isa leaned her head against Bailey's shoulder. Bailey rested her palm on Isa's hip, pulling her closer. Olivia reached over and pressed play on Isa's playlist, the small but mighty speaker filling the air with strains of Beyoncé's "You Won't Break My Soul."

The dancing started slow at first, a little shaking of the shoulders by Olivia, Delaney shimmying all the way up until she was standing, Isa pulling Bailey to her feet...but once they started, and the music reverberated in the air and through them, there was no stopping them.

THE END

ACKNOWLEDGMENTS

This book came from a lifetime of watching teenagers trying to figure out a world where the people they trusted most exploited that trust. I wrote it for all of them.

I couldn't have done it without my early readers and the people in my life who give me space and time and encouragement to write. The list is long. To Sandy Sackman for all the days in Avalon, for the quiet, for the laughter, for the tears, and for dancing. Thank you. Sandy, Stacey McGonigle, Syd, and Greg, you were there when I typed THE END (I know it's silly and corny but I always type The End even though it was the first of a gazillion drafts.) Thank you for cheering and then waiting four years to read it haha.

My parents, Merle Molofsky and Les Von Losberg, as incredible poets and writers, you inspire me. Thank you for being early readers and fixing most of my mistakes before anyone else had to see them!

Laura Carraro, our writing days mean everything to me. Your exquisite clarity of language and sentence structure inspires me and your keen eye made this a better book.

Patty Gillette, if you didn't read the first page and tell me to keep going I probably wouldn't have. Those critical voices in my head needed to be calmed with the brightness of your voice.

Carol Marie Lynch, Mellissa Smith, Carol Maria Dawley, Amy Bogusz, Jillian Marra La Porta, thank you for being early readers. Your friendship keeps me going not only as a writer, but also as a human.

Susan Freedman, your wisdom, and knowledge have been invaluable sounding boards whenever my characters search for justice. Alexandra Farina, your eyes on these pages made a tremendous difference and I am grateful for your time and attention to this book. Laura Schaefer, I wouldn't be here without you and I am forever grateful to you for giving readers and authors and bunnies a home at Scattered Books.

Whenever I started to really procrastinate (which was every day) I heard my father Dominic Chianese's words…keep writing. So I did.

Carley Moore, my writing boss, thank you for believing in these characters and for making this story stronger with your compassion and commitment to storytelling. Your novels, and poetry, and blogs, inspire and help make sense of a world that would be lonely without stories.

Caroline Leavitt, your brilliant guidance brought this book here. Thank you for believing in it and in me.

Penny Eifrig, your commitment to books, to stories, to justice, to the environment is unparalleled. I am lucky to work with you and am grateful that *Pinned* exists because of you.

Mallory Rock, I am deeply grateful for your profound ability to create beauty and capture the essence of this book in design.

To my children; Anthony Jr. your expertise was vital to this story and I thank you for taking my calls in the middle of your workday because I had questions, Joseph Michael, this book would not exist if you didn't keep encouraging me, you have taught me so much, Elijah, you were my muse for much of this story, your strength and sensitivity and belief in yourself inspire me every day, Grace Clary, daughter of my heart, your careful eye on these pages and your deep understanding of how to inspire me to keep going are part of this book, Arielle Scarpati, daughter of my heart, you are a light in my life and you inspire me every day. To my granddaughters, Sovay Lena and Esme June, my little bosses, you are my everything. To my husband Anthony, we were nineteen when you first read my work, and I've felt your love and support for every moment after that. Thank you for believing in me.

What people are saying:

"**Pinned** is simultaneously haunting and prophetic, and dear to me for its honest, riveting depictions of troubled parents and their children. Set in the wealthy suburbs of New York City, Chianese exposes what Americans get up to when they have too much time, money, and all the wrong priorities. At the tender heart of this novel is a community torn apart by sexual violence, secret keeping, and unexamined trauma. Chianese has written a perfect book for our current political crisis. You don't want to miss it."

~Carley Moore, author of **Panpocalypse** and **The Not Wives**

"**Pinned** is a novel filled with portraits of powerful family dynamics and issues of corruption and the wellsprings of victimization. It surveys the conundrums faced by Emmett Ainsworth and other characters who find their personal values and objectives clashing with forces outside of their control.

Readers will find **Pinned**'s focus on how predators are born and evolve frighteningly realistic. This is the mark of a well-done plot which pulls readers into the real world of threats, predators, and survival tactics.

These very elements are a huge draw, not just because they emerge within well-crafted, believable characters and situations, but because they provoke much food for thought as the story forges unexpected new territory.

Rebecca Chianese is adept at juxtaposing the perceptions, concerns, and motivations of a disparate group of characters. She creates important opportunities not just for individual reflection, but for adult and teen discussion groups."

~D. Donovan, Sr. Reviewer, **Midwest Book Review**